LEVEL
ZERO

DAN MCDOWELL

Black Rose Writing | Texas

ISBN: 978-1-68433-704-0
PUBLISHED BY BLACK ROSE WRITING
www.blackrosewriting.com

Printed in the United States of America
Suggested Retail Price (SRP) $19.95

Level Zero is printed in Book Antiqua

*As a planet-friendly publisher, Black Rose Writing does its best to eliminate unnecessary waste to reduce paper usage and energy costs, while never compromising the reading experience. As a result, the final word count vs. page count may not meet common expectations.

Praise for

LEVEL
ZERO

CURATED BY EDITORS AT BOOKBUB as a
FEATURED NEW RELEASE FOR HORROR (2021).

HORROR FINALIST FOR MAXY AWARDS (2021)

BEST THRILLERS BOOK AWARD NOMINEE - HORROR (2021)

"*The Shining* meets *Dante's Inferno*. *Level Zero* is brimming with sinister surprises sure to keep horror fans up at night. Hellish hospitality awaits... McDowell's portrait of two self-absorbed, morally-challenged men -- and the price of living life without empathy - is hard-hitting and utterly believable." *-Best Thrillers*

5/5 Stars.
"A solid chilling horror. McDowell builds a world of betrayal, dark intrigue, decay, and uncanny in this tightly constructed horror. Dark and often bone-chilling, the novel generates both chills and thrills." *-The Prairies Book Review*

5/5 Stars.
"Creepy and bizarre; a combination of elements makes *Level Zero* an intriguing read for horror fans. Unreserved and disturbing, this is a gripping tale from Dan McDowell." *-Reader's Favorite*

DEDICATION

FIRST:

To the one who took my breath away.
You always shoot straight, calling my bluff when I don't realize it,
and motivating me every step of the way to be a better man.
I wouldn't have it any other way.
For my love, Tiffiny.

SECOND:

To my children and all that pick up this book:
Keep dreaming.
Keep believing.
Keep learning.
Keep creating.
Find your purpose and run like you never have before.
It's all but temporary, our existence. Make it meaningful.

LEVEL
ZERO

WARNINGS AGAINST FOLLY

PROVERBS 6:12-19

A troublemaker and a villain, who goes about with a corrupt mouth, who winks maliciously with his eye, signals with his feet and motions with his fingers, who plots evil with deceit in his heart — he always stirs up conflict.

Therefore, disaster will overtake him in an instant; he will suddenly be destroyed — without remedy.

There are six things the LORD hates, seven that are detestable to him: haughty eyes, a lying tongue, hands that shed innocent blood, a heart that devises wicked schemes, feet that are quick to rush into evil, a false witness who pours out lies and a person who stirs up conflict in the community.

SUMMER 1982

CHAPTER ONE

The service was elegant, and the chosen photo was perfect, but the late Helena Reinhold remained dead. CHRIS WILKERSON stood fifteen feet from the casket next to his grieving spouse, Katrina, reflecting.

I don't know what to say. Eight words from Katrina since Helena passed, and they were something to the effect of "change those pants," and "that's the wrong colored belt." No way to a smoother landing, is there?

He stood tall, handsome, and well-dressed while Katrina donned a beautiful black dress with hints of lace and a matching head covering. With Helena's death, the Reinhold legacy hung in the balance. Despite the continued support of her benefactors, the late Mrs. Reinhold was never likable, nor respected.

She lay motionless in the blue dress Katrina picked for her. Though bold in contrast to the mahogany box surrounding her body, the mortician's exceptionalism in prepping Helena to match up with her best photographs was admirable — even working to choke the stench of formaldehyde from the room with hints of potpourri. The classic eye-makeup and lipstick matched her blushed cheeks while the diffused lighting illuminated her corpse in a natural color.

Her service went by with just the pomp and circumstance the elites of Riverton expected, and in a defining manner that only the prosperous could afford. With their hands separated, Chris and Katrina paid their final respects before giving a cue to the funeral director to close the lid. The pallbearers moved into position, and the rest of the room scattered. Exiting the rear of the facility, the funeral home staff escorted them toward the hearse.

He reached out to hold Katrina's hand. She ignored him.

I'm searching for words, but I have nothing meaningful to contribute, he thought.

As they loaded into the back seat of the hearse, Katrina spoke to Chris, peering into his periwinkle eyes, "I really can't believe this."

Chris rolled the window down a notch and mumbled, "A means to an end."

"You don't need to say anything. Unless you're going to work for a greeting card company, you can stop with the generic remarks. They got old twelve years ago."

"You're right. I'm sorry."

The graveside service ended in a blur, leaving Chris in an unshakable haze as he and Katrina drifted further apart.

．　　．　　．　　．　　．

Time went on, the bereavement leave dried up, and CHRIS WILKERSON returned to work at WGBO 530 AM. Wayne Wallace and Ramblin' Ron sat in the studio chattering away as the ON AIR light flashed above their heads. Chris fell into the producer's chair just outside the studio for the first time in weeks following time away to mourn Helena and support Katrina. Both men in the studio waved.

Yeah. Yeah. Nice to see you, too. What's on the agenda this afternoon?

He studied the paperwork on his desk as the wall's countdown clock hinted at the approaching commercial segment.

Ron came out of the studio and patted him on the shoulder. "It's good to see you. We've missed you. If you need anything — anything at all, let me know."

"I appreciate that," Chris said, more muted and subdued than usual. He rifled through the stack of paperwork accumulated on his desk.

"You want to go out for a smoke?" Ron asked. "Wayne's going to run with the next segment. We're due a good catch up."

"I haven't even been here five minutes, but, why not?"

They walked past a poster for the Dynamic Duds show as oversized caricatures of Ron and Wayne yelled into illustrated microphones, one across from the other.

Ron stopped in front of it. "I always thought they made me look like a doppelganger to Nixon...Wayne's fat chin's too chiseled."

"Ha. I love that poster," Chris said. "I think it's a fair likeness. It's great to be back."

. . . . .

Arriving home later that day, Chris recounted the escapades of his return to WGBO with Katrina while they shared a slice of pizza at the oblong Reinhold family table. Katrina had yet to acknowledge him after several minutes of after-work chatter.

"Were you paying attention to anything I just said?" he asked.

"Whatever. I don't care about what you do at WGBO. You just go on and on about it whether I want you to or not, so why should I bother acknowledging your wacky-pack stories."

He squeezed Katrina on the hand, and she pulled away. "I think it's about time we get out of the house a while. A little time in the sun could do you good. I'd like to see that nice figure of yours gallivanting in that number we got you last summer."

"Are you flirting or flattering?"

"What's it to you? I haven't applied for a job in the greeting card business yet. Can't a man hit on his wife a little now and then? You deserve the truth."

"Whatever. I'll pack up." Katrina exited the room. A minute later, she called from around the corner, "Wait a minute. You're going to take off work as soon as you get back? That doesn't look good on you. Why don't we wait a couple of weeks?"

"Not necessary. I arranged more time off. We can stay at the rental cabin if you want to hang around a few days."

"Good enough for me," she said.

CHAPTER TWO

TODD ADAMS and his girlfriend, Lorrie Hatcher, smoked a cigarette together outside the Bridgewater Restaurant on Oak Hollow Lane. As their date night neared its end, they stared at an aged hotel building that towered over the block, puffing smoke into the sky one after the other.

"What a waste… they should demolish that place," Todd said.

Lorrie looked at her leather watch. "Yeah. Right in the armpit of Riverton, and you still bring me *here* to eat."

What's on your mind? Spit it out already, Todd thought.

"Come on — the food's spectacular," he said, "I saw you hesitate. What was that about?"

"We used to sneak in there at night when we were kids…"

"We? Who else would go with you? What was it like?"

"Oh, I don't know. A safe-haven for lowlifes and thugs to screw around. Some kind of sanctuary the cops in Precinct Three turn a blind eye to. Who knows what councilman they paid off for the arrangement?"

"You ever hook up with one of the… the residents?"

Lorrie's eyes widened as she slapped him. "You know I'm not that kind of girl. I can still picture the needles in the walls and scattered all over the floors. You had to kick the freaking things out of the way to walk the hallways. All those bums living in there were better off dead.

It was weird. I felt unwelcome when I went in and cursed by the time I left. They say buildings can't talk. This one did, Todd."

"What are you saying? When was this?"

"It was about twelve years ago. Just the kind of crap teenagers do. Can we talk about something else, please?"

"Okay, let's…" he said. "What about my learning to fly? I've had my license for months, and you still won't go up with me."

"I don't want to. You need more time."

"It's not that big a deal. I've been flying these little planes with Stu in the cockpit for over a year now. You haven't encouraged me a single time, have you?"

She shook her head at him. "I won't let you throw your life away in the sky. I've always had a bad feeling about *you* flying."

"*Me* flying? What's that supposed to mean?"

Lorrie scrunched her nose as she took another drag and blew it in Todd's face.

You've got to be kidding. What a jerk move.

"I don't want one of us to end up dead," she said.

"We've discussed this before. Statistics don't lie. We're two-thousand times more likely to die on the highway than we are in the sky."

She flung her cigarette on the ground, smashing and extinguishing it under the heel of her sandal. "Don't you remember the Halloween party last year? You checked out on me, and I thought I lost you."

He donned an unnatural set of pearly whites. "What? At Creensteen's? Are you kidding me? That guy's duller than a used eraser."

"You're changing the subject. Dale's your manager. You ought to show more respect."

"Maybe I will one day. Once he does the same for me."

She grabbed him by the arm. "That's not what I'm getting at. I didn't know who you were. How many other times is that happening when I'm not around?"

"It was just an episode. A momentary lapse of judgment. Let it slide, Lorrie."

"Judgment…? Or sanity? What if another of these *episodes* happens in the sky?"

"That's what the lithium's for," Todd said. He put one of his hands in his pockets, fidgeting with loose change. "I crush up my little pill, dump it in my coffee, and my troubled world melts away."

Lorrie scoffed, twisting her hair around a bare ring finger. "You aren't a spokesperson for the stuff. Hell, you don't even take it half the time. You can't expect results just pissing it away like that."

"Pissing it away?" Todd pulled at the top of his belt, swiveling side to side. "That's right. Nineteen-hour half-life and eighty percent of it comes right out when I drain the lizard. I knew we were hooked up for the right reasons. Nursing school's done you some good after all."

"Stop it, Todd. Shut up."

Todd reached over and put his arm on Lorrie's shoulder. "Look, I know I'm not a perfect man… and you're not a perfect woman, but our offspring could be something special."

"You can't keep playing with my emotions this way. Four years we've been together. One empty promise after another, and we've gotten nowhere. Maybe we'd be better off…"

Todd interrupted, "You know that's not fair."

"Forget it. Take me home."

"You got it, ma'am."

Lorrie grabbed Todd by the hand to hold it as they walked toward the truck. "I'm not sure about this. The life you've got planned for us. Maybe we're not compatible?"

Some nerve on her. I'm raging.

Todd stopped and froze in the middle of the sidewalk as they strolled under a busted out street lamp. "Not compatible? You're such a tease. One minute you're doting on me like I've discovered the dadgum Pythagorean Theorem, the next, I might as well be working for Satan himself."

"Well, are you?"

"Of course not. I'm a decent man. You know that about me. Tomorrow morning, we fly."

"Fly? What are you talking about? There's no plane rental on Saturday."

There we go — uncertainty in your eyes. That's better. Todd 1, Lorrie 0. Time to make the vein in your forehead show.

"Our savings account. I finally bought us one."

Lorrie's face reddened. "No, you didn't. We're going to pretend this discussion didn't happen." She pulled her hand away from Todd, glaring at him as she grumbled, "Let's say it did... You better get your sorry ass back to whatever goon sold it to you, return it, and get our money back immediately!"

"Give me a break. You know who's pitching in the bulk of the cash in the account. Get in the truck, now!"

Todd opened the door, and Lorrie climbed in, staring back at him.

"Are you raising your voice at me?" she asked.

"And if I am? What you gonna do about it?"

"Raise mine. I like a man who gets authoritative!"

That's more like it. I'm a man in control. It's better that way.

He walked around the front of the vehicle, hopping into the seat as he reached across to buckle Lorrie's belt.

"How presumptuous. What else do you do on impulse?"

"You'll find out soon enough, sweetheart. You'll find out soon enough."

Several minutes later, they pulled into the parking lot outside the apartment.

Putting the car in park, he placed his hand on Lorrie's arm. "How about a caffeinated nightcap?"

"I'll permit it this once," Lorrie said, jabbing at him. "I really hope you were joking, Mr. Adams, because if you weren't..."

Todd stared at the sky a moment and replied, "Come on. Let's go inside."

CHAPTER THREE

LORRIE HATCHER awoke duct-taped to the seat of a plane.

What's going on here?

Commotion came from behind. Todd walked around from the rear, bellowing in a masculine morning voice, "Had to get her all fueled up. Now we're ready."

Why can't I focus? I feel like I'm going to faint.

"Did you... drug me, Todd?"

He smiled. "Guilty as charged. I crushed up a few pink pills in your coffee. You need to see me fly. We'll keep this between us, okay? Don't you trust me?"

Lorrie scoffed as her mind wandered.

Why I've wasted the time on you I have is beyond me. I guess I'm just that desperate.

"You wish..." she said. "I was kidding around about your impulses last night. This isn't right."

"Impulses? You mean like the way you floozy around with the medical staff at Riverton General?"

"What are you talking about?"

He's got me so messed up, I can't get angry. What's going on?

The plane escalated to several thousand feet as they drifted further from civilization.

"I hate you!" Lorrie fumed, punching Todd in the arm. "We're done."

She peeled at the duct tape covering the top of her legs.

Layered with care. If this discolors my denim, I swear I'm going to freak.

"What were you thinking, taping me down like this? You are some kind of crazy, aren't you?"

"Oh, don't worry about that, Lorrie. Watch and learn. The only way to fly... is to fly high."

Lorrie remembered the adage her father taught her years earlier. *A man caught in personal calamity can only be a shell of the man he was created to be.*

She and Todd made eye contact. Her mind screamed.

You're not the man I love. I don't know who you are anymore.

Todd spoke in a sweetened, artificial tone, "I made you something to perk you up, sweetheart. Have a sip."

His hair stood straight up and unkempt as he sported an unfamiliar smile — the polar opposite of his typical refined and well-kept appearance — a handsome man in high finance where the stakes were high, and the paydays were higher.

"You know I can't trust you anymore," Lorrie remarked as she continued removing the tape.

Todd slammed his fist on the center console. "Just take a sip, airhead."

"I won't."

"Suit yourself. Percocet is the way I'm going, baby. I feel it kicking in now. Nine little pills crushed up in a mimosa, and I'm off to the races."

Lorrie scoffed. "You lifted my samples? How could you? You're my rule follower. What the hell is going on?"

Todd glanced toward her, speaking in a deadpan tone, "Never when I'm manic, honey... Never when I'm manic."

The plane ascended in haste as Todd and Lorrie peered over Riverton County.

Todd's voice grew playful, "Look over there, dollie. There's Richland Lake. Or wait, is it Barton Hills?"

He has absolutely lost it. These are my final moments, and I'm wasting them with this nutjob.

Her face became more flushed with the passing seconds. "I've had enough. Take me down now."

"Are you ready to admit I can fly yet? That I've got what it takes? Or is your pride gonna get in the way? You just can't stand to see your sweetie succeed at something, can you? Hey... what are those little things dancing on the windshield?"

Todd's eyes glossed over as he peered toward Lorrie.

"Todd, you mixed the Percocet and the lithium, didn't you? You're going to pass out any minute."

"That's the idea. I'm ready for this to be over."

"These medications are messing you up. Let's get you back on the ground, and we'll get you some help."

"I'd rather be in the ground." He laughed in an uncontrollable loop.

"Todd, you are scaring me. Dear God, you're really scaring me."

"I'm sorry, Lorrie. It's um... it's um... oh gosh... not another one. I'm clammy."

"Do not faint. Do not faint on this plane, you hear me? Take deep breaths. Breathe in... breathe out... If you kill me in the air, I swear I'll haunt you."

Todd's face grew pale, the plane plummeted, and he fainted. Lorrie lurched over the console to take control of the aircraft with only a couple of pieces of tape stuck to the top of her blue jeans.

"Oh, please God... Give us another chance... Give us another chance," she cried out.

•   •   •   •   •

KATRINA and Chris Wilkerson traversed across Richland Lake in their speedboat. Katrina searched for aquatic inspiration for an art project as their stereo played *Billy Squier*.

It's time to call it quits, she thought. *I can't take the impulsive decisions and disregard for others any longer. Scaring everyone significant in our life away… day by day. Life apart will be better. He can keep the townhome. I'll take the estate. We'll take some time to ourselves and regroup later.*

An escalating noise came from the sky as a small plane took an unnatural nose dive toward the shoreline. It crashed into the trees about a mile away.

"What was that?" Katrina asked. "There's no landing strip out this way, right?"

"I don't know. Let's go back to shore and check it out."

They headed toward the site of the crash at above-average speeds. Katrina attempted to stabilize her art collage in momentary frustration with Chris's reckless boat navigation.

Son of a gun. This guy can't do anything safe, can he?

They sped across the top of the water, breezing toward the shore. Katrina lost her footing twice.

"Come on. Be careful!" she yelled.

She scurried across the deck as she carried the project. They continued to speed up, and she slipped, hitting her head as a cascading world of fog surrounded her.

Just like mom. Trauma to the head.

Chris jogged across the boat, raising his voice to get her attention, "Katrina! Katrina! Stay with me, honey."

He tried to wake her, but there was no response. She lay on the boat deck facing the sky, eyes open, her body motionless.

Chris hovered above. While trying to give her CPR, beads of his salty sweat poured from the top of his head onto her face, and the plane crash became insignificant. Loading Katrina into the black Town Car, Chris laid her out across the rear seat. Without a single pay phone in reaching distance, he would have to rush her to Riverton General Hospital (RGH) on his own. By the time they arrived, Katrina was unconscious.

FALL 1982

CHAPTER FOUR

BOB "LIVEWIRE" JAMES remained busy wiring intercoms for RGH's new emergency announcement system. He maintained a look he considered well-defined — black jeans, a matching t-shirt, and a tight ponytail. His eyeglasses were reminiscent of John Lennon. He tested the speakers as a nurse exited a room with her head hanging low and dejected.

What's her deal?

He peered around the corner as he pulled the wire through the exposed ceiling tiles. Within the room, a man trembled, staring at what Livewire assumed was a significant other lying in bed, unconscious, hopeless, and helpless.

The man talked to himself or prayed. "I will do anything... anything to have my Katrina back."

I guess I'll go see what I can do. The guy don't have no one else to talk to.

Livewire walked into the room, never acknowledged by the distraught man. Peering around the room, he struggled to see the patient behind the slew of medical equipment and devices as their hum and beeps sustained her.

Looks like this chick's got no chance.

As the burly red-headed man wiped tears from his eyes, he interrupted, "Has she been out a while?"

"It's been a little while now. Boating accident."

"Well, at least she ain't dead... yet. There's always hope."

"I'm sorry. Who are you?"

I hope he can't smell the Old Tymer's. Bein' snakebit by whiskey at 2 in the afternoon will be the end of me.

Livewire extended his hand toward the man to introduce himself.

"Bob James, Riverton A/V. Just call me Livewire. And you?"

"Chris Wilkerson... Livewire, huh?"

"Yeah. Just a nickname the guys at the shop call me. It's nice to meet you."

"What are you doing in here?"

"Sorry." Livewire walked toward the doorway and turned around. "Say, I don't know if you're much of a believing man. You know... about the things and powers that are beyond this world, but I've heard of a place. Somewhere you should see, you know. Where she might be... healed — where some kind of higher power can help."

Chris's eyes squinted as he aspirated. "God? A church? Is that what you mean? This is a hospital. Isn't this where a coma patient should be? Isn't *this* the place?

"Oh, no. No. There's an urban legend about a place over there in the Oak Hollow District. You much into superstition?"

Chris looked up at him, his eyes rolling. "Oh, I don't know. I guess I'll believe just about anything that gives me hope at this point. I'm all for clinging to that... however I can."

"There's an old building over there. Used to be a hotel, I think. God knows what it is now, and I'd advise not explorin' much into that. There are some dark things that have gone on over there through the years, but there've been miracles, too. You know, special things. Maybe they really do have healing water. Maybe it's all just folklore. I don't know. I'll leave what you do for you to decide. Like I said, I haven't had much to do with the place, and I'm not sure I *ever* want to."

Chris looked over at Katrina, pale and motionless in the bed as steady beeps pulsed from the heart monitor.

"Not much she can say to stop me, right? I'll go check it out. Oak Hollow District, you said? Old hotel?"

"Yeah. I think it's all boarded up now. For all I know, the joint might even be for sale. Wait until it's good and dark, and snoop around a bit. Riverton PD's got better things to do than torment some coma patient's husband hopin' for a miracle. Godspeed."

"I don't see a career in social work for the likes of you. Thanks for the encouragement, guy."

Despite Livewire's collectedness during the conversation, addiction called his name.

I need another drink.

He walked down the hall toward the broom closet and took another gulp of his *Old Tymer's.*

About time I replace this old flask. Never cared much for the Mardi Gras symbol on it anyhow. Pitiful thing's discolored from years of blood, sweat, and tears.

Livewire wrapped his lips around its curved top as he inhaled the drink in a rush. Footsteps approached.

Who's there?

He pulled the closet door closed, chugging the last of the whiskey. The handle turned to open, and he pitched the flask in the corner.

Somethin's not right.

"Livewire, you in there?" the voice called out.

He fell to the floor unconscious.

CHAPTER FIVE

CHRIS WILKERSON exited the hospital as it turned dusk, and he walked a few blocks toward the Oak Hollow District. He and Katrina had dined on the block a few times at the Bridgewater Restaurant, the area's last hope for a revitalization of any sort.

I guess this is it. Chris Wilkerson, I hope you know what you're doing.

Walking toward the extensive building, he peered up at it, catching glimpses of silhouettes engaged in questionable behaviors. He moved toward the entryway and noted an etching in the stone of the building's outer wall.

THE OAK HOLLOW HOTEL — ERECTED 1926 BY DON WASSERMAN... MAY OUR FOLLY NEVER LEAD US ASTRAY. FOR W.W.

Never stepping into the building, Chris opened the door and looked around a moment.

What a sad decline. This place must have been so much more.

A voice called out from behind, "Not going to get very far, sir. You can't just come snoop around over here. Can't you respect the hallowed ground you're standing on?"

Who is this guy? Give me some space.

"What are you talking about? Hallowed ground? This place is a dump."

"Watch yourself. I've managed a pawn shop down the block for a while. There's something that just ain't right about it. I best get back over there. I was just on an evening stroll."

"It's a good night for that. I'm Chris Wilkerson."

The man extended his hand to shake Chris's, "Steve Renzell. Nice to meet you. Steer clear for your own good. I can't put my finger on why I feel implored to tell you this. Call it an intuition. I get 'em from time to time. I ain't no caretaker or wet nurse, though. I don't want you to get the wrong idea."

"Thanks for your concern. Have a good night," Chris said as Steve strolled the block toward Bridgewater. He walked away from the building in misdirection. Steve turned around to assess his whereabouts.

Go on now. Get out of here, Steve. I'm a grown man. Leave me be.

After Steve was out of sight, Chris moved back toward the door and entered the building's lobby. An older black woman draped in loose fuchsia-colored fabric approached Chris. She spoke in a Cajun accent, "Can I help you with somethin', honey? You look lost."

"I don't know. Maybe… I was told this building might help me…"

"Darlin', this place will do whatever you need it to if you treat it right. You hear me? Smoke one with me, will ya?"

"Sure. I could use a drag."

Let's see where this takes me.

"Oak Hollow. It's an area of many successes and failures. People grade a place based on its surroundings. I know the verdict on this joint may not be that great in *your* social circles, but there's a whole 'nother thing going on here behind the scenes. You know what I mean?"

Chris studied the room in enchantment. Despite mediocre maintenance through the years, it had good bones. The ground floor possessed an open layout with dried out fountains, worn tapestries, weathered pool tables, and red felt chairs. Clusters of people hovered in each corner. Some had fires lit and burning near busted out windows. Others hummed and chanted incantations. The peculiar place captivated Chris.

It's like another world in here.

17

"Did you hear me, honey?"

"I'm sorry. I was just looking around. Can I rent a room?"

"By the hour?"

"No. I'm a married man. What about for the month? What would it cost?"

"We own this place," she said. "The Wasserman's built it, and now it's mine. Daddy didn't last long in here. It was too hard on him after everything that happened."

"Riverton City Council hasn't shut you down yet? Looks like the place could use a major facelift. You must be failing auditor regulations a mile long."

"You don't know Precinct Three very well, mister."

"I'm sorry, I don't follow."

"We run Oak Hollow, man. The Wasserman's made a slew of deals back in the 20s and got us zoned in our own special way."

"You still haven't answered my question. Can I rent a room?"

"No, you can't rent a room. If you want to buy me out, I'm easy. Cash deal. No realtors."

"Buy you out? I just asked for a room. Not the building. What's in it for me?"

"There's a lot more to offer, darlin'. Let's just walk around for a minute. I'll show you. Back over here, northwest corner, we tell fortunes. Does that interest you?"

"No... no," he answered. "I'm a believing man. I want nothing to do with the spirit world."

"Suit yourself. Let me take you over here to the bar. Isn't it marvelous?"

Chris ran his hand down the side of the polished but dusty bar top.

"Yep. It still has the original cherry wood," she said. "Take a seat and pick your poison."

"I gave up the bottle. Too many men dead in my family from it."

"Fair enough, mister morality. Let's go over here — The Table of Vice. I've got more opportunities for pleasure."

"I'm sorry. Miss...?"

"Greenwich. Sylvia Greenwich."

"Miss Greenwich, I've got my own selfish agenda."

"I know you do. My only rules, whether you 'rent a room' or you take the entire building are simple, and they've *always* been the same. Don't you go having a lying tongue with me... Ain't no room in here for a false witness. There sure as hell ain't no room for stirring up trouble in the community or any damn haughty eyes. You respect us as if we are royalty answering to a higher power, you hear? You best not set your feet where you ain't welcome either. They'll rush to evil faster than you can count to three. I promised there wouldn't be any more innocent blood spilled here, either — no more wicked schemes. You get the idea. You said you're a believing man. This might even sound familiar."

Chris nodded. "Yeah. I catch your drift."

"Just sign the dotted line, honey."

What's going on here?

"I'm sorry? You have the paperwork ready already?" Chris said. "Something's not adding up. We only just started talking. I think it's time that I leave."

"Let's not stop what we've already started," she said. "Oak Hollow's been waiting for a visionary like you for ages. Don had the paperwork lined up long before he passed on to the next life. We just haven't had the right one come through the doors. Breathe some new life into us, and we'll get out of your hair."

"Give me a second to think."

"Okay. I'll scream at Katrina for ya."

What the...

"How do you know about Katrina?"

"Doesn't matter. You're here for help, aren't ya?"

"It does matter," he said. "I want some answers."

"Don't get testy with me! You can have her back. Now sign the dotted line."

Now you're just getting me angry, lady.

"What are you saying to me? Why should I trust you?"

She laughed. "You've got nothing to lose... but your wife... or your mind. Riverton's got plenty of those people running around already. Why add yourself to the list when you've got the opportunity of a lifetime right in front of you?"

"What are you talking about? This is weirding me out."

He heard a mysterious voice speak in a gruff tone, "Just sign it while you're still on this side of the headstone."

Sylvia smiled as she made eye contact with Chris. "Take a look around if you're not ready. I just have a feeling about you, Chris."

He grabbed her by the arm, pulling her toward him. "I never told you my name... or my Katrina's."

"You didn't have to, honey... Your beautiful soul screams it loud. Here you are."

The room remained dim. Chris grabbed the document from Sylvia, noting its peculiar resemblance to the texture of skin.

Is this grafted together?

Despite his reluctance, his desperation to give Katrina another chance overarched any rational thought process. He signed the document, and the entire room went dark without a soul in sight.

"Sylvia? You in here? My lighter's at the hospital."

The mysterious voice spoke again, appearing as a shadowy figure in the room's corner surrounded by cigar smoke. "Don't sweat it, Wilkerson. You're on my terms now — Sylvia's nothing more than a distant memory, all but dust and ash. I'll leave you alone. Just uphold the warnings Sylvia spoke earlier."

Lights and incandescent lanterns illuminated the space as Chris studied the large room. The Table of Vice had disappeared, there were no signs of the fires lit, and the bar was empty. The dated tapestries and fountains were full of garbage, syringes, and vermin. Chris walked across from one side of the ground floor of the building to the other. He found remnants from years earlier, but the appearance of the room had changed. Reaching in his shirt pocket, he examined the document he signed.

What do you know… the deed to the property. Too easy. What am I mixed up in now?

Struggling with the disorienting reality of his experience with Sylvia and the mysterious figure, he concluded, *Yes. This will be Creepy Nights. I love middle of the night epiphanies.*

Despite elements of good buried deep within, his seasonal appreciations for the dark became unhealthy fixations. Creepy Nights would be the place his unmentioned dream to sell scary stories would become a reality.

CHAPTER SIX

Just beneath the hotel, CREEPER JOE BONSALL lurked the fated Oak Hollow property's abandoned tunnels. He was not a towering presence, nor did he possess a notable girth. His skin became paler with time as he remained confined and away from the familiar scorch of the Texas sun. Isolation stripped the vivid blueness in his eyes. They now matched his pupils, and he had a pronounced hobble. He was dressed in a shredded burgundy toned bellhop uniform — ragged with scraps missing and chewed into by rats and years of wear and tear. Dust lingered in his pores, refusing to wash away despite many tireless efforts. He sat in silence, waiting for his next assignment from the one who kept him captive, the Shadow. Tormenting voices whispered in his head, one after another.

Forever trapped. You damned fool. You never listened and you'll never leave. Your mother is disgusted with you, now and forever.

The Shadow emerged. "You should have listened. You know what this place is?"

"A subway tunnel," Joe uttered in dejection.

"No. You're mistaken. It's much more than just a tunnel, and we both know that."

Joe remained silent. His look hinted at the tantalizing isolation he faced in his earlier years.

"It's a gamble messing with the likes of you, Joe," the Shadow said. "Thing is, I'm tired of seeing these tunnels so devoid of life. Sylvia and the other restless fifty-three are out of the way, and the folly business has dried up." They walked through the tunnel side by side until Joe separated himself, pulling further away from his captor.

"We'll turn this tunnel into a lair — a proper resting place for all fifty-four of them," the Shadow said. "Leaving them to haunt the hotel would not be fair to Chris after he signed the dotted line. They've toiled for ages in the lobby above, waiting for a redeemer. A redeemer, Joe." He kept on, "As long as you play by 'my' rules, I'll help you get them here, but you'll have to capture them. Let me be clear, I forbid you from taking out your rage like you have in the past. You've been damned in here a long while, and you know something… that was all *your* doing. I'm going to let you loose."

"I've been trapped. Maybe I deserved it," Joe replied.

They came toward a waterfall. Joe dunked his head into the spring just beneath to exit the conversation. His face and movements became youthful and recharged as he came up from beneath.

"That's better," the Shadow said. "The Spring of Life will have its way. Don't expect involvement from me beyond giving them a nudge. We can't keep welcoming ghosts down here. It wouldn't be right. Get Chris more invested in the property up top. Leave him a few bread crumbs. As for the tunnel, I'll leave that to you. We'll give these weary souls what they deserve, a second chance at life… not in 1928… but in 1982, linking them up with fifty-four of the most vegetative beings on this side of the grave. I needn't say more."

Joe remained uncertain of the future. The tunnel could be a place for joy and for sorrow — two absolutes well solidified in his mind for years as he remained far from civilization. This sentiment was not all dark and sinister, and neither was he. But when nightfall struck, he struggled to control his sick impulses — a problem carried since his youth in an unraveling ritual that was always the same. He would light a fire in the tunnel, chanting unfamiliar words as he circled around it in a way that only he could — speaking in a glossolalia that grew louder and louder with time until he would fall to the floor unconscious. This was all in a momentary darkness in the brain that led to the hours where the Creeper within him and the darkest parts of Oak Hollow came to life. Their entanglement remained incomprehensible — but youthful defiance came at a cost. Life was different, and he remained trapped in a state of being far worse — in a fate that would lead him to places he should never again go.

Joe Bonsall's rapid decline from being a spry, seeing young man to a tormented and lifeless soul gnawed away at him without mercy for years — like a rotting wood susceptible to the worst of termites.

CHAPTER SEVEN

As the night sky shined upon him, CHRIS WILKERSON inspected the back of the hotel property. He stared at the stars hovering above until he tripped on an unmarked panel raised slightly above the ground.

What is this?

He collected a crowbar from the adjacent, cream-colored storage building and worked to pry it loose. The small building's positioning seemed to serve as something of a cover for the panel and the entrance and exit of its visitors. Chris gritted his teeth as he lifted the lid. Looking down into the hole, he noted metal rebar steps protruding in a well-defined line. Deliberating a moment, he descended into the tight, dark space, scaling its twelve steps toward the bottom. He arrived into the lower part of the shaft, staring upon the multi-footed gap to the floor. An open hatch led into the area below. Dropping to the ground level, he grunted.

Ouch. That was further than I thought.

He studied his surroundings. It was a long and dark tunnel with only the faint glow in the eyes of an unintroduced acquaintance and a few dim lights lining the ceiling.

This place is huge.

A scratchy and whiny voice called out as clammy hands grabbed him by the arm to pull him off the ground, "Let me help you, Chris. What brings you here? I didn't invite you here now, did I...?"

Who's this guy? I don't know him.

Chris shook his head. "I guess not. I didn't realize anyone was here. I was just exploring the property. I'm starting a new business. Creepy Nights... Riverton will be better off because of it... just you wait."

"Creepy Nights, eh? I like a good creep out. As for Riverton, I don't doubt your impending success at all," the mysterious tunnel dweller said. "I admire your... ingenuity, but you have to admit... you know what this place was before, right?"

Chris ran his fingers through his thinning hair while pondering on the question.

"A hotel?"

"Ding ding ding! You have any idea how many terrible things happen in hotels? Any idea at all?"

Chris shook his head. "I guess not. Just what I've seen in the movies and read in a few of my favorite books. It's fiction."

The whiny-voiced individual grinned. "Well, I've been here much longer than I want to admit, and I've seen an awful lot of things, and let me just tell you. The reason... the reason this place is no longer a hotel anymore isn't pretty."

"What do you mean?"

The character motioned to Chris to move down the tunnel as he showed him around. "October 29th, 1928... Blood and screams. Lots and lots of them."

Get real, weirdo.

"Okay, well... that's in the past," Chris said. "What's fifty-something years got to do with me?"

"Fifty-four years! Trust me, I would know better than you!" The creep clicked the back of his teeth with his tongue. "Arrogance. Or, perhaps you're just..."

"Just what?"

He slapped Chris on the back. "Brushing off a spree of deaths on a property is a slippery slope. Especially, if your business is going to specialize in telling stories that revolve around such — death, that is. Don't you think?"

Chris's stomach bottomed out. "Deaths? What are you getting at? I didn't even explain what my business was. What's going on?"

"That's for me to know and you to ponder. Maybe the title gave it away," the weirdo remarked.

Fear crippled Chris's mind.

Talking that way to elevate yourself makes so much sense. Doesn't it? Who am I kidding? I'm humoring him.

The creep put his arm around Chris as they continued to walk. While moving through, Chris reviewed the various pipes that ran across the ceilings and the drips and trickles of the tunnel.

Stay cautious. Something's not right.

"Sure... Okay," Chris said. "What did you say your name was?"

"Just call me Joe. I was a bellhop at the hotel back before the Great Depression hit us full force."

You don't look too bad for being alive way back then. Then again, there's no way you'd still be this young.

A gulp engulfed Chris's throat.

"There's more for you to see in here," Joe said. "I know it's dark, but your eyes will adjust."

·　　·　　·　　·　　·

The pair visited for hours. Joe was a character full of stories, all the while keeping a mysterious allure. Most of which were more twisted than Chris ever wanted to hear or know about. Despite this, it was apparent that the gruesome details delighted Joe.

Joe's voice echoed down the tunnel, "Yeah, so that's when I put them in the furnace and admired their shrieks of terror. It was quite satisfying. The smell of searing flesh... the sounds of shrieking sinners... and the retribution for the worst kinds of people to walk this beautiful earth."

I can't take any more of this.

Chris felt himself gagging as he pondered upon the vivid and grotesque descriptions.

"Really? Joe, are you that proud of these situations? I like scary stories because they are fiction. I want nothing to do with them in reality."

Joe popped a peanut in his mouth. He crunched its shell and spat it toward a neighboring fire pit that glowed. After a moment of silence, he hoisted the pewter cup full of unshelled legumes toward Chris.

Chris waved it away.

I don't want anything from your filthy hands, he thought.

"You'll never understand the world as I see it," Joe said. "I've always seen it differently. I'm a seer. No. I don't have visions flashing before my eyes like the privileged few that do. It's just human behavior. Body language. Tone of voice. Hobbies. Interests. It's called acute observation, better known as paying attention. Something very few of us do anymore. You could benefit from learning the art form if you apply yourself. Don't expect any help from me, though. Heh-heh."

Chris stopped the conversation. "Okay. I think I've heard enough today."

"Why don't I make you something to eat while you're here?" Joe said. "You know… to make your trip worthwhile. Hell, it might even motivate you to come back and visit again. I get kind of lonely here."

He stepped away to the opposite side of the tunnel, revealing an access door to a giant freezer stored behind the walls.

"It's all linked to the bottom of your building," Joe said.

My building… I like the sound of that. Finally, something that's mine without the Reinhold family crest plastered all over it.

"Chris… Chris… Your mind must have been wandering…"

How did you know that?

"There are a few passages and connections in the basement level of the hotel leading into this place... into my place," Joe said. "That is, if you know how to get through, and I'm the only one that knows that. As a matter of fact, this used to be the hotel's overflow freezer. They relocated it back in the 50s, right before it went under. The best part of it… it's still connected to your electricity lines, partner. You ever have quail before? It's a bit of a delicacy here. I save only the best for my privileged guests!"

Chris remained upbeat, despite a growing fear and eagerness to leave the strange labyrinth. "Sure, why not?"

Joe brought over two of the frosted birds from the freezer, striking a match on the front of his teeth and lighting a nearby grill.

"Don't worry. No wind in the tunnel to snuff it out."

"Yeah, but what about the fumes? Couldn't that hurt us?"

"Not a chance. Did you not see the fire lit over there? Same idea, genius," Joe said, taking a whiff of the smoke from the match. "Ah, nice. We have two miles for it to dissipate. Besides, I've got it vented in strategic spots — you just have to trigger it to make the vents open."

"And how do you do that?"

"Now, if I revealed all the secrets of this place to you now, wouldn't that take away the fun for us? I'm not going to tell you... yet. I'll give you a few projects, and then we'll see if you're up to standards. Then, I might tell you more. I'll tell you this much, the tunnel is full of more fun, terror, and creepy than *you* could ever fathom. That's all *you* need to know."

"Okay then, fair enough. I might as well." Chris clasped his hands together and sighed.

Joe dropped the quail onto the grill top. "The bird's got to get nice and charred. You learn to eat different in here. More like God made us to, you know? None of that refined 'big city' eating in fancy restaurants. Just two guys having high-quality bird in an abandoned subway tunnel."

"Subway tunnel? *That's* what this was. I remember hearing about that in grade school. You got anything to drink?"

"Of course I do. The question for you, Mr. Wilkerson — Do you want the stuff for the boys or the stuff for the men?"

Chris slicked his hair back, trying not to show impatience. "I don't know anymore. Surprise me."

Joe laughed, eking out a few words, "Okay, I'll *surprise* you."

He proceeded to the south end of the tunnel with two pewter cups. Chris continued to monitor the birds as they cooked.

How long are you going to be gone? I don't want to screw this up. Who knows what you'd do to me?

Chris flipped the birds over so the other side could crisp.

Joe arrived back with drinks. "Now, that's a foul! Fowley boy... I never told you to do that, did I? Making hasty assumptions. Ah, Ah, Ah!" He shook his finger at him and said, "I'm just kidding. That was a test, Chris, and you... passed! If you'd left the bird to cook and burn all the way through while I wasn't here, you would have failed, and we couldn't be sharing this splendid meal together. I mean, I wouldn't have any use for you. You'd be a dummy. Heh-heh."

Chris struggled to fake a laugh.

Who is this weirdo?

CHAPTER EIGHT

The pair dined and deliberated over the bird as CHRIS WILKERSON forced conversation to ease his anxiety.

Is it just me, or are his eyes getting bluer and brighter?

"You're looking a little different already," Chris said. "How often do you eat?"

"When I need to. Being malnourished and away from people for a while will do that to you. I never left since... since I decided to call this home."

"Why not?"

"I like it too much."

"Like what?"

"Never mind that," Joe replied. "Quit grilling me and eat up."

After Chris munched on the quail a bit, he spoke again, "Not bad. Not bad at all. You know, I kind of like this. Peeling back the wings and everything was weird at first, but I'm a strange guy, and I think you are, too. Just the way the Good Lord made us, right?"

Joe's pale face soured. "No. That's the depravity of man. The fall. You know, Garden of Eden. The whole sin shebang." He picked a shred of the bird's flesh from his teeth.

"That's one way to look at it," Chris said, taking a sip from the pewter cup.

This stuff tastes odd. Thought it was just water.

"Well, let's get to work," Joe said. "I want to do more in here. The city doesn't even acknowledge the tunnels anymore. What a failure to Old Town Riverton, not to mention the associated expense of keeping the unworthy dodos out. The outer entry points are sealed, and I've never been bothered. You came down the street level's only way in. There are other ways out, though. The doors only open one way, and they're engaged from the inside out, masked and hidden away. There are a lot of areas to spread out. It's not just straight lines either — there are little passageways throughout the place engineered to minimize flooding... you know, that sort of thing. I'm making modifications to it. I intend to exploit people in town to get the supplies I need. You know, the various things I'd like to have — to tweak and make this place more enjoyable. They won't know the difference, just ignorant imbeciles. That's all they are."

"You intend to exploit them? It seems to me like you're well on your way already." Chris dropped the pewter cup to the floor. "Hang on a minute. From all you're telling me, you've been here for years. Why haven't you made more progress?"

"Calm down. I'm not comfortable talking about my time in purgatory. He wouldn't... I couldn't do what I wanted for those years. Let's just leave it at that."

What are you talking about?

"Purgatory? You dead? Because last I checked... I'm not," Chris said.

"I'm not going to discuss that with you any further. Now, about my tunnel..."

Chris interrupted as he looked around for an exit, "Okay. Look, I'm sorry I've upset you. What about more lights? It's too dark. I'm guessing you must see a lot better than me or something. I can see you're into the whole hermit in the ground motif. I hate to break it to you, man, but you're not the first."

I've got to get out of here now.

The glow in Joe's eyes brightened. "Thanks for noticing. I do see well," he said. "I really do. I don't like it bright. There ain't no one that wants to see these pores any brighter than they are. I've got a new vision for this tunnel now while I pay off the rest of my penance."

"Penance?"

"I'm challenged to collect a specific group of lesser people to make up for the sins of my past."

Chris furrowed his brow. "Lesser? You mean like the indigent and the destitute? Or something else?"

"Think more in terms of purposeless people because of life's unexpected setbacks."

"You're speaking as if you're expecting *me* to help," Chris said. "What's it to me? Is that fair to me, God, or Satan, or whoever the hell your master is? Are we partners now?"

Joe stared at Chris. "Is that what *you* want? I swear I'll make your business something special if you want me to. Shake on it?"

I can't control it. He keeps luring me in. Sad thing is, I drank the kool-aid, too. I'm just enamored by the mystique. Get cautious, before it's too late. There goes my right hand, anyway.

The two shook hands, and the tunnel thundered with a loud clap as Joe clawed into Chris's wrist with his unkempt fingernails.

"Ah, shit! You cut me."

"Total accident," Joe said. "Here, let's wring the blood out in this pewter cup. It'll stop before you know it. Would you look at that? It's filling up quick. Let me just run this over here and get another. I'll be right back." Joe disappeared into the shadows of the tunnel.

The date of Chris and Joe's peculiar union was October 29th, 1982.

Joe returned with two pewter cups. He handed one to Chris and he sipped from it. Joe poured the clear liquid from the other cup onto Chris's bleeding wrist. The penetrated skin soaked it in, healing in a moment's time.

You've got to be kidding me.

"What was that?" Chris said.

"Take another drink and see for yourself."

Yeah, right. I'm smarter than I look. Who knows how long it will take before this stuff wears off?

"And why should I?"

"You'd be a fool not to, Chris. You're my guest, and I welcome you to consume it. Don't you like what you see?"

Chris drank the semi-sweet liquid again and the pain in his body dissipated.

"A path to relief. Know the pain… and learn the contrast. That's the best way." Joe spoke lingering words that would hover in the back of Chris's weary mind, "I like to call this place, 'Level Zero.' Since *you* are going into the scare business, we can make it out to be one hell of a ride. That would be fun. Wouldn't it? Heh-heh."

Struggling not to slur his words, Chris raised his voice, "Stop laughing and let's get down to business." An otherworldly inebriation took hold.

What's happening to me?

Creeper Joe's eyes turned yellow, and his voice became an octave deeper. He grew stronger and more energized as he transformed. "Don't you order me… You're going into business with me, dummy! Not the other way around. I can give you a taste of scary if that's what you want… Is that what you want?" He leaned in close, breathing in a savage fury toward Chris's face as the warmth of his breath hit the whites of his eyes. A brass syringe fell from Joe's pocket onto the floor. He kicked it aside.

Timidity lingered in Chris's voice as he backed away, "No. I don't want that. I'm sorry. This whole situation is a little… out of my comfort zone."

"*You* are going into the business of scaring people!" Joe yelled. "There's no such thing as a 'comfort zone' anymore. You're professionally committing yourself to forever staying *out* of your… comfort zone and vowing to do that to as many others as you can. Why is that, Chris? Why is that? Oh, I know, maybe you're just old-fashioned? Perhaps, two men having a meal together in a dark room seems odd to you. Not much of an '80s man, are you?"

Chris shook his head.

You have no idea.

He looked at his restored arm and said, "No, no. It's not that. It's you. You're not meant to be here. You've admitted that already."

Joe's demeanor changed as he massaged Chris's shoulder. "I have? I already told you more than you needed to know about me. Some mysteries are best left unexplained. I can help you benefit from some of these… mysteries — if you play ball with me. Will you play ball?"

I feel like I'm going to be sick.

He maintained his composure as he replied, "Okay, yeah. Sure thing."

Another thunderous clap knocked him to the ground, unconscious. The tunnel brightened as he and Joe appeared in a baseball stadium. A surrounding crowd of flat people watched them from the stands, accompanied by a dull hum of stadium noise. The exhibition was already in progress, and the score was five to four. Joe had the lead.

Chris stood hovering over home plate, mystified by the transformation.

What was in that drink? Good grief. That's the last time I ever accept anything from a stranger.

"What do you think there, Chrissy boy? Let's play ball," Creeper Joe bellowed from behind the pitcher's mound as he donned a red catcher's mask.

The organ played, and the crowd roared. Joe wound up, preparing to pitch.

"I'll give you a fast ball. Right down the middle. You better get a home run."

He delivered the pitch, and Chris's swing missed the ball.

Come on, now.

"Strike one, sucker! How about some pin stripes? Your uniform's looking a little dull," Joe said.

The next ball dropped from the sky into Joe's hands.

"Same pitch. Don't blow it… You can do it, buddy. I'd hate to call you a loser. You don't want to be a… loser, do you?"

Cheeky dickens. Not going to trash talk me.

He gripped the bat — his fury increasing as he prepared to swing. Creeper Joe delivered the pitch. The ball flew across the left of home plate at an obnoxious speed, striking Chris in the chest.

"Oops. I'm sorry about that!" Joe said. "I could see the rage in your eyes. Don't stir up trouble in the community with your anger. That's one of the Cardinal Rules here, you know. Your anger will lead to that, even to having hands that shed innocent blood, you creep."

"What?"

"I said… it's a Cardinal Rule. Don't you read the Bible? Proverbs 6. I would have pegged you for some kind of Bible Trivia champ. Or wait, are you more of a chump? Heh-heh. I'll give you another. It could be the most important swing of your life — what you have left of it, anyway!"

Joe raised his eyebrows up and down a few times before hurling the ball. Chris swung early, catching a piece with a familiar crack. It soared through the sky toward the right-field fence.

"Going, going, gone! Home run for Chris Wilkerson! Time for the crowd to go wild! Oh, wait," Joe paused. "I'm sorry. The perfect score is five to four — not five to five. You're not allowed to change that. I should have told you. Oops."

What the hell is going on?

Without warning, balls plummeted from the sky toward Joe as he flung them full force at Chris, pelting him mercilessly. Creeper Joe grew animated and moved, resembling an over-caffeinated pitching machine. The pelt-a-thon continued until Chris dropped to the ground. Soon after, the stadium's lights went out, and the synthetic crowd faded away. Chris lay flat on his back, dazed. After taking a few minutes to recover, he came to his senses, staring at the tunnel's ceiling as a rat ran across his chest.

"Loser. Loser. Loser! Sorry, Chrissy boy. I rigged that game. My stadium, my rules. Capiche? My tunnel, my rules!"

I hope I'm seeing the glorious light. Heaven help me.

Chris passed out.

CHAPTER NINE

TODD ADAMS awoke in RGH.

Crappy room. I'm not that important, am I? Not a single card or flower to wish me well, either. Nope. Not even one visitor...

He pushed the panic button on the remote attached to the bed, staring up at the television in the room as the evening news played. No significant stories, nothing to pique any interest. He yanked the IV from his arm and sat up, feeling a numbness below the waist.

I guess I didn't miss anything important. Where's Lorrie? I'm the one that should be dead.

A full-figured woman entered the room. Her forehead wrinkled as she squinted to study Todd.

Aren't you going to say something? Stop staring...

"Hi, I'm Nurse Rickle. We weren't sure if you would *ever* wake up. You are one lucky man."

"Lucky? Why do you say that?"

"They say your plane was all but burned up on one side," she said. "Something snuffed out the fire closest to you. I'm very sorry, sir... but your other passenger didn't make it."

He scoffed. "And *you're* the one to tell me? Some night shift nurse? Is this as good as it gets?"

She nodded. "You'll get enough bumps and bruises in your life to appreciate it more one of these days. I'll let the doctor know your back with us. I've got to get to my next patient. Must be something in the water around here today. She just woke up, too. You two both arrived on the same day. Never seen that before. Strange coincidence. Mercy. It's time for a night off. This is a little stranger than I'm up for." She walked toward the door.

Todd's mind raced as he looked around the room, hoping to find some clarity. Memories of the event all seemed a blur.

I need a method. A plan. Some way to rationalize and justify what happened. At least I'm not handcuffed to the bed yet. The amnesia's got me scatterbrained.

Todd Adams was nothing more than a broken man with a fractured mind. *Enraptured by struggle, he glimpsed a piece of an unfamiliar past.*

A ribbon-cutting ceremony at a hotel hinted at an unfamiliar period and life. He stood in front of the building, clipping the ribbon as onlookers applauded.

Good Lord, they're going to have to up my dosage. I've gone mental.

As he came back into the moment, the door to the room squeaked open, clanging shut behind a doctor in a lab coat. He approached Todd's hospital bed, extending his hand to introduce himself.

"I'm Doctor Hicks. To be frank, I never expected to have this conversation with you. All tests told us you were brain dead. Perhaps it's a blessing in disguise that *you* get a second chance. I wish Lorrie had that chance. I expected the toxicology screen on you to be nothing short of questionable, but, somehow, it came back negative. The odds are in your favor, though. I have no doubt in my mind that you were in any sober condition to fly that plane. Your story's been all over the news. All I can say is… this is your time to shine bright."

Todd studied Dr. Hicks.

Look at you. Thirty something… A nice bird's nest on top of your head. Tall and slender. Intelligent. Single. Who knows what else you did with Lorrie? If I had my wits about me, I'd slug you now. Stop thinking that way. Play it smarter, Todd.

"I… don't remember a thing I should."

"It'll be fuzzy for a while. I would expect nothing less from a coma patient arriving in your condition. My bigger concern is the risk you are to yourself and to others."

"Risk? What do you mean?"

"You're going to need a lot of therapy. We have to get you physically and mentally back into shape. A brain injury is no overnight recovery."

"Doc, I don't know. I feel different. It's hard to explain. Can you let me walk?"

"Walking is weeks away. Just be grateful you're alive."

Todd's mind drifted.

He stood in a large hotel lobby packed with guests dressed in fine garb surrounded by ornate décor. He explored the place of intrigue within his mind, despite having never been there.

"Todd, Todd, you with me...?"

"I'm sorry, doc. I'm just trying to wrap my head around things."

"You know Lorrie worked up here... and off the record, we had our share of chats the last year or so. She told me how you were sometimes. I'll do my best to avoid the conflict of interest because I'm the only double duty shrink and MD in this hospital. There's not enough evidence to lock you up, but then again, *I'm* not the one carrying the guilt. We'll get you back on your feet... Questions for me?"

"I don't remember much, doc. Only messed-up fragments. When will it come back?"

"In God's time. In God's time. Let me be clear, I'll give you fair treatment, regardless of how *I* feel about the situation. RGH could use some good press given our recent wrongful death suits. Keep in mind, I'm the one to discharge you, so be wise."

CHAPTER TEN

CHRIS WILKERSON awoke on the eighth floor of The Oak Hollow Hotel building (the soon-to-be home for Creepy Nights) — a place that would claim him as its own.

How did I end up in here? Good grief.

The area was wide open, once a ballroom of sorts responsible for hosting the most exquisite parties. The space still housed various pieces of dusty furniture left over from the hotel. There were red felt chairs, tapestries, and bear skins strewn about the floors and walls. He walked around the dark room as the moonlight shined through the windows. Magazines in the room dated back to the 1950s, spread across the top of a worn coffee table. To its left, there was an end table with a few tobacco pipes and a Tiffany lamp on it. He laid down on an old blue sofa, checking out a few minutes before he reflected upon his encounter with Joe in the tunnel.

It was a weird night, but I'm inspired. A new perspective won't hurt. The fifty-four fast ball pelts scared the hell out of me, though.

The loneliness he felt was eerie, leaving him unsure if it was the silence, the isolation, or the emotional toll of the day that wore upon him.

Daybreak arrived, and Chris walked several blocks toward RGH.

Katrina, let's see how you're doing.

When he arrived at the nurse's station, Nurse Rickle's eyes lit up.

"Chris, you've got to hurry down the hall. She's awake! We were calling you all night, but the line just kept ringing."

"Wow. Yeah, I didn't make it home. Stayed at a hotel down the street."

Maybe there was something to last night. I never expected that.

As Chris strolled past other hospital rooms, a man moved back and forth in the hallway, relearning the mechanics of walking.

Nurse Rickle stopped and spoke to the man, "Keep up the excellent work, Todd. Dr. Hicks will have my hide for letting you out of bed so soon, but your progress is remarkable."

"Thanks," he said.

"Who could have imagined it?" Nurse Rickle said. "This guy was in just as bad a shape as Katrina, and he's already walking overnight. I suspect she'll be right behind him. Don't ask me why… It's just a feeling I have."

Chris came around the corner and looked at Katrina. He gazed into her eyes, and a chill ran down his spine. It seemed impossible that a person's soul could alter their appearance. The woman he gazed upon was only a shell of Katrina. Something had changed.

"Chris!"

CHAPTER ELEVEN

Weeks passed by, and CHRIS WILKERSON was ready for adjustments. He and Katrina sat on the ground floor of their townhome apartment. Her eyes glimmered with an unrecognizable perkiness while she recounted her latest dreamy experience. Reclining in one of the plaid printed easy chairs; he watched her mouth move but missed the words.

I'm ready to hear myself think again. Day after day, she goes on and on about another life, and I can't stand it anymore. How many hours are we going to waste talking about her eccentric and excitable dreams? I used to think I was too much that way. It's like I'm dealing with a different person, now. Talking about the things like they were realities. Vivid visions of the roaring 20s and stacks of cash. I'm sick of it.

"Chris, you didn't hear a thing I said, did you?"

"Of course I did. You were telling me all about the grandiose 1920s. I hate to break it to you, but we're not living in a world of Gatsby. The Reinhold legacy is nothing to sneeze at, though. This is an enjoyable life."

"No. I was telling you to call me 'Sylvia.' Sylvia Greenwich."

What the…?

"What did you say?"

"I said, call me Sylvia Greenwich, darlin'. You've got your own selfish agenda, don't you?" She chuckled and placed her arm around Chris as she kissed the top of his head.

Who are you? This can't be real.

Chris stood up, proceeding to the front door. He called out to Katrina, "I can't have this conversation right now. I need some fresh air."

"Take all the time you need. I'll be waitin'."

She grinned at Chris. The eyes of Sylvia Greenwich looked back at him through her.

He dashed several blocks from their downtown townhome, making a beeline toward The Oak Hollow Hotel, the new home for Creepy Nights.

Dear God, help me. I'm too young to be losing it.

He raced toward the lobby as a record player played *A Flock of Seagulls* tune.

"What do I do?" Chris yelled. "I don't understand. How did I end up in this situation?"

The Shadow emerged and said, "You got yourself into this, Chris. It's only fair that you pay up. You know what to do with her."

Chris hurled a rock from one of the lobby fountains at the record player, and the ambient music stopped upon impact.

Swirls of thoughts raced within.

What am I supposed to do with this? Some unexplained figure is giving me marching orders now. No matter what I do, I'm screwed.

The passing seconds seemed endless.

I shouldn't have had that third cup of coffee.

The Shadow spoke again, "You know what? This land has much to offer you... if you'll let it."

Beads of sweat streamed down the sides of Chris's temples as his heart pulsated faster.

Call the undertaker now. My mind has checked out of Riverton. I can't handle this anymore.

He ran outside. Katrina stood there waiting.

What do I say? Crap.

"What were you doing in there?" she said. "You can't just run off on me like that and not expect consequences."

"Katrina, what else can I do? All this talk of the roaring 20s... and now Sylvia Greenwich. It's making me feel like *I'm* the one who's cuckoo."

"Cuckoo?" she said. "What are you trying to say about me? What is this? Are you hiding something from me? You got a fling on the side going on?"

Chris struggled to reply to the barrage of questions, pivoting toward misdirection, "You know good and well what it is. Get in there and see for yourself, *Sylvia*! They've got medications for identity crises like you're facing. I think it's time we get you some help, honey."

Gazing into her eyes, he realized it was no longer Sylvia he yelled at, but Katrina. Her tears welled up.

"What are you trying to do to me? You know my recovery will take some time," she said. "What were you messing around with while I was away... or *who* were you messing around with? Is there something else you want to talk to me about?"

"I don't know anymore," Chris said. He ran his hand down the wall of the building as the hair on his arms stood up.

"You better shoot straight with me, or we're done. I don't have to put up with this. You know how well off mother is.... was."

"You know what? I think it's best if we take some time apart," Chris remarked.

Katrina scoffed, cocking her fist back. "So, you are hiding something from me, then? What's her name?"

"It's not like that. Nothing at all like that. You wouldn't understand."

"Try me."

Chris sighed. "I'm launching a new business called Creepy Nights. Maybe after a break, we can team up again."

"Creepy Nights? What kind of name is that? Some kind of strip club for vampires?"

Chris laughed as they walked through the ground floor, studying the remnants of the place's former radiance. They stopped in front of a weathered and worn painting of a man in a suit and top hat with a pipe. The nameplate beneath read William Wasserman, 1856-1910.

"Of course not. Look around the building. I know it's not much yet, but I'll be fixing it up. Creepy Nights is a pay by the minute call center hotline. People will pay hand over fist for horror stories. Trust me. I know this will sell in Riverton. You've seen how the people flock to the horror films. It'll be just like taking candy from a baby."

"I'm sorry, Chris. Yeah, we need to take a break. I'm not feeling this right now. How much did you sink into this? All I see are construction bills, repairs, and dollar signs."

"I'd rather not talk about it. Money was never a worthwhile point in this deal."

"Says you. It was *mom's* money. If we're not talking about finances anymore, then we've got no business being shacked up. I'll get our divorce papers started right away. Are you going to fight me on that?"

Chris brushed a layer of dust from the painting and they became choked up by it as it spread across the room.

"Forget it. Let's separate awhile. I'll check on you in a few months. If you get a little antsy, you can do the same. I'm gonna take residence up top."

Katrina grinned. "Suit yourself. Chris Wilkerson, the high and mighty — towering over Riverton and looking down on the rest of us in his dilapidated building. What about WGBO? You're just gonna leave the radio station behind to manage itself?"

"Wayne and Ron will take it over. I've already discussed it with them."

"Those guys couldn't tell their left foot from their right. Are you going to trust them to keep *you* afloat?"

"See you later, Syl… I mean Katrina."

Katrina looked back at him in an unfamiliar manner as Sylvia's eyes emerged. "You can call me Sylvia. I like that." She grabbed him by the arm and pulled him close as she kissed him on the cheek. "Speak to you soon."

CHAPTER TWELVE

After continued struggles with Katrina, CHRIS WILKERSON moved the bulk of his personal items from the Reinhold estate and townhome, relocating much of it to Creepy Nights. Late one evening, after several nights away from Katrina, he walked the floor, peering out the windows studying Riverton and its changing skyline.

Katrina, I wish you were here. I miss you. Not Sylvia, just you.

Wayne and Ron had taken over his job managing WGBO and the associated responsibilities, only calling a few times for guidance. Things appeared to be working out okay as he began a new chapter in his life.

I'm not going back to the tunnel anytime soon. Joe's a little too far out there for my liking. We'll catch up one of these days. No harm... no fowl... wait... no harm, no foul!

Time went on, and Chris continued to improve the Creepy Nights facility, even going as far as having an express elevator installed on the east wing of the building linking Level Eight to Level Zero and an alternate express route that ran from Level Zero to Level Six. He informed the installation crew that it routed to a small storage container in the basement. Within the elevator, Chris had a key panel installed for the Level Six to Level Zero express ride. He wanted to fend off the risk of Joe or other vagrants getting into Creepy Nights without his approval.

Hoping to grow awareness toward the business, Chris brainstormed commercials. Advertising would be his first venture in getting the word out to the surrounding area. Resting in an office chair near an old desk in the room's corner, he leaned back and propped his feet up.

How did that song on that movie go? Man, that was terrible.

Something catchy would stick best… just like that one had with him. The tune would become stuck on a loop in his mind for hours. The short jingle was far more effective than its producers could have ever imagined. Perhaps, even more memorable than the film itself. It may have been stupid, but it worked well. And then, that's when the missing piece hit him, just like he hoped. He jotted it down.

Scary, scary, that's what we do. Scary, scary, we say boo. Scary, scary, we'll make your dreams come true! NIGHTMARES! HAHAHAHAHA! 1-800-SCARE-ME.

He played an improvised tune on a dusty *Yamaha* he brought from the townhome. He sang to himself. It was short, goofy, and effective. The KISS method worked just fine. Keep it simple, stupid.

I know what I'll do. I'll make a fictionalized version of Joe and play him myself. We'll do the split-screen thing they are doing on the movies and music videos nowadays. I'll call him… 'The Creeper.' That's a shtick that's sure to win. I can see it now. Throw on a little costume shop makeup. Dress up like a bellhop… Hell, I can even sing the theme song for Creepy Nights in a voice like Joe's. I've got it.

WINTER 1982-1983

CHAPTER THIRTEEN

NANCY HELBENS pulled the car into the large lot next to the Creepy Nights facility. The building was odd considering its surroundings, sticking out above the abandoned warehouses and storefronts. The pastel purple accents with darker tones across the structure made it unique.

Is this it? Man, it needs some help, a woman's touch. The paint job is fresh, but it's awful. That's for sure. Just another receptionist gig, Nancy. No big deal. Answer a few phones. Greet some customers. Shine the big man's shoes. Maybe use the lint roller every now and then. I need this job.

Comatose for three months, her accident left her out of sorts. Nothing was quite the same since her waking. Her ex-husband, Chip, left her, and her confusion and disorganization worsened. The hardest part of the breakup was moving back in with her mother, who paid little attention to her. Nancy struggled — being enlightened in unusual ways. Despite these challenges, she was able to keep up appearances.

I guess I'll go into the lobby, then. I'm fifteen minutes early. I'm sure they'll send someone to greet me soon.

She sat down in a chair just inside as a lesser-known song from *The Police* came through a speaker. She studied the room, noting nothing but dust, a small container of unopened window cleaning solution, and a yellow squeegee bucket — ever-apparent reflections that no one cared. The clock on the wall remained stuck on 1:23 — its second hand ticking, yet never moving forward. As she settled in, the lobby remained empty. Feelings of anxiety crept up upon her.

Maybe I'm here on the wrong day... or I'm here at the wrong time. No. Wait, is this even the right address?

Nancy pulled out the loose-leaf paper folder assembled with the interview details, recalling the strange phone call with Chris Wilkerson the previous day.

Yes. Correct place. Correct time. That's a relief.

Minutes ticked away. Still, no one appeared to greet or welcome her. A ringing startled her as it chirped behind the receptionist station. She walked over and answered it.

"Hello. Creepy Nights lobby, this is Nancy."

"Oh, good. It's Chris Wilkerson. Glad you made it... Monday-Friday, 10AM-6:30PM. We'll be in touch. Welcome to the team."

Nancy picked at her teeth as she replied, "Wait, you're not going to interview me?"

"Na... I have too many other things to do. I'll touch base with you when time permits. Five an hour sound okay?"

That's a pleasant surprise. My last job paid $3.35.

"Absolutely!"

"Good. Well, get busy. Tidy up down there. There's a filing cabinet full of stuff to organize. I have a few house rules that I'll have you post throughout the facility. They've been here longer than you or me. Make the lobby your own. Make it homey. I'm good with whatever you decide. After all, that's part of what I'll be paying you for. There's a kitchen around the corner from the reception. Help yourself to a drink anytime. I'll call in a lunch order for you to pick up soon."

"Sounds good," Nancy said. She sat down at the cluttered desk as a smile overtook her.

"By the way, I don't have anyone taking calls yet. I'll start recruiting soon. If we get anything, just get their information and tell them we'll call them back. I've got to go. Talk soon. Bye."

"Bye."

I'm finally going to get a routine and make some money again. Two months of interviewing, and then this materializes in moments. It's too good to be true, she thought.

Nancy peered around the room as she acclimated to her surroundings. Other than a few misplaced calendars and forgettable taxidermy, she had many opportunities to bring the lobby to life.

So much to improve upon, but mountains of potential, and plenty to keep me busy. I can move out of mom's. Thank God. Job security!

The phone rang.

It must be Wilkerson.

"So, what'll it be for lunch, boss?"

The voice on the line crackled through the phone, "Huh? I want a story. Transfer me to option one, please."

"I'm sorry, sir. We don't have anyone available right now to help. Can I get a callback number? We'll get someone in touch with you."

"334-7812… My name's John."

Nancy prepped to hang up the phone. "Okay. Thanks, John."

The line went dead.

Oh… no. Not again. Should have gone on the medicine, Nancy. It might have helped.

Nancy went catatonic as she had another of her spells. Memories misfired and jumbled up in a tangled up mess as she struggled to remember the difference between her dreams and realities. Despite an unexplained familiarity, the distant past was overwhelming. Memories poured into her like they were her own as her body and mind waged an unbeatable war against her. Her date of awakening, just like the rest, was October 29th, 1982.

CHAPTER FOURTEEN

TODD ADAMS exited Riverton Financial, walking a few blocks toward the Bridgewater Restaurant. He glanced at the aged hotel building as the flickering purple of the Creepy Nights sign glowed in the evening sky.

Lorrie, you are some kind of saint looking down on me now, aren't you? he thought. *What is that atrocity?*

He stepped into the restaurant.

"Good evening, sir. It's been a while," the host welcomed.

"Evening, I'll take a seat at the bar. Dining alone tonight."

"Very good, follow me this way. Take a menu."

Todd took a seat, studying the back bar and its multicolored smorgasbord of paths to inebriation. An attractive woman sat to his right. She smiled at him, and he returned a grin.

Who's this foxy lady?

"Hi there. I'm Todd."

He extended his hand to introduce himself. She held on, lingering longer than he expected. Her perfume was strong and southern, her voice — silky and smooth.

"My name's Katrina."

"It's nice to meet you, Katrina."

"Likewise, Todd. Charm me, please? I'm having a rough day."

Todd rubbed his chin and contemplated, "Hmm... Where do I start? You look beautiful tonight. That's not a pickup line. I mean it."

There's a diamond ring on her finger. Don't do it, Todd. You're trying to be a better man, remember?

"That's good — an impressive start. First round's on me," she said.

"I'm uh... not sure about this conversation anymore. Married?"

Katrina's eyes squinted. "And if I am? What's it to you?"

"I'm trying to get my life in order. Vice isn't something I need to explore anymore."

"Why are you sitting at a bar next to an attractive woman, then?"

"That's what the voice in my head just asked me. Are you two acquainted?"

"It's very likely. Mine sure is screaming loud about you, handsome."

Todd struggled to hide a smile. It had been a rough recovery, and Katrina was a breath of fresh air.

"Well, I'm not one to just waste time with chitchat," he said. "What do you make of that joint down the street?"

"Creepy Nights? Don't get me started. That's why I'm over here drowning my sorrows with you — my husband, my soon to be ex, Chris, is to blame for the awful purple. That jerk ruined my life."

"What do you mean?"

"He was a good guy, and for a long while, we had an enjoyable life together. One night, something inside him just flipped. He never lost his temper or went manic. He just became a different person set on scaring everyone. I watched it become an unhealthy fixation — frightening people, I mean. The clown petrified my poor mother so many times, he might as well have killed her. I mean, he practically did. Chris was all about the jump scares. He'd just go around the corner and *pop* out in front of her like he was twelve years old all over again, picking on the girls at recess. Mom's health wasn't that great. Her constant anxiety left her blood pressure sky high around the clock. Chris got a rise from that. He'd do little things to get on her nerves before his... transformation. I never thought much about it. Eventually, the little things kept getting bigger and bigger."

I might get along better with him than I should. Stop it, Todd. You're not that way anymore.

"Sounds about like a psychopath to me," Todd said. "You into *that* kind of man or what? There's plenty of 'em. Think it's that Y chromosome. Sometimes has an extra hint of evil just behind it. Don't get me wrong. I'm no feminist. The X chromosome isn't much better off."

Katrina laughed and said, "Point well made. Point well made... He bothered mom all the way up until the day he killed a deer and smeared its blood all over the inside of her Mercedes. This idiot told her he killed a deplorable man and used her vehicle to transport and dispose of a body as some sort of sick joke. For the record, he killed no one. Unfortunately, my crazy but well-intentioned mother was such a clean freak she couldn't stand the thought of her vehicles being used for such a despicable act. Don't misunderstand. She wasn't a humanitarian, not by any stretch of the means. She was much more concerned about the overall cleanliness of her vehicle than any victim. When she spotted the car and the shape it was in, she collapsed to the ground and fainted. Damned jagged rock on the edge of the driveway did her in when she slipped and hit her head as she passed out from the rush of overwhelming panic. The autopsy report showed the trauma to the head did her in. Poor, lonely old bag."

Katrina's emotions peaked, and she teared up, scratching at her scalp. "Must be the alcohol talking. I don't know. I miss her."

She raked her fingers through her well-kept and dyed auburn hair in its radiance. Her beautiful almond eyes enchanted and entranced Todd. His mind drifted a moment. He returned, following a moment of shameless desire for her.

"Well, I'm sorry about all that. Guess there ain't no easy way to bring momma back. I can't blame you for considering a divorce," he said. "What's really working on you, though? That can't be it. I've got an intuition for reading beautiful women."

"Well, what do *you* think?" she asked, rubbing her brow with her nail-bitten left hand and shaking her head. "Can't you see my struggle? My mother's death. Wouldn't you think that would have caused some tensions? My stupid... idiot... knucklehead for a husband basically killed her. He didn't give a care, though. Mother was worth a lot. A whole damn lot. He was always wasting money on horror movie props, posters, anything like that. I bet our garage had $60,000 of that shit... pardon my French... before my accident. It just gets me worked up thinking about it! And now..." Katrina slammed her fist on the bar and scoffed. "We own a damn building that's Riverton's biggest eyesore — in the scourge of the Oak Hollow District. The jackass did the whole thing while I was in a coma and just goes and buys the place on a damn whim."

Coma? I guess I'm not the only one. Maybe I'll tell her. Maybe I won't. Tucked in my back pocket for safekeeping.

"I still don't really know how or why. It's just been too much for me... for us." Katrina stopped to sip on her Old-Fashioned. "I couldn't stand thinking about the terrible thing he did to mom and to me. Even if it was a second or third-degree sort of thing. Yeah. I'll admit her death wouldn't have bothered me as much had it happened differently, but Chris's juvenile antics just drove me up the wall. I can't trust him. We escaped a while to cope with the loss, and I worked on an art therapy project. I never expected Chris to be so reckless, but he was, and now, he *is*... more than I could have ever imagined." She pinched at her wrist as if her nerves and frustration overwhelmed her. "As you could guess, I'm completely against the purchase of the property, but he signed whatever papers there were while I was comatose and won't even show them to me. I don't know whether to resent him for it or not. I may be better off not knowing how much he paid for it. It was too much."

"I'm sorry. It sounds like it's been quite a ride dealing with a complicated guy like that. We're all a little that way, aren't we?"

Katrina took a deep breath as Todd stared into her eyes. "Whatever. Do you actually know anything about Oak Hollow?" she asked. "Chris just turned a blind eye to the history of the block. So much blood shed in the area for many generations — no point in talking any reason with him, though. Chris can really fixate. In fact, he can be flat-out obsessive when you let him. Could probably even call him clinical."

Cut to the chase, lady.

"I got you. I know the type," Todd said. "Too well. Bartender, I'll take the check. Katrina, it's been a pleasant chat. I'm sure I'll run into you again one of these days. I'm a little old fashioned. I don't feel quite right shooting the breeze with a potential divorcee. We can talk on the other side of it if you want. I *am* attracted to you, but I want to do things right this time."

Katrina's makeup ran down the sides of her cheeks. "This time? Don't you want my phone number?"

"You know what I meant. I'll talk to you later."

Todd exited the Bridgewater Restaurant and headed down the block toward his pickup. He circled around and drove past Creepy Nights. All the lights in the building appeared off except the top floor. A silhouetted figure stood near the window.

A man hobbled into the road as Todd's eyes studied the building. He came up next to the truck as it rolled and tapped on the glass.

His voice was scratchy and whiny. "You've got to help me. Help me out. I need money."

"How about a five spot? That's the best I can do."

"That'll work. Thanks, Todd."

"Not a problem. Wait a minute. Who are you? You don't know me."

"That's okay. I'll see you later. Heh-heh."

The peculiar individual disappeared before Todd could speak to him. He vanished behind the Creepy Nights building.

People are strange.

CHAPTER FIFTEEN

CHRIS WILKERSON targeted the streets, recruiting select numbers of the area's homeless to work for him based on their imaginative states of mind. The individual's coherence and conversational skills drove Chris's decision-making process. He assumed many of these types would be well-immersed in alternate realities and fantasies because of their hyperactive imaginations.

Wrapping up morning recruitment, he sent them on to the Creepy Nights lobby, where a slew of the unshowered guests would later bombard Nancy. He carried a soup and sandwich out from the Corner Brothers Deli down the street, and walked back toward Creepy Nights. Creeper Joe sat on the sidewalk as a youthful homeless man in his first street-level appearance in over fifty-four years. Something had changed, and he blended in with the others that loitered in the area well.

I should talk to this guy. He might be a good fit for us.

Joe held a pewter cup in the air, as if expecting a donation.

"Have any spare change for me?" he said in a disguised and upper-Midwestern accent.

"Are you looking for work? I'll give you part of my sandwich? Here you go, friend."

Oh boy… it's him.

Joe grinned. "Nope, but thanks for playing. Any thoughts on my costume? I clean up alright, don't I?"

Chris rolled his eyes. "If you call smelling like garbage and looking like you haven't bathed in weeks, then… yes. You clean up excellent."

"No poking fun. That's not fair."

"Whatever you say."

Joe stood up and wrapped his arm around Chris's shoulder while they walked back toward Creepy Nights. He took the sandwich from him, biting into it.

"What's this about?" Chris asked.

Joe led them into an adjacent alleyway.

"It's about time we have a chat. *You* are going to have to fulfill your commitment. I want you to collect Dale Creensteen. He's an easy target. The type that pays no attention to whom or what's around him — lost in his own little world the times he does. Here's the address. Take this bottle of chloroform, too. Snitched it from someone at RGH the other day. It should help. Heh-heh. The signal fire's lit. Now go get him before time runs out. I'll meet you behind the building after dusk to assess your hunt. Don't worry. He's an easy capture. It's the soul I'm after, not the man. That makes it more palatable."

Chris scoffed, stopping in the middle of the alleyway. He studied the area for onlookers. "Joe, I don't know why you think I'd go along with this. I'm a man of many convictions."

Joe's eyes yellowed, his voice grew fierce and more profound, and he yanked him closer, cutting into the side of his arm with his sharp fingernails. Blood dripped, and Joe dropped his pewter cup beneath it.

"We wouldn't want to get the alley all dirty, now, would we? Dirty boy. Let me help you with that. A little Indian sunburn should do the trick." Joe alternated his hands over the wound as the blood drained into the cup beneath. "Right as rain. See?"

Chris looked at his arm. The bleeding had stopped and coagulated. *Too weird.*

"You want to ask me 'why' you would go along with it again?" Joe asked. "You know why. Don't squeak or squawk to the cops, either. Otherwise, I'll show you a whole new meaning to damnation! That goes from this point forward, pushover! Do as I say, so I don't have to."

"I need some time."

"Time for what? Creensteen's a pencil pusher. He won't put up a fight. You're a big man. Aren't you, Chris? From head to toe! Heh-heh."

They exited the alley, walking down the street together, and Joe mellowed.

I can't handle much more of this. God help me.

The pair walked to the front door of Creepy Nights, bidding one another an awkward farewell.

"Aren't you gonna come in?" Chris said. "You'd blend in just fine with the rest. I could use someone with your storytelling prowess."

"Who said they were only stories? I don't have any business being in there. I'll see you later tonight. I'm told Creensteen drives a black '82 Prelude for what it's worth. Good luck."

Creeper Joe maneuvered toward the Level Zero entrance behind the building as he called out to Chris, "Catch you later."

"I don't know…"

The color of Joe's eyes changed again as he clicked the back of his teeth loud enough to echo off the side of the dated structure.

Chris sighed. "I'll see what I can do."

"See you later, Chrissy-Chris. Don't forget about our agreement." Joe dismissed himself.

I guess it's about time I pack heat.

Chris stormed inside after the unsettling run-in with Joe. He walked past Nancy, and she motioned toward the lobby packed with unannounced guests. Riverton's finest panhandlers, street philosophers, and hobos would soon have a chance at being low-cost storytellers.

"Any messages for me?" he muttered.

"Not really. Are you going to tell me what this lobby full is about?" She popped a Reese's peanut butter cup in her mouth as a dull hum of incoherent chatter surrounded them.

"Not really or no? There is a difference. Just give me a damn answer!"

Nancy sighed, dropping her fist on the desk in a less than silent protest. "Okay, fine. Katrina called. She's going to sue you for the mismanagement of her mother's trust fund."

One minute Katrina's pleasant. The next, she's suing my ass. Can't a guy catch a break?

"That's quite enough," he said. "We have guests here. I'll be in my office upstairs. Send them up to Level Seven, Surprise and Scare. I'll meet them there for a debriefing."

She glared at him a moment. "You mean... they're going to be working here? You got cots and a soup kitchen up there I don't know about?"

"And if I do? What's it to you? I'm not paying you to judge my impul... my choices. There are showers up there. We'll get them cleaned up. Everyone has a story to tell, Nancy."

"I'm due for a smoke break," she said, "This is stressing me out."

"Go ahead. I'll speak to you later."

•   •   •   •   •

Chris sat at his desk, reviewing the latest stack of résumés. He kept pitching more of them in the trash pile.

"Nothing special... unqualified... too showy... overqualified..."

He stood up and walked toward the elevator, going down to Level Seven. The group of homeless recruits stood clustered together. Some were chatting. Others stared at the ceiling. The rest chattered away to the air.

Find your voice, Wilkerson. Rally the troops.

"Alright, thanks for coming in today. Here's a quick pep talk. The job isn't that difficult. You receive a call, you collect the customer's information, and you tell 'em a story."

He stared into their eyes as they processed what he said. There were only blank facial expressions.

Not getting it, are they?

He sighed. "It's the same way you get yourself off the hook with the cops when they bug you... or you lie to a person in a car on the street corner to get money. Throw in some blood and guts... a little scandal. Boom! You've got yourself a Surprise and Scare. Level Seven is all about surprises. That's why I think your spontaneity is your best asset. The west wing has the original rooms with beds, showers, and a kitchen. They are a little dusty and could use some cleaning, but I'm sure you guys can make it work. Make yourself at home. I've got some chili and *Flitz* in the refrigerator to keep everyone at bay. I'm no micro-manager. Just do the job I'm asking you to do, and I'll take care of you, no questions asked. I'll come down tomorrow and we'll get you started. I expect everyone to pull their weight if they are going to stay here. Don't get lazy."

"Chris... my name's Ebony. Thanks for the job. I won't let you down. I'll keep an eye on things."

Chris looked at her and nodded. "I saw imagination in your eyes when we spoke. Show them how it's done. We already set the phones up. Have them push the green sign-in button and take a call when it arrives. Keep it on target."

"I got it. No frills or thrills without some chills!"

Chris laughed. "That's right. Thanks, Ebony."

CHAPTER SIXTEEN

CHRIS WILKERSON exited the room and went toward the elevator.

No frills or thrills without some chills. That's actually pretty good.

When he arrived to the lobby, he walked past Nancy, staring at her in a sullen gaze.

"Are you okay?" she asked.

"Yeah, I'll be alright. Need to run over to WGBO and check on Wayne and Ron. Some of the bills aren't being paid like I've asked them to."

"Alright, then. Your poker face needs some work. See you later."

Keep your comments to yourself!

Chris proceeded to his vehicle and drove toward Riverton Financial. He staked out the parking lot, eyeballing the black '82 Prelude while his stomach remained in knots. Employees exited the building for about two hours until it was the only vehicle remaining in the lot other than his Town Car.

It's bound to be time, soon. Where are you, Dale?

Chris pulled out of the lot and parked across the street. He walked back to the Prelude and opened the passenger door. After leaning the seat forward, Chris crawled in the back seat, waiting for Creensteen.

I'm too big to squeeze in back here, who am I kidding? He'll see me.

He staged the rag and chloroform. His nerves tingled while he studied the sag of the car's cloth ceiling.

A bit of an odd problem for a new model…

The car door opened as a shrimp-figured man climbed in. It was Creensteen. Stuffing his hand in a space above the ceiling, he pulled out a stashed pack of cigarettes and lit one up. He started the vehicle, adjusting the mirrors to his liking.

"What's that smell?" he muttered.

Chris lurched over the seat and smothered Creensteen's face with the rag. After only two seconds of struggle, Dale Creensteen had passed out.

"Dale? Dale?" Chris whispered, verifying his consciousness.

No reply. Chris studied the area.

Looks like the coast is clear.

Once he determined there were no onlookers, he left Dale in the Prelude and walked back to his vehicle. He started the Town Car as a police cruiser approached. When he saw it, he spewed a barrage of profanities.

Keep it calm. Keep it collected.

The officer slowed and rolled his window down. Chris leaned out the window toward him and waved, unable to hide his nervousness.

"You doing alright tonight, partner? Lookin' a little pale," the officer said.

Chris faked a grin. "Yeah. Had a late night at Riverton Financial. Markets are tanking again. Not looking like a pleasant week for me. Got to pay the mortgage. You know what I mean?"

The officer chuckled. "I suppose. My name's Officer Penske. Take my card. Let me know if you need anything. I'm up for a promotion soon and may have a shot at bigger opportunities than routine stops before too long. My gut's telling me you could use a little help. You being harassed? Got a boss committing fraud? What's going on? You can trust me."

"No. No. Nothing like that. I'm fine, officer. Thanks for checking. Have a good night, and thanks for your service to the community. We need more dedicated guys like you." Chris waved at him with the wrong hand, dropping the rag he used on Creensteen onto the ground. He cursed under his breath.

Way to go, idiot.

Penske looked at the rag and back up at Chris.

"Spilled the coffee on the dash, huh?"

Wilkerson's heart pounded as he nodded.

Penske grinned. "Happens to the best of us on the night shift. Take it easy, guy."

Man. That was a close call. I've got to get back to Dale quick before this stuff wears off.

Officer Penske drove away as Chris wiped the sweat from his forehead and climbed out of the vehicle to retrieve the soaked chloroform rag. Waiting until the cruiser's taillights were no longer in sight, he shut the Town Car's headlights off and drove back to Riverton Financial. Approaching the Prelude, he pulled Creensteen out and dropped him into the trunk.

Chris drove several blocks and drove into the Creepy Nights lot.

Hope the night shift crew doesn't see me. Dale's going to wake up any minute.

He pulled toward the back of the lot near the storage building as Creeper Joe's glowing eyes glared at him.

He climbed out of the car, walking toward Joe.

"Well, I'll be," Joe said. "Chris Wilkerson is coming through in the clutch. Would you like to shed a tear with me? Our first capture's kind of special, isn't it?"

Chris scoffed. "He's in the trunk. You can have him."

"Alright, alright," Joe said. "I'll help you this time, but there's fifty-three more. Don't get too cozy. I'll bring you some more names and locations tomorrow. That wasn't so hard, was it? Trouble is, Creensteen was easy… Easier than a floozy in a red-light district. It's going to get a little harder, but so will you. It becomes impersonal, and before too long, it's just a job. 'Got to pay the mortgage,' right? Heh-heh."

"You freak," Chris said. "I should kill you now while I have the chance."

"No. No. We had a deal. You've got to deliver, or I'll slit Katrina's throat. Heh-heh. What's it to you, anyway? Aren't you separated? A little trouble between the sheets? What's the dealeo?"

"It's complicated."

"I know. I can't help but laugh at what a sorry sucker you are — a pathetic excuse for a man. You weren't enough for her. Were you?"

Chris looked over his shoulder. "That's enough. I see a cruiser on patrol. We need to break this up."

"*You* do… I can disappear in the blink of an eye when I want to. I'll take Creensteen. Ta-ta!"

Chris closed the trunk of the car and moved it toward the front of the building. The police car circled around and pulled up next to him. It was Penske again.

"What are you doing over here?" Penske called out. "Your headlights were off. Trying to hide some doobies or what? I expect that out of a teenager, but you're like forty, right? Come on, man…"

"No, nothing like that. Just had to lock up the storage shed out back."

"You live here or what? Isn't this the creepy story place?"

"Yeah, it's a side venture. Got to make ends meet. Got an apartment upstairs… the rent's cheap."

"You don't have to lie to me," Penske said. "Have a good night. Next time your gonna light up a joint, don't do it in a dark corner with the headlights off… That's too obvious, man. Don't sweat it. I'm not gonna say anything."

"I really wasn't…"

"Whatever," Penske said. "Take it easy. You have my card if you need anything. By the way, I like the commercials. A little makeup on your cheek bones makes you pretty." He drove away.

Yeah. Get on out of here.

Chris walked up to the building, studying the empty lobby and the flicker of the new fluorescents.

Looking better already.

He proceeded to Level Eight to turn in for the night.

CHAPTER SEVENTEEN

Pondering on the days ahead, CHRIS WILKERSON admired the progress and handiwork across the lower floors.

Level Seven's under control. I've got better things to do. I remember learning the value of the laissez-faire management style. I'm ready to get down to my graduates. Body Horror will be fun. We'll see who makes their way to the front of the pack.

He entered the lobby to greet his new hires, keeping introductions brief. "Good morning, welcome aboard. It's sure to be quite the ride. Follow me to the elevator."

They climbed on, studying one another, and remaining quiet through the ascent.

No more damn smacking. What a nightmare.

"No gum chewing in here, please, miss. Spit it in the garbage bin to our right. Here we are, Level Three, Body Horror. We'll circle around and tour the floor and cubicles, then we'll get going. There's not much of a training program. We're a seat of the pants style operation, and it's been working well on the other floors. As you can see, it's a sick place to be in the most artificial of ways."

They walked around the room, each reacting a bit differently to the macabre and artificial scenery.

Break up the awkward silence, Chris.

"For inspiration... Fake blood, fingers, toes, bones — in jars, on shelves, and dangling from ceiling tiles. I even added every tool that could inflict harm from a garage — everything from lawnmowers to socket wrenches and tire irons to fence post drivers. Any questions?"

The gum chewer spoke, "I want the desk by the Northeast window. For good luck."

"Superstitious much? What makes it any better than the rest?" one of the others asked.

"That's enough," Chris said. "Don't badger each other because of eccentricities. For the record, my preferred corner of choice is southwest. From all I've been able to gather and read in the papers, The Oak Hollow Hotel was once the crown jewel of Riverton. I've sunk my fair share into it to get it looking more presentable over the past couple of months. I hope that information only helps you appreciate it more. Follow me over here, and we'll take a call. We're going to bring the building back to life with our collective vitality, aren't we? It's been purposeless a little too long. Logging onto the phone is simple. Just follow these button sequences on the instruction sheet and the assigned code on each desk. What do you know? We have a call waiting."

I'm coming across too excited. Mellow out, Wilkerson. Pull yourself together. This is your stage.

He looked around at the four others sitting beside him and pulled out his black-inked *Bic* and a ream of dot-matrix paper from the desk drawer. "Make sure you take notes as you go. You don't want to get too lost along the way. You have to be able to tie it all back together."

Deep breaths, Chris. Deep breaths.

"Thank you for calling Creepy Nights. My name's Chris. How can I scare you today?"

"Chris, I think I've got the wrong number."

"No, no. I don't think so. We have a story for you today. I can feel it. That's our trade."

"Okay, fine."

"Our fee is ninety-nine cents per minute. Got it?"

"I'm not going to pay for that."

"Alright, fine. Just stay on the line. This one's on the house."

"Get on with it."

"1971. There once was a twelve-year-old boy named Bill. He walked home from school slower than he should have. When he came down Elm and Maple, he walked across from Roger's Barber Shop and later past the tax appraisal office. He noticed a small blue shed behind the building and wondered what it might house. Storage, perhaps? It wasn't weatherproof by his own estimation. Maybe something else? He wasn't sure. He observed the chief appraiser, Mr. Beldon, locking it up as he prepared to leave. Bill slowed down, waiting until Beldon vacated the premises. After this, he backpedaled and headed toward the shed. It was off the main street — its rooftop visible over the small fence next to the building.

The padlock on the shed was unlocked. Bill took it off and stepped inside. Looking around, he noted a series of glass jars on the shelves. One was full of fingernails from top to bottom. He glanced at the next one and noticed another full of toenails. Then, he peered down and saw a jar full of toes. They were all large *Vlasic* pickle jars. It was almost like the junior-high science lab he had been in just two hours earlier, but this was something more disturbing than frogs or cow hearts.

Mr. Beldon was known around town for being particular with his accounting practices as a quiet man. He lived alone but often spent most of his waking hours at the office and a substantial amount of time 'working' in the shed after hours. The boy unscrewed the jar full of the toenails as he heard commotion outside the door. There was nowhere to go, and the shed was small. He knew he was nothing more than a meddling kid trespassing. Just as he thought the door was about to open, he heard the padlock click, and it closed. It became pitch black inside. He hadn't looked around enough to identify his surroundings other than the jars. What could he do to avoid bringing attention to himself? Perhaps Mr. Beldon hadn't seen him.

His eyes adjusted, and faint shadows and shapes became more visible. There was a small vent at the back of the shed where he could get someone's attention if he could bend it back, but he couldn't reach it. He stacked the jars full of extremities, one on top of the other, hoping to push the vent open. He climbed until the first glass jar cracked. Naturally, it was the jar full of toes. He crashed with his meager 106 pounds bearing down on it as glass shards cut into him. Sandals were a poor choice of shoe that day. The side effect, his big toe being sliced. The severed tendons dangled as his blood spilled out. He didn't know if he had another jar to put the spilled toes into. It was his mess to clean up. If he had not been in there, he could have avoided this PICKLE altogether. From the smell of things, Old Beldon just used pickle juice to cure the toes. He heard the padlock being removed as the door opened, obviously alerted by the commotion.

The older tax appraiser spoke in a mysterious tone, 'Kind of ironic, ain't it? Your toe comin' off, and my jar full of toes spillin' all over the floor? I was in the mood for a fresh one, anyhow. Give it here, and I won't tell your ma and pa.'

The boy yanked off the remnants of his toe, and Beldon bit right into it.

'Mmm... just what I was hoping for, son. I didn't even have to solicit it this time, either. I know. I'm an odd one. I'll let you out of here after you eat one yourself and swear to me you'll tell no one else about this. We best get you to the hospital. Here, I'll give you another toe from my jar. I bet the doc can sew it on.'"

The voice on the other end of the phone interrupted, "Okay... okay. That's enough. I don't need to hear any more of this story. You are good, Chris. Very good. I'll pay you for it."

Chris concluded the call and said, "Pass on the word. I'll transfer you to our account representative to firm up the billing. Speak to you soon!"

"Goodbye."

Chris turned around to the new employees in training who clapped for him before he spoke, "And that, folks, is a Body Horror story. Who's up next? I'm off to lunch. I think I'll go for some pickled pig's feet. Haha!"

• • • • •

Only a short time following lunch hour, a myriad of personal struggle swept over Chris. Chilling memories resonated within his mind as he reflected on the capture of Dale Creensteen and three others.

They're all in there suffering — what a mess. I'm in deep kimchi.

The horrific images of each altercation flashed in front of him more and more often as his stress increased. Each one lent itself to a peculiar interest in blood and gore, leaving his mind wandering to unhealthy places.

It's the contrast I love. Blemished and unblemished skin and the associated scrapes and nicks running amuck from their point of origin. Change the subject now. What am I going to do with the tunnel?

He threw a stress relief ball in the air in a repetitive motion. A slew of troubling thoughts left his conscience conflicted and shackled by Creeper Joe's unrelenting grip. His mind raced.

I want eyes on it. If I get implicated in someone trying to escape while Joe is out and about doing whatever he does when he's wandering, there's no telling what trouble I'll end up in. I've got a reputation to protect.

CHAPTER EIGHTEEN

LIVEWIRE's employer, Riverton A/V, did him no favors while comatose. Instead, they enabled him. He remained employed, even after his drunken incident. His gracious manager covered it up to keep the RGH contract afloat.

I'm not sure about this assignment. I have no idea what to expect.

Despite being months since he kicked his addiction to alcohol, the scar on Livewire's forehead reminded him of his dangerous habit. Numbing the pain of his past through booze was no longer an option. Outleting his feelings and emotions via other channels would now be a requirement. Confusion and disorder remained a struggle for him, though – always finding some kind of solace in the hair of the dog. His issues further compounded themselves upon his awakening from the blackout on October 29th, 1982. Ignoring them to the best of his abilities, he ran from his unruly feelings. The booze had wrecked him. Still, he acknowledged his commitment to sobriety was essential to the next chapter. He pulled on the handle to Creepy Nights and took a deep breath.

I'm not ready to be back yet. It gives me the willies.

He entered the building and approached Nancy.

"Can I help you, Bob? I'm sorry. I mean… Livewire."

He looked up at her and gulped before speaking, "Uh... Yeah... uh... Mr. Wilkerson... he... um... asked me if I would come to speak to him about another job he had for me."

"Another job? Really? I don't know anything about that."

Get on with it. I don't have time to waste.

"Okay," Livewire said. "Well, can you please check with..." he gulped, "him?"

I can't get the words out. Just a stomach bug. It'll pass.

"Can I sit? I'm not feeling well."

"I'm sorry to hear that. Sure, go ahead. I'll call Mr. Wilkerson and let him know you're here. Let me know if you need anything."

He experienced the strange and queasy moments about once a week.

It's just phantom withdrawal symptoms again. A medical professional would say as much, too.

Until this incident, he was at home and in bed during the overnight hours when the events occurred. This time was different, like a waking nightmare in his mind.

The subway tunnel collapsed in front of him as smoke overtook the space and surrounded him in a heaping pile of burnt ash. He smelled his skin as it burned.

Let me out of here. Let me out!

His mind ran wild.

I shouldn't have lit the dynamite. Shouldn't have done that.

He sat there convulsing as Nancy looked away, snapping out of it when she beckoned, "Mr. Wilkerson will see you now. Go ahead... around the corner, and to your left, you'll find his private executive elevator."

He entered the elevator as *Duran Duran* piped through the garbled speakers.

"Ugh. Euro-trash. I'm All American. Yep. Baby, I was born to run."

He muttered to himself, "I know where the elevator is, genius. I wired the friggin' thing up myself. Don't you remember? I set it up so Chris could play whatever he wanted throughout the whole building. Speakers already sound like crap."

Talk aloud to yourself like you're mental. That makes sense.

Still feeling uneasy, he waited for a moment of clarity on the ride up.

His mind balanced.

There we go. Just in time.

Nothing had been the same since he sobered up. The elevator doors opened to Level Eight. Livewire had never seen much of the floor other than the select areas he installed the speakers and sound system before. Chris had not permitted it, remaining elusive and secretive.

Entering the vast area, he observed Chris's empty desk in the building's southwestern corner. Clutter overwhelmed the area as items and hotel furniture from years past remained scattered. The music from the elevator followed him into the room at an intolerable volume. He looked around to see if he could locate Wilkerson.

"Hello. Mr. Wilkerson? Are you here?"

The fool's gonna blow the speakers out.

He raised his voice, "Hello! Mr. Wilkerson?"

Livewire walked toward Chris's desk and sat down at the chair in front of it, assuming he would make his way over soon.

CHAPTER NINETEEN

LIVEWIRE continued to study the disordered room full of old hotel furniture, movie novelties, and other miscellaneous objects, and his mind wandered.

I'm not gonna waste my entire day waitin' on this guy. I got stuff to get done. Two minutes and if he doesn't show. I'm out of here.

A short time later, Chris Wilkerson emerged, straightening his collar out and walking out with a superficial confidence. The pair shook hands, and Chris spoke, "Oh, I'm sorry to keep you waiting, Bob. I'm glad you found a seat. Let's get down to business, okay?"

"Yeah. Sure. Sounds good. I prefer it if you call me Livewire."

"That's right. Apologies. Beneath my building is a large tunnel. I don't know if you remember hearing much about the abandoned Riverton subway project before the Great Depression? It was quite a production back in the 20s."

Livewire nodded.

What's this guy trying to get at? Time's a-wastin'.

"Anyhow," Chris said. "There was a substantial amount of work completed on it before the city scrapped it and left it behind."

"Yeah, I think I've heard something about that before. I didn't know that it was still... a 'thing.' I assumed the city filled it in with dirt after the... the..."

Chris shook his head, fidgeting with the *Bic* on his desk.

"That seems to be what everyone recalls. It's still there. I want to contract you to do some more work for me. This time we're going to take it a step further — speakers, microphones, surveillance cameras, the works, all throughout the tunnel. Let's make it high tech. Money is no object, buddy. However far a half-million will take me. I've got access to a trust fund that runs pretty deep, but I may lose that soon so we need to move quickly. There are two miles of tunnel. I know it's going to be a costly and time-consuming project. I assume you'll need to quit your job and come to work for me if you elect to move forward with this. Are you up for that? I imagine it'll take you some time."

Livewire crossed his arms, taking a breath before replying, "Why are you doing this? What's the catch? I'm not gettin' it."

Wilkerson picked up the tie-dye stress relief ball from his desk and tossed it to him.

"I'm doing it because I can. That's all you need to know. No catch. You'll need to live there while you work, though. Don't worry. I've got a small apartment setup in the basement that leads in there. You can stay put. Please be aware, I consider this a top-secret operation. No one else needs to know what you're working on. Don't give your bosses a reason for quitting. Just call up the supply list, and I'll send whatever you need down to you so you can work your way through with minimal disruption. While you're at it, map it out, too. Flag it the way you would a corporate enterprise, would you? It's dark in there, so you'll want to make sure you're prepared for that. I have electricity and water running there already from sometime in the tunnel's original design. It's all tied into the Creepy Nights utilities."

Livewire stared at Chris a moment before speaking again, "What the heck you plannin'? You buildin' a haunted house or what? This sounds like a much larger project than anybody needs. Can I bring my crew in?"

Wilkerson shook his head. "There are endless opportunities for it. And no... No one else can help on this one. It's a one-man show. How does twenty an hour sound?"

Holy Moses! Twenty?

He stood up and reached out to shake Wilkerson's hand. "Sounds great. I'll take it."

"Good. Can you start next week?"

A rush of nausea hit Livewire.

Not ready to feel this way again. Please, not right now.

The room caved in around him as Chris's speech came to a momentary halt. Despite never going inside, his strange bond with the tunnel left his mind jumbled.

The dust and ash clouded his eyes as he heard other men screaming in their torment.

"Why'd you do that? We're all gonna die."

How could this be possible? I was born in '52. No… wait, 1902. No, that's when Grandad was born. He worked these tunnels. Ugh… I don't know anymore. Am I losing it? I'm thirty-one. I knew I shouldn't have messed around with that psychic medium back in '78. Now I'm payin' my friggin' penance. That's got to be it.

Chris waved at him. "Livewire, are you there? Hello? Let's get you some sunshine. Can I get you something to drink?"

Wrong question for a drunk… A drink. Oh, yes, a stiff drink. That would be nice. I hate these feelings. I hate 'em.

Only in his imagination did he answer this way. He articulated self-controlled, as his mind remained plagued by thoughts of his addiction. "No. I'll be fine. Thanks for the job. Let me get some personal affairs in order and turn in my notice. Then, I can start estimating the supplies and tools needed to make it happen. You've got to clue me in soon, though. I'm intrigued."

Chris grinned. "All in due time. All in due time. I stock the basement refrigerator with *Flitz* beer. Help yourself."

Gotta stay on the wagon… gotta stay on the wagon… Livewire thought. His mind had reset.

"Thanks. See you in a couple of days."

CHAPTER TWENTY

After a brief wait in the Riverton Behavioral Therapy Center's lobby, TODD ADAMS stared into Julie's eyes, hoping she could help him.

I'm not going to write her off. I have to change for the better if I'm going to get it together, he thought.

His cynicism toward therapy lessened as his medication mellowed him out. Coping with life after the accident and losing Lorrie was not an option. It was a necessity. Todd's mind checked out a moment while Julie chattered.

Man… Where was my head at?

Her emerald eyes and sandy-colored hair kept his attention. Even her jewelry matched perfect to his liking.

She's a decade too old and two degrees too smart. Forget it. It's some kind of conflict of interest.

"Therapy is not something for the faint of heart. It took some real guts to get you in here, didn't it?"

Todd nodded. "Yes, that's a fair assessment. I don't think I can ever find normalcy again. My inner peace. You know what I mean?"

"Manic depression is not something you can fix with only pills. It takes a lot more than that. Self-discipline, self-care, and a lot of therapy."

Here we go. I didn't show up to get lectured.

"You don't get it," he said. "These feelings aren't always mine."

Julie smiled, taking some notes in a leather-bound notebook. "Todd, it's easy to separate ourselves from the part we hate the most. You can't do that, though. See through the eyes of 'Manic' Todd. The Todd on the airplane that day."

Go ahead. Keep talking to me like I'm four years old — the 'Manic' Todd. God dealt me this hand. Let me play it my way.

Todd twisted his college ring around as he replied, "It's… it's not a memory I relish upon. I'm a different man now. This coma changed me. I hope for the better."

"Todd, it's a great thought. We can't totally unprogram our brain chemistry, though. I want you to do like we talked about. Find some new hobbies. Collect things you enjoy. It doesn't have to be anything conventional. In fact, I'd encourage you to make it unconventional. Integrate it. Find your Feng-Shui. Set a budget and make a plan. It'll do wonders for your home décor. It did for my husband."

"*Did* wonders? Is he gone now?"

"Yeah. He walked out on me a month ago. I don't know what to say." Tears welled up in her eyes. "I'm coping with it as best as I can."

Todd shook his head and gawked. "And they sent me to *you* for therapy? Come on, lady. Take a break and grieve your husband."

"Grieve him? I didn't say he was dead. I don't know where he is, but I don't think he's dead. The best thing I can do for him is let him breathe." She looked at her watch. "Well, that's all the time we have for our session. I'll send the report to Dr. Hicks to let him know your progress. RGH wants us to have at least six sessions a month for the next three months."

Exactly the way I want to spend my time…

"Fine. Thank you, Julie."

Todd walked out of the Riverton Behavioral Therapy Center and headed toward Riverton Financial.

Some kind of lunch break that was… shit.

SPRING 1983

CHAPTER TWENTY-ONE

CHRIS WILKERSON picked the phone off the receiver and rolled the rotary dial.

It's time to call Katrina. It's been five months.

The line pulsed several times before she answered, "Hello?"

"Hello, Katrina. I'm sorry I'm just getting back to you. I wanted to talk to you about something."

"Hold it," she said. "I'm the one that's been calling you. You just took months to return my calls. I want to say my piece first."

"No. Let me."

Her voice raised, "No. Shut up and let me talk."

"I've got a business prop...."

"What part of 'let me talk,' don't you understand, idiot...? I'm not putting up with this crap."

Are you shaking the phone at me? Seriously. Pull it together.

"I'm sorry," Chris said. "Hey, let me talk to you about my proposition before you say anything else."

"Fine. You have one minute. Don't waste it."

"Okay. It's about Creepy Nights — I want you to come partner up with me and lead the Space Fiction floor. Don't worry, I won't micromanage or bother you. I know how much you've always liked those stories, and I don't know which direction to take them. I know you'd do great at it."

"Why in the world would you think I would want to come and work for you? You've done nothing but cause grief and stress in my life. We both know our separation was for our own good."

Good question. Do I have an answer?

"You won't be working for me. We'll be 'business... partners.' I'll split the proceeds from the sales with you. It'll be a good thing. Trust me."

"You keep forgetting that I don't need to work again to make it. The main thing I'm unhappy about is what you've taken and squandered away on this Creepy Nights business venture. What's going on at WGBO? Those guys have turned it into a big disorganized mess."

"I don't want to talk about that right now. As for Creepy Nights, trust me. It hasn't taken long for me to realize there's an enormous market for this, and I am all in. You know how I get with my projects. Come give it a trial run. And for Pete's sake, drop the lawsuit talk."

Katrina replied calmer than she had been in the previous minutes, "Okay. I'll give you a month, and then I'll decide from there. I owe nothing to you. Nothing at all. You stole mom from me with your nonsensical shenanigans. Innocent prank or not, she's gone. She's gone."

Here we go again. Alright, then. The pleasantries are out the window.

"Stole her from you? Come on. You never liked her that much. What good was she as she moseyed about and withered away, yapping on the 'ol horn to everyone but you? You can thank me later."

"Screw you! I'd slap you right now if I were standing next to you. I'll show up next week for your Space Fiction floor. If you are just doing this to manipulate me, I'll wear you down until you've got nothing left. Nothing!"

"See you next week, sweetie!" Chris said.

CLICK.

CHAPTER TWENTY-TWO

KATRINA WILKERSON hung up the phone. Pacing back and forth across the living room of the Reinhold estate, she studied the coat of arms, the historical weapons of war, and the various art pieces gracing the walls. She fell to the floor in a moment of anguish.

Yes, I've still got a soft spot for you, Chris Wilkerson. You don't deserve it, but I can't help it.

After taking a bit to regain her composure, Katrina stood up and walked to the garage. She headed toward her steel-gray Firebird, got in, and drove away.

She talked quietly to herself as she drove along, "Chris, you sure wear me out sometimes…"

Cruising across town toward Oak Hollow, she psyched herself up.

I'll just catch him by surprise. See if he means business. I could use a competitive advantage. I'm here to set up my desk early. That's all I have to say, right?

Katrina parked and looked up at the Creepy Nights facility in disgust before proceeding to enter.

Don't look around too much. It will just make you angry. Pull it together, lady. You're in control.

She entered the lobby.

Well, aren't you a pretty little broad? A little plump in the middle, but you've got a nice face.

"Can I help you?" Nancy asked.

"I'm Katrina Wilkerson. I'm here to work on the Space Fiction floor."

"Space Fiction? I didn't know…"

"Chris told me he had it ready for me," Katrina lied.

Nancy bit her lip and said, "Okay. Yeah. Go ahead. It's just behind me."

She took a deep breath and prepared to push the door to the area open. When she looked back, Nancy picked up the phone and whispered.

Inner turmoil had overtaken Katrina since her awakening as Sylvia buried herself deeper into her troubled psyche.

Why am I even doing this? This guy is nothing but a hassle.

She studied the room, noting its refreshed look, and the modernized call center setup.

Looks pretty close to standards by my estimation. Fine… I'll give it a shot. Why do I feel so peaceful right now? It makes no sense. My mind at rest… in here, of all places?

Chris rolled around the corner in an office chair from an adjacent cubicle space. "Hey, it's nice to see you again. You're a few days early, but I've got no qualms with that."

"I'm not sure I can do this. My gut told me to, but my heart's just not right. I don't want to be here with *you* at *your* company."

"Katrina, I told you. It's *our* company. Stiffen that upper lip and toughen up."

Damn. He knows me too well. I can't quit now. He never forced me to do anything.

"Okay, so explain this to me then," she said. "I know you're telling scary stories, but how does it work?"

He clasped his hands together and unclasped them twice before looking at the ceiling and responding.

"Look at *me!*" she yelled.

"Oh… Well, it's easy. We tell genre-specific spooky stories. Like the paid '900' numbers, only the focus is on scaring people, nothing else. I don't tolerate any other kind of thing around here. We're a classy club for classy people. We link each floor number to an option on the telephone. Look at this flyer…"

CREEPY NIGHTS
5454 Oak Hollow Lane, Riverton, TX, 78731
CHOOSE FROM ANY ONE OF OUR OPTIONS BELOW!
Option/Level One- "Space Fiction"
Option/Level Two- "Creature Features"
Option/Level Three- "Body Horror"
Option/Level Four- "Manic Panic"
Option/Level Five- "Campy Corny"
Option/Level Six- "Apocalypse and Alternate Reality"
Option/Level Seven- "Surprise and Scare"
1-800-SCARE ME
Call us today for the thrill of your life for only 99 cents a minute.
CREEPY NIGHTS provides original, scary stories 100% of the time, or we'll give your money back. We guarantee it!

Katrina smirked as she studied the flyer. "You don't have much of an eye for design, do you? You called these folks 'classy' people? Classy creeps, you mean? Look at this place. It seems like you're making some progress, but I'm not sure about the posters. I'm going to freeze you out of mom's trust fund. How much have you squandered in here?"

"A lot less than you think. Katrina, this is your floor. You change it up however you like. Just set it up to inspire stories. Remember, none of that space opera crap, just scary stuff. That's my only ask."

"I understand… but if this is *our* company, *I'll* bend the rules as *I* see fit, and *you* will tolerate it. Otherwise, I'm gone. I can run this place straight into the ground, force bankruptcy, or take it over easily if that's what I want to do. It's a good idea — but it will soon be mine if you as much as screw a single thing up."

"Katrina, *you* are calling the shots. This floor is all yours, *baby*. I'll give you the 'space' you need to do your space thing. Partners? We'll shake on it."

Did this jackass just call me baby?

She reached out to Chris's hand, pushing it away.

"Partners... temporarily. Let's regroup in a couple of weeks."

"Sounds like a plan. Here's a key. Take one of the basement apartments if you don't want to go all the way home. That's totally your call."

"Why don't you walk me down like a proper gentleman? You used to be..."

"Sure."

CHAPTER TWENTY-THREE

Chris and KATRINA WILKERSON conversed as they explored the basement. The lighting was minimal and its musty smell lingered. Wood panel walls choked all life from the corridor as old church pews lined empty spaces in disorder. Katrina noted six apartment spaces and another unmarked room.

"Are we going to pay someone to clean this mess up down here? This place could be a lot nicer with some elbow grease. It's obvious we've had some dead animals in here at some point. Ugh."

"We? I like the sound of that. I reckon I'll get around to it... eventually."

"I bet *you* will." She scoffed. "I hear you're quite the philanthropist now - cleaning up the riff-raff downtown. Anyone else free-loading down here yet? You were always too nice for the wrong reasons."

"Too kind. That's a loaded question."

"What?"

"Forget it. You're the only one."

Why won't you look at me? Something's not right.

"Okay?"

"Don't you remember? When this place was a hotel, the staff quarters were located here. I told you I've been sleeping up top. Level Eight is my floor."

"Yeah. Stay in your penthouse and leave your lovely ex-wife to rot in the basement with possum corpses and vagrants. You're so sweet."

Chris didn't react to the comments and continued, "I have a couch, a refrigerator. Nancy gets me take out. I don't really need to leave anymore. Not only that, I've got this killer sound system. I mean, why should I leave, you know?"

I can't take it anymore. You annoy me, and I annoy you.

"Okay," Katrina said. "We're not that casual these days, are we? No point in faking it. I don't need every waking detail of your life. I guess I'm happy that *you* are happy. Let's get a couple of weeks under our belt, and we'll evaluate from there."

"I'll leave you to explore. I need to go check on some things upstairs. Let me know if you need anything. Thanks," Chris said.

What else is down here? Are you hiding something?

Katrina made her way into each of the dusty and unclaimed apartments before claiming one as her own. She gathered cleaning supplies, hoping to tidy up. Walking to another unmarked door, she turned the handle.

It's locked.

She entered back into the room she wanted and straightened it up. While dusting one of the nightstands a few minutes later, movement caught her eye in a darkened corner of the room. A pair of eyes glowed an iridescent yellow.

Who's that over there? Am I being watched?

Her nerves heightened.

The figure pulled a brass syringe from his arm, sighing in satisfaction.

"I... I wasn't expecting anyone... now. What do you know, Katrina with a K?"

"Excuse me?" she said. "Who are you?"

"You were hoping I'd show, weren't you?"

What a creep-o.

"Ew. Get out of here, now!"

"I thought you might like the whole 'mystery man' mystique. I guess I was mistaken, *Sylvia*. Do I have to dig around your murky soul to pull it out of you?"

She shook her head, elevating her foot in the air toward him.

"It's Katrina! Now, get out!"

The creep's eyes yellowed brighter as his rage intensified. "What gives you the right to order me around? I own this place, you know? I'll call you what I want when I want!"

"No, you don't. Chris and I own this place."

The creep gawked, "*Psh...* you own nothing in this game we call life. I scratch your back... only after you scratch mine. You understand me? It's not a pretty arrangement we have."

Chris, you've outdone yourself. You've found someone weirder than you.

"Pretty arrangement? What does that even mean?"

"Interesting you should ask. What is it now, 1983?"

"Yeah?"

He chuckled as he pestered Katrina, "Personal question... how was *1982* for you? I'm guessing it was... restful? Heh-heh."

"What are you talking about, creep? I'm getting out of here. You don't know me."

You're a little cunning, aren't you? Mystifying...

"Quite the contrary. I know you very well. For all you know, I was creeping on you while you were sleeping. You and a few others. Chris was checking this place out before... you... woke up. He knew no better. We hadn't met yet."

"Ugh," she grumbled. "What's your problem?"

"My problem is you. People like you. You think you can just come in and disrupt my plan. My master plan. Do you have any idea what *I* am trying to do? Any idea at all? Of course, you wouldn't, too dumb to have a clue."

"Excuse me," she said. "Don't insult my intelligence. I'll make you regret talking to me that way before it's all said and done."

"Prove it."

"Fine. Show me around, and we'll see what happens."

He took her around the corner, showing her the entrance into the southeast side of the tunnel of Level Zero via the former wellhouse room. Katrina walked past the inner part of the building's cornerstone, stopping for a moment.

"Wait a minute..." she said. "Cardinal Rules? What's this?"

1. NEVER DISRESPECT THOSE THAT ARE LESSER. PUT THEM ON A PEDESTAL AS IF THEY WERE ROYALTY ANSWERING TO A HIGHER POWER. (DON'T LET YOUR EYES BE HAUGHTY. LOVE THEM LIKE THEY NEVER WERE.)
2. NEVER TALK ABOUT THE UNEXPLAINABLE THINGS THAT YOU SEE TO STRANGERS. IT WOULD BE TOO EASY TO BE A FALSE WITNESS.
3. DON'T STIR UP TROUBLE IN YOUR COMMUNITY.
4. NEVER SET FOOT WHERE YOU AREN'T WELCOME... YOUR FEET WILL BE QUICK TO RUSH TO EVIL.
5. DON'T RECYCLE ANYONE ELSE'S WORDS AS YOUR OWN. A LYING TONGUE ONLY LEADS TO TROUBLE.
6. NEVER SHED INNOCENT BLOOD.
7. NEVER HAVE A HEART THAT DEVISES WICKED SCHEMES.

The creep tried to breeze on past them. "Oh, you know, rules of the house. Most people aren't so... clandestine in their lifestyles. Well, except the ones that say they can follow them all the time. You know, the publically religious types. It's all about how they look in front of everyone else and nothing more. No one does anything for the genuine good of another anymore. It's all about making themselves look better than the rest. Selfish. Selfish. Selfish! Damn them all to hell! I despise that. Why can't there just be good people that are good for no reason? There are plenty of bad people that are bad for no reason, and of course, there are bad people for good reasons. The gray area is the part that chaps my hide. The question for you, Katrina... what are *you*?" the creep asked. He stroked her on the side of the arm, smiling with a harrowing menace.

She scoffed. "Get your greasy mitts off me!"

"You didn't answer the question."

"The kind of person who doesn't tell a freak like you! I've seen enough. I'm having trouble believing *you* follow these so-called Cardinal Rules. This all just seems like middle-school kid antics to me. What did you say your name was?"

"Just call me Joe."

He lunged toward her, hurling her to the ground.

"Never call me a freak again. This will teach you a lesson!

He slashed his finger across her shoulder as her lacy shirt sleeve tore and blood oozed.

CHAPTER TWENTY-FOUR

CHRIS WILKERSON sat in his office, reflecting. He propped his feet on the desk.

Wilkerson, what are you getting yourself into now? This is getting complicated quick.

The office phone rang.

"Chris, it's Nancy. Katrina never came out of the basement. You want me to go check on her?"

"No. I'd rather you stay in the lobby. Let me go. That's longer than I would have expected her to stay."

Chris rode the elevator to the basement level.

Where is she? What is she? I turn my back on you for one minute... and...

The elevator door opened. Creeper Joe stood there waiting.

"Talk about curbside delivery. Thanks a lot, Chris!"

"What have you done?"

Joe donned a Cheshire cat smile. "What I knew you never could. You two were never the best of friends. You know who she really was. Just like the others, she's one of ours..."

"One of yours," Chris corrected.

"No. You're mixed up in this, too. Don't think otherwise."

"You freak... what the hell did you do to her?"

"I'll give you a hint... the better question is how? Heh-heh. You weren't watching the cameras to... how would Katrina say it? To get your jollies?"

Chris cocked his fist back and steadied his feet, staging himself to knock Joe to the ground.

"Of course not. I don't think Livewire's even finished yet. Katrina's my problem. Mine! You have no right!"

"You gave up that right," Joe said. "We all know it. You signed the dotted line, made a pact, and took over Oak Hollow — the street level of it, anyway. Level Zero's all mine."

"What are you saying? Where is she?!"

"Not far at all." Creeper Joe smirked. "A little super glue on the eyes. A few fish hooks in the skin. A scorching iron to the legs. Just wanted to make her feel welcome. Don't you feel relieved? She ran the hotel into the ground. We've all got reasons to resent her for that."

"I'm calling the cops."

"Ah ah. We've discussed this already. Why would you do a stupid thing like that? Creepy Nights is doing very well. You think a business that ridiculous could have the success it has without my help? Guess again," Joe pulled out a piece of Katrina's blouse from his pocket. "I liked the black lace. It was very flattering to her... matronly figure. Thing is, you don't have any kids, do you? Poor baby. I'd hate to kill her. It would be your fault. Remember, you have control of your own destiny." Joe walked away from Chris. He turned around. "Oh, by the way, I might have snitched a surveillance tape from Riverton Financial the other night. Let's just say if you do squeak... RPD *will* get a delivery. The license plate of your car is right in the shot. I'm always a step ahead. Don't bother trying to catch up."

"What's your deal with Katrina? *Sylvia* ran Oak Hollow into the ground, not her. She admitted as much," Chris said.

"There's no difference between them anymore. They're one and the same. She's on the list. I never showed her name to you. Level Zero beckons all of them like a lighthouse beacon bringing its wanderlust ships home. Don't worry. I made everything better. She's not screaming anymore. A dunk in the spring did her good. I just had to tease a minute and soak in the fear."

"The spring?"

"The Spring of Life. Haven't we been over this? Don't you remember playing *ball*? Never mind, we're out of time. Ta-ta."

Joe exited the basement into an obscure passage. The wall closed up behind him. Chris approached, finding no point of entry. He cursed.

There's no way in.

Tears welled up in his eyes and he buried his head into his hands. A few minutes later, he studied the basement stumbling into the wellhouse room. An unfamiliar doorway at the rear looked to lead into the tunnel. Chris struggled to move toward it.

What have I done? Dear God, what have I done?

He sank to the floor with his back pressed against the cornerstone.

CHAPTER TWENTY-FIVE

LIVEWIRE emerged from the tunnel into the lobby, breezing past Nancy. She threw a pen at the back of his head.

Not gonna turn around, Livewire thought. *Keep going. I don't want to talk to her anymore. I've had more chit-chat with that girl than I ever should have. She can't ever take a hint, can she?*

"Where are you going, mister? I haven't seen you in a while?"

He entered the elevator and pressed the DOOR CLOSE button over and over. Nancy approached behind him.

"Wait a minute," she called out. The door closed.

Good riddance.

He pressed the Level Eight floor marker, proceeding to the penthouse level of the facility.

Time to pass on the good news to Chris. What can I say? I've outdone myself, haven't I? He'll be happy as a lark.

The elevator doors opened. Chris stood there to greet him.

"Hey. How's the project going?"

"Well, boss, I've just about finished. Let's go to the basement, and I'll give you the grand tour of the control room."

Chris blinked his eyes, leaving them shut a second longer than expected. "The basement? I never told you to set it up there."

Livewire scoffed, wiping some black dirt from his nose. "Where else was I going to put it? I thought you wanted to be discrete? I'm sorry. It just made little sense to me to put it anywhere else. Running the equipment cabling all the way up here seemed to go against the cost-effective approach. I know the money hasn't run dry, but we wanted to do this smart, right?"

Chris nodded. He reached into his pocket and squeezed on his stress relief ball. "Yeah, I'm sorry. I should have clarified. That empty back room in the lobby would have been fine, too. I'm not real thrilled to be in the basement."

"And why is that?"

"No particular reason. I just prefer life above the surface. I get a little claustrophobic. It's fine. Climb on the elevator, and we'll go down."

Livewire pressed the zero button. "You feelin' alright?"

"I'm fine."

"I don't mean to pry. I just hadn't heard much from you since I started the project. Making me go through Nancy for everything was... interesting."

"Did you two get frisky or something?" Chris asked. "I don't know what you want from me... If you're looking for an apology, you're not going to get one. I've got my own cross to bear."

"Hell no. She ain't my type, too chatty."

"Really. I hadn't picked up on that. She's all business with me. I guess she likes you." Chris poked Livewire in the ribs.

Really, dude? You're crampin' my style.

The elevator doors opened, and they walked toward the control room closet.

"Here we are..." Livewire said. "It ain't 1984 'til next year, but Orwell would be proud."

"Livewire, are you telling me *you're* literate?"

Jerk...

Livewire opened the door. "Why wouldn't I be? Come on in. I'm literate enough."

"Take a look. I've got fourteen monitors to cover the zones you requested. Each camera has built-in microphones and night vision cameras when it gets dark. Use the little joystick and these levers to maneuver around. The buttons allow you to place any of the cameras on the larger screen. The audio activates on that channel automatically."

Livewire whirled the swiveling chair around.

"Look back here. You can even throw an eight-track or cassette in the deck to play music in the tunnels. I figured it would be a nice touch if you ever do run with turning this into a haunted house one of these days."

"This looks great. Wow. Livewire, you've really outdone yourself. Music in the tunnel, huh? Maybe even some WGBO? Nice touch."

Chris studied the video displays again and scoffed.

"What's wrong? Livewire asked. "I thought you'd be pleased."

"I'm sorry," Chris said. "I know you've done a lot of work. I don't see a camera on the south end. You haven't run into anyone... have you? I mean any... *thing*. Vermin? Anything like that?"

"Not really. Just me, myself, and I. I may have seen some critters here or there. About what you'd expect... There *is* a camera on the south end, but the screen's blacked out. Dad-gum rats must have chewed the cable. I wrapped most of 'em in conduit. I'll go back down to check it out. What are you going to do with this, anyway?"

"I've got to stay a step ahead."

"Step ahead of what?"

Chris rubbed his hands together as the glow of the monitors illuminated behind him. "I... uh... have a business reputation to protect. Creepy Nights is catching on quick. It won't be long before kids, vagrants, and vandals snoop around. I can't be having that."

"Hey... what was that? I thought I saw somethin' on the screen."

"Probably just a glitch," Chris said. "I wouldn't worry about it."

"Critiquin' my work, huh? I guess you're payin' me for it, so what gives? I won't press you any harder. It's your tunnel. What you do with it is your business, not mine."

Livewire studied the monitors. "I thought I saw it on zone four. There's an old freezer link up. Looked like the light flickered for a second. I'll engage the audio."

"We need to get you back in the sun," Chris said. "You're seeing things. Security is just something I take seriously. Thanks."

Whatever you say. Something about this just seems off.

"Not a problem. I'll get back there to the south end with a new cable run, and we'll get that section back online."

Chris walked out of the room without a proper goodbye.

Just my luck… Almost done with this joint, and I still end up with the short end of the stick.

CHAPTER TWENTY-SIX

That should just about do it, LIVEWIRE thought as he pulled the cable through the tunnel.

He gulped down another can of *Flitz* before pitching it into a dark corner. A sniffling sound became audible. He moved toward it.

Who is that? Is someone there?

He ran his fingers down the side of the wall and sniffed at them.

"I smell you. I know a woman's body odor a little too well. You're trespassing. I'm going to have to tell Mr. Wilkerson. If you leave now, I won't say anything."

Sure enough. Look right over there.

A woman was sitting in a dark corner crying. He called out to her, "I didn't realize anyone else was here. I was just kidding about snitching. You okay?"

You've got to be kidding me. It's Chris's wife. He is some kind of freak, isn't he?

"No. I'm not okay. Of course he didn't. He hasn't once tried to come and get me out of here."

"What are you talking about? Are you trapped or what?"

The woman scoffed. "What's it to you?"

What's your deal, lady?

"Let's not drag this out," he said. "Seriously, just come out with me now. No woman in her right mind should lollygag around in a dark tunnel. Bound to be bats, rats, God knows what else is in here."

He grabbed her by the hand and she shrieked.

"You mean... Who else!" A bizarre figure leapt out from behind a dark corner. "She's not going anywhere. And neither are *you*! All those visions... those unexplainable feelings. I see it in your eyes!"

"What?"

"You're one of them, and guess what... We've got room for you, buddy! And you know what? Your hands shed innocent blood. Those animals never deserved to die. You know that."

"What's wrong with you?" Livewire quipped back. "What you talkin' about? One of what...? We weren't workin' out."

"A likely story. An animal's innocence isn't worthy of our bloodthirsty hands. Come on, now... a housepet? You should know better! Back off the wagon, I see. What a booze-brained loser." He bonked Livewire on the head with the *Flitz* beer can he pitched. "And a disrespectful litterbug. Why don't I just rough you up a little?"

Who does this guy think he is?

The creep twisted the beer can in circles until it split in half and he spread it out.

"What? What in tarnation you doin'?"

"That's for *me* to do and *you* to find out. Hold out your arm."

Katrina spoke up, "This creep's name is Joe."

"Katrina, thanks, but, I'll do the introductions. You just stay right where you are."

Creeper Joe lurched toward Livewire as he wrapped his left arm around his neck.

"Get on the ground!"

Livewire fell to the floor. "Ain't gonna get a fight out of me. I just want the hell out of here. Let the lady and me out, now!"

Joe raked the can across him as he cut into the top of his wrists.

"Just gonna mess you around a little. Heh-heh."

"Please stop," Katrina said. "Stop it before you kill him!"

Blood dripped from Livewire's wrists onto the floor.

"On your knees…" Joe ordered. "Lap it up. Lap it up. Like a dog… Like the mutt you killed… Don't make me keep cutting you."

Livewire knelt, licking the blood off the floor and consuming the dirt and tar. He gagged, growing sicker from the torture. Drifting in and out of consciousness, he mumbled in incoherence, "You want me to… what? Want me to what!"

I'm as good as dead.

"That's enough. I'll take care of the rest," Joe said.

Joe whacked Livewire in the back of the head hard enough to render him unconscious.

•   •   •   •   •

LIVEWIRE awoke, and his thoughts raced.

What a freak. I've gotta get out of here. At least the blood's scabbing up now. I thought I was dead.

From the dark corner ahead, a pair of yellow eyes glowed. The creep lunged toward him. He cursed under his breath.

Not again.

"What's your deal with me, man? I'm just here to do a job. I didn't do nothin' to bother you."

"Forget it," Joe said. "Let me pour this on you. It'll make you right as rain. You know, I think you're alright. Your story might even make 'honorable mention' up top on Level Seven, Surprise and Scare. Let's dig up your wife's parakeet and dog, give 'em to Chris, and have him stuff 'em and put 'em on the floor for inspiration. Taxidermy and Texas go well together, don't they? If you're lucky, I might even pump your useless behind up with formaldehyde and stick you in a glass case, too."

Livewire studied the cuts on his arms, watching them heal as Joe poured a clear liquid over them. Creeper Joe grinned as he stared at Livewire.

"That's better, isn't it?"

"No, no… This ain't right. I ain't got no business messin' around here."

"Take a swill while you're at it," Joe said. "I'm sure you'll see something worthwhile..."

"Nope," Livewire said. "What's going on here?" He tried to stand up and Joe knocked him back to the floor.

"Healing water..." Joe said. "Isn't that what you called it?"

I don't believe this.

"Say what?"

"Spring of Life. You give to Oak Hollow. It gives back to those it deems worthy."

"Say no more."

I've got to stay in good graces with this guy. I bet I can get on more comfortable terms treatin' him better than he deserves. The freak's never had a support structure a day in his life. There's somethin' strange about him. Some kind of aura... I don't know.

CHAPTER TWENTY-SEVEN

TODD ADAMS looked into Julie's eyes as his next therapy session went by at a snail's pace. The rearrangement to the room since their previous session unsettled him.

Find a distraction. The time will go by faster. She's an airhead. Did she change the order of her degrees on the wall? The doctorate used to be on the top.

She continued her discourse, "The thing about the manic and the depressive is that they are day and night with each other. Yin and Yang. Sometimes, I'll see a patient, and they'll be a lovely spring lily, standing out amongst a field of others that are all the same. The next time I see them, they're withered away, flat, and out of the frame while the others grow and blossom. Fast forward another session later, and I see an entire field... dark and charred, no lilies in sight, and then the strangest thing happens... a fire poppy grows amidst a field of ash."

Why do you have to be so good looking? Your analogies could use some work, though...

Todd smiled. "And what's that to me? Why do you feel the urge to tell *me* this?"

"I think you have the potential to be all of them. You've got to watch yourself so you can sense when the seasons are changing. Most folks bob up and down near the middle, about like a metronome, up, down, up, down. Being cyclical in our mood isn't a foreign concept.

For others, the cycle is more chaotic, up, up, up, up, down, down, down, down, up, up, up, up, up, up, up, up, down, down, down, down, down, down, down. Then just when you're expecting to go back up again and find a normalcy in your cycle, you get a burst of up or down so high or low, you feel you're going to fly right off the rails."

So deep. This talk is lib...erating.

"Todd, look at me. Where's your head? There are solutions buried deep within you. You're already helping by talking to me and taking the medication. Now you've just got to connect the dots with where your mood is. Neutralize the worst parts of yourself when you're out of sorts and capitalize on the very best of yourself when you're on top of your game." She adjusted herself across from one side of the office chair to the other and sighed. "Listen, I'm not here to sugar-coat anything. I'm here to help you improve your life."

Todd smirked. He flung a magazine off the table into the floor, knocking over Julie's glass of water.

"Todd, what's going on?"

"And just like that, she explains why the world spins at an angle... when we all knew that already. Look, I appreciate what you're saying and you trying to help me pull it together. The thing is, I'm dealing with something worse than a little mania here, Julie. It's a fu... it's a nightmare."

"Say it how you feel it. You don't have to censor yourself around me. Let out that pinned up emotion. This is a safe-haven."

I can't say it how I feel it. Are you kidding me? Self-control. Good man. Good man.

"How I feel it? Okay, then. I think you're beautiful. I think this relationship could lead me to trouble. I think that I'm capable of a lot of things I want to be capable of, and even more that I don't. What's the point? How do you fix that? I take my medication. I do my exercise. I even went out like you told me the other night and met somebody. Just as luck would have it, she's a soon to be divorcee with a chip on her shoulder the size of Alaska. So... what the hell do I do with that? You got a solution for me?" Todd's voice rose to an excessive yell, "Does your little DSM tell you how to deal with this shit?" He flipped the end table over and stood up, towering over Julie.

Julie reached her hand out and grabbed his arm. "I don't appreciate the damage to my office, Todd. We'll get to that later. It's okay. I'm here to help you."

Todd's mind raced away, and he glimpsed into the past through another man's eyes.

A middle-aged man stood in the middle of a pasture, staring down at him. He was soft-spoken. "Don, I've never seen richer, more fertile soil, son. Look at these lush oak trees. The grass is vibrant. Every single spot I place my poles reflects astonishing amounts of energy. I have visions this property will be something beautiful once it's developed. An area for people to come together at every phase of their existence. One day it will be yours. Promise me you'll take care of it," the man said.

"I promise, father. I feel it too," he concurred, standing a mere 5'4, still dressed in his Sunday best.

He glimpsed the father strolling with his arms behind his back, keeping his hands clasped together, and trusting his legs to never fail him. It must have had something to do with his feet and its steady link with the ground below — that feeling of gravity forever pulling to make the person above prepare to be one with the earth it walked on.

Their rods met the spot where the depths of the earth screamed the loudest, and the father and son penetrated the soil with their shovels several minutes.

"I didn't expect us to hit fresh water this soon. We aren't that deep yet. Let's keep going... I expected harder soil. Lay those boards on the edges, son."

•   •   •   •   •

"Todd, come back to me. Where are you?" Julie was snapping her fingers at him, trying to get his attention.

"Oh, I'm sorry. Where were we? You didn't hypnotize me, did you?"

"No. Tell me where you were."

"I can't recollect it, but it's there. What's wrong with me? Am I losing it?"

"I pushed you too far today. I'm sorry. Let's regroup next week."

"Sounds like a plan, pretty pe-can."

"Say what?"

"Sorry, my… dull attempt at humor."

"I like that smile," she said. "Remember, stay in touch with yourself. Don't be afraid to slow things down when it feels like everything is crashing down on you. That's what hobbies are for. Call me if you need anything."

"Thanks. How's the situation with your husband? He ever make it back?"

She looked away from Todd and sighed.

"No, he didn't. I'm trying to move on with my life. I can't change what I can't control."

No, you can't. So why are you trying to change me? All that education, dollars spent, and the best you can do is… tell me what I already know…

"I'll send some positive thoughts his way," Todd said. "Don't give up hope."

Her face soured. "Thanks. Have a good afternoon."

Back to the grind… What account can I exploit today? They make it too easy to take advantage. I'm no savant, but no one pays attention to anything. Double dose ought to straighten me out.

Todd grabbed his bottle of lithium pills from the glove box and dropped two into his car temperature coffee.

Come on now! Pull it together.

CHAPTER TWENTY-EIGHT

WAYNE WALLACE and his radio partner, Ramblin' Ron, prepped to exit the WGBO studio upon concluding the evening's episode.

"That was a good show tonight," Ron said. "I like what you did with that whole fish out of water theme and the gags…"

"Want to go grab dinner together?" Wayne asked.

"That sounds good. Meet you at Bridgewater?"

Wayne collapsed to the floor and convulsed.

Ron lunged toward the studio floor. "Wayne? Wayne? Come back to me. Come back to me, man. You alright?"

Wayne's eyes remained catatonic.

A terrifying memory rushed in front of him while he laid flat.

He stood in an old farmhouse as he entered a boy's room. He studied it, before gravitating to some loose floorboards, and yanking them up.

"Get out of there, Joe. Right now!"

The young teenager's little burrow was five feet deep. Knowing he acted out, the boy avoided his father. The man lurched to pull his son up.

"I have no words right now! None!"

Grabbing his son by the arm, he dragged the teenage boy across the floor, its splinters piercing his back as bruises formed from his tight grip. He scolded his son without mercy, "Your feet will never be quick to rush to evil again, boy. Never… I'll slow you down for this. Why did you do that? Why did you do that, son? She was undeserving! What were you thinking, knucklehead?!"

He chugged ounces of his *Old Tymer's* whiskey, slamming the glass bottle on the back of Joe's knees.

"None of my children will serve anyone but God. None of you. You spawn of Satan! Turning that cat into a marionette… *What* were you thinking? S-I-N. Can you spell that? Huh? Huh?"

He got right into the boy's face. "I didn't think so, dummy."

The liquor on his breath permeated the room.

He wiped his face and said, "I'll beat you 'til there's nothin' left, boy. Don't you ever 'mess nothin' around like that ever again, you hear me…? You might as well be dead for this God-awful act."

He pulled out the pistol he kept tucked in the back of his pants.

"Lay down on the ground, son, face down. I'm not going to allow any spawn of Satan. I'm not going to do that. You hear me, boy?"

He grabbed the revolver by the barrel, pistol-whipping his son behind the knees until they turned black and blue. The boy would never walk the same — his stuttering gait, forever scarred as a stark reminder for his misdeeds.

"There! Now we're done. That'll teach you a thing or two about respecting others the way God made you to."

The man hurled his son into the corner of his bedroom as the entire house shook.

"Go back into your hole. Maybe Satan will yank you straight to hell where you belong! I'm not much for giving second chances, but, your hussy for a mother wants me to take you to Reverend Selsky. Maybe he can talk some sense into you. I sure as hellfire ain't qualified."

· · · · ·

Wayne returned to his senses, realizing the memory was never his. Nothing was the same since his car accident the previous year. Though comatose a mere two weeks, he faced a slew of mental and emotional problems post recovery.

"You okay? What's going on?" Ron asked.

"I'll be alright. I had one of my... moments again."

"The lightheaded thing?"

"Yeah, something like that. I'll recharge over the weekend and see you on Monday. Have an extra drink at Bridgewater for me," Wayne said.

"Yeah, will do."

CHAPTER TWENTY-NINE

Chris Wilkerson popped into the lobby to greet NANCY HELBENS. His face showed no emotion and his voice remained flat, "Do you have a second? Let's find a conference room."

Nancy grew pale.

Gah. The petty cash... I'm such a dummy.

As Chris motioned toward her to sit, she studied the side of her arm, refusing to make eye contact with him. The chair she sat in squeaked as silence held the room its invisible hostage.

Chris sighed, collecting his composure before speaking, "I'm really sorry, Nancy, but I cannot, and I will not tolerate a liar. Nor can I stomach employing a thief. At the root of all evil is deceit. It's a shame I have to do this because you were doing some good things for us. You've left me with no other choice, though. Pack your belongings and get on. How long has this been going on? I hope the Reese's were worth it... You want to talk about it?"

Of course I don't want to talk about it, she thought. *Get on, and I will, too. I'm such an idiot.*

"Alright, then. That's how it's going to be? Good luck." Chris stormed out of the room.

"So... I can't be trusted with petty cash, and I've got a sweet tooth. Give me a break."

She slammed her fist on the table.

That was too loud.

The door to the room squeaked back open. "What was that noise?" Chris asked.

"I was just packing my things."

"Take care, thief. If money was really that tight, you should have said so."

• • • • •

After taking a few minutes to pull herself together, NANCY HELBENS walked out of the Creepy Nights facility. She moved toward the parking lot where her navy, wood-paneled station wagon was parked.

Can it get any worse? Momma's gonna freak. Dummy... dummy... dummy... That's me.

It was a rainy Tuesday night as she cranked the volume on her car stereo to the maximum.

"Folks, we interrupt our Two for Tuesday classic rock-and-roll mix to announce another disappearance in Riverton."

She changed the station as she cruised down the street past the Bridgewater Restaurant at an increasing speed. Three blocks later, the business district ended, and it led into an area surrounded by Oak trees.

"Who's there?"

Holy...

An unidentified pedestrian charged toward Nancy's vehicle, running her off the road straight into a tree as her car wrapped around it.

• • • • •

She awoke in a dark and unlit area with staggering ceilings, hearing the faint sounds of dripping and the chirp of smaller life creeping along. A chilling and whiny voice reverberated through the tunnel as she looked around. The creep spoke with exceptional confidence, "Alright then, Nancy. Let's throw law enforcement a bone. They're hungry for one, aren't they? They'll never find you. All they do on the

110

news in these situations is sensationalize. They love to create a narrative, a story — where pictures, faces, and names become nothing more than statistics. I won't let you become one of those. This isn't the same. Far different from any trail that those sorry dogs can sniff their way into."

He pulled out the bent nose automotive pliers from Honest Steve's and yanked back and forth until he ripped her implanted tooth out, stripping it away from the mounted screw. She could only scream a moment before seeing stars as she writhed in excruciating struggle.

Oh God, have mercy on me and my life. If you take me now, know that I'm sorry.

"Didn't belong in there anyway, did it?" the tormenter continued. "It was a phantom tooth… just a façade, nothing more than that. You should know about façades, shouldn't you? Heh-heh! What do you have to hide? The implant has a serial number. What do you say? Should we give them a little nugget? That'll be enough to keep things interesting, will it not? Everyone's going to assume you were just depressed. I mean, losing a job is one of the top five traumas experienced in a person's life, right? Especially since you worked so hard for… Chris. The guy raked you over the coals, didn't he? You know, people make so many assumptions. Most of them will be out there thinking you'd run away of your own volition to stay out of touch with the rest. It won't take long for them to give up hope and move on with their lives." The creep hovered above Nancy, his breath escalating as he continued his monologue and held onto her arm.

Get your hands off me. I can't stand the slickness.

"You have something you want to say, sweetness? Oh, I know how it stings, but it's the truth. You know you belong here. This place has been tirelessly pining for you. Thing is, most of life's important lessons happen in tumultuous times, don't they? There's power in numbers. So many missing pieces. And now, I'm bringing you all back together where you belong, tangled up in my web. It hasn't been easy collecting you. Remember? Can't you remember? Look into my eyes, dear child. You will see. *You* will see! Remember? You've got to get a hold of yourself! Otherwise, this place will eat you alive if you let it. It's a cruel dark world out there, my dear, but you won't *ever* have to worry about that anymore, will you? Who knows? You might even thank me later. Heh-heh."

The creep handed her a drink in a pewter cup.

"Take a swill of this. It'll cure the pain."

Please be poison. Please be poison. Just kill me.

She drank from the cup in one long-winded gulp.

Why do I feel relieved?

Nancy tried to speak but found no words. The bright glow in the creep's eyes radiated as he celebrated her capture.

"Call me Joe. I don't always introduce myself, but you're a looker. I always liked a round middle on a gal. I'm just going to bag the excess and take it to storage. Make yourself at home, because you won't be going anywhere soon."

Joe grinned as he stutter-stepped away into the darkness, toting a sack of Nancy's blood.

I feel like I'm going to faint.

The tunnel brightened up and an eleven year old Nancy appeared in her childhood backyard, lying short of breath in her sandbox. Her mother sat on the porch sipping on a glass of spiked lemonade while she crocheted.

"Walk like a crab, kid. We've got to burn some more calories. The damn sun sure ain't cooking them off your big behind."

"Momma, I can't do anymore. I just can't."

"I don't want to hear that. Get your lazy butt up now, before I make you eat more sand."

Nancy began to cry.

Bobbie Helbens stood up from her chair, chunking her glass against the brick wall of the house. "Stop that. You took too long!" She walked toward Nancy, cocking her fist back. Bobbie's face morphed into Creeper Joe's while her voice remained. He waved his hands side to side mimicking patty cakes.

"Nancy, Nancy. You're so fancy. Get it together so you can fit your pantsy!"

Her world went black.

CHAPTER THIRTY

Passing on Ebony Ivory for a promotion seemed the logical solution to CHRIS WILKERSON.

Too nosey and self-centered. I don't need any more of that. I'm just about running a charity for her anyway. Self-righteous and self-assured. No room for that in my management team. If Creepy Nights is a field of baseball players, she plays soccer — skilled in her own way, but not up to my expectations for Campy Corny.

He prepped to close out the interview in the small conference room behind the reception area, lighting a cigarette, and taking a drag. Looking away from Ebony for a moment, he puffed smoke in the air before turning back to conclude. He straightened her hand written résumé on the desk under his interview notes.

"Ebony, I want to say thanks again for your time today. It was an interesting interview. We'll be in touch as we make a formal decision on the manager role. I'll continue interviewing in the coming weeks and let you know… should we elect to offer you the job. I've always held my Level Seven staff in such high esteem. I really don't know what would attract you to a management role on Level Five. You are fundamentally doing the same thing already."

"For a fraction of the cost… Mr. Wilkerson," she said. "Is this your diplomatic way of telling me you're still weighing out your options and saying I don't measure up?"

"Ebony, that's not a fair question to ask. I've already gotten you off the street and given you a chance to get your life in order. Don't put me in an uncomfortable position."

"So, you're telling me someone else will get the job?"

Chris's face reddened. "No, I'm telling *you* to give *me* some time."

"Okay, well, I hope the candidate you find works out, then. Have a nice day."

Chris dropped his pen on the desk in front of him, slapping a hand on top of it.

Stupid little b...rat.

"Ebony, you're still under consideration. I take these decisions seriously. I don't know why you continue to be so combative."

She challenged Chris, leaning in closer toward him as she whispered. "I know how the business world works. I didn't fall off of the turnip truck yesterday. I've hired people before."

Stop talking now before I can your sorry ass.

Chris rubbed his eyebrows and sighed. "Ebony, this is a unique environment that requires a variety of talent pools and experiences. I wouldn't sell yourself short or make any hasty assumptions about what you don't know or understand."

Ebony shook her head. "I just sense it. You're going with someone else."

Chris inhaled as the embers on the tip of his cigarette glowed. He dismissed Ebony, blowing smoke in her direction. "Okay, then. Don't listen to me, and by the way, don't let the door hit you on the way out."

"Useless hag," he muttered as she walked out of the room.

FALL 1983

CHAPTER THIRTY-ONE

The clock buzzed.

Is it morning already? I've got to get myself to bed earlier.

TODD ADAMS slapped the noisy timekeeper from his nightstand onto the floor. Fumbling for his pills and the stale mug of lukewarm coffee, he twisted the lithium medication capsule in half and poured the contents into his drink.

Ah… that's the ticket.

He dragged his feet through the apartment, passing by a growing wall of lawn equipment partnered with some autographed *Boston* vinyls. He dug through his laundry basket, looking for his least wrinkled shirt. Upon dressing, he grabbed a bagel from the kitchen and pulled out his day planner.

Employee Assessment Meeting with Dave Rigson, Oak Hollow Country Club, 9AM

"Forgot about that… ugh… Guess I'll dress for the green today."

He stumbled into the bathroom, still neglectful of the stubble spread across the marble countertop left over from his previous week's touch up. Clumps of deodorant stuck to the floor just beneath as toothpaste crust lined the base of the mirror. One of the two bulbs above the smudged self-reflector illuminated as he studied his veneered appearance — a testament to masking his troubled past. He kept a manicured, but well-past five o'clock shadow, plastic-framed glasses, and a shapeless and poreless hairline purchased from a mail-order catalog in Beverly Hills. Despite maintaining a pretty boy image to match his career in finance, Todd Adams lived like a bum. He could afford more and do better. He just didn't anymore.

·   ·   ·   ·   ·

He and Dave Rigson stood on the green of the ninth hole as the sun beat down on them in an uncommon October heat.

"Adams, I hope you have a better week soon. We all have our slow times. The thing is, your recent performance is crap. I don't remember it being this bad for a long while. Probably since Gerald Ford was still president and Creensteen was passive-aggressively jabbing our asses away to meet quota."

Todd pulled out his putter and focused on the pin, positioning his feet in alignment with the hole. "Oh, Dave, it's just a phase." He putted the ball as it dropped straight into the hole. "We all have our difficulties. I'm waiting for that next manic burst of energy. Usually kicks in around this time of year."

"What are you talking about, Adams?"

"I've said enough. I'll get things in order, Dave. That's fifty-four strokes on the front nine. Fifty-five, and I would have said I'm gonna call it a day. Not a pretty first half for either of us. Let's say we mulligan the tenth with a hole in one and hit the clubhouse for some cold ones. My treat."

Todd flashed a grin at Dave as they boarded the golf cart. He drove a few seconds and then clammed up.

"Dave, I need you to take over. I'm not feeling great today."

Dave took control of the wheel as requested.

Todd's mind drifted elsewhere.

The hotel appeared in vivid detail. Tapestries and whirlpools, men in bath caps, and beautiful women in bathing suits that looked like outdated pajamas. He stood behind the lobby welcome counter as he popped open the hotel's cash register.

.   .   .   .   .

"What's going on, Todd? Where's your head at?" Dave asked.

"Forget it. I need to unwind at the bar for a bit… take my mind off things."

"You know we've got EAPs for this kind of thing. Company rules… I'll always be your boss, first. Your friend, second."

Todd picked up the bottle of *Flitz*, guzzling it a little too casually.

"You do know we're on work hours, Adams. Drinking on the job? You sure you're alright?"

"Dave, I'm fine. Thanks. You just had to bring up Creensteen, didn't you? I've been perfectly okay with him being gone. Just the kind of loser this area's better without."

"Todd, that's not fair. Dale's missing. You can't make light of these things. That could be *you* one day."

.   .   .   .   .

TODD slammed his fists on the steering wheel as he studied the gridlocked commute home.

Why do I even live here? This place is a wasteland. Nothing good ever comes out of this city, except smog and unemployed hippies. I'm sick of it! What a wilderness.

He inched down Riverton's crowded interstate with his radio tuned into WGBO 530 AM.

A voice boomed through the car speakers, "The thing I love about this strange city, Wayne, is its desperation to become larger when they never planned it to be. Council thinks if they just lure in a few corporations, throw up some high rises, and bring in a fancy port-a-john, Riverton becomes the hippest place in the Lone Star State overnight."

"No, Ron. We're not traveling that road again. I'm of the thought we'd be in better shape... if this entire town ceased to exist, just the way God made it, and before all of us... weirdos invaded."

I have to agree with you there.

"Weirdos? Wayne, I... am no weirdo. You are, though. I saw you go into one of those fancy port-a-john's the other day, and ladies and germs. It looked like he... liked it. You know what I mean...? Just picture it, a street-level port-a-john, fully equipped with the vented windows at the top... all that cheap, frosted plexiglass where you can make out that someone's in there, doing whatever it is they're doing... right in the middle of Eighth Street. Isn't it lovely?"

"Ramblin' Ron, folks... Ramblin' Ron. He's a deplorable guy, just like the rest of us."

"And what are you, Wayne?"

"More deplorable than you, Ron. More deplorable than you. And as for the port-a-john... of course it was me. Where else was I going to go? Under the bridge like everyone else around here?"

WAH... WAH... WAH... A horn audio cue played in the background.

"Haha. You are such a character. Hey... Let me tell you about my friends over at Blue Mountain Vision Center. They have changed my life..."

Enough. I hate commercials.

Todd shut the radio off. The WGBO Dynamic Duds radio program entertained him daily on his afternoon commutes. The thing that kept Todd interested was their notable clash with the rest of Riverton — a quirky pair always quick to disrupt the airwaves miles and miles in every direction. He glanced over at his Dud-Head baseball cap laying in the floorboard of the passenger seat.

Backstage passes to see minor celebrities are... never overrated. Yes, Lorrie... I'm still trying to justify the $50 subscription fee, but a shot to meet Ramblin' Ron or Wayne Wallace at the Wilker Park Chili Cook Off later this year just might be worth it. I love those guys.

After moving a mere thirty feet heading northbound, he noted an offensive billboard advertisement to his left. He looked below as his eyes met the flickering red letters at Honest Steve's Pawn and Loan —

one of his frequent after-work hangouts. Despite not being his exit to go home, he put his turn signal on, progressing toward the exit ramp. One sarcastic thought after another raced through his mind about his disdain for the troubled city and its traffic. He came off the interstate, turning into the pawn shop parking lot. While pulling in, a homeless man stood near the entrance in a blue hoodie. He held a torn paper sack over a beer can and a cardboard sign covered with permanent marker.

Need booze. Please help. I lost my job.

"Yeah. You lost your job *because* of booze, is what your sign should say," Todd said under his breath as he straightened a shoddy parking job.

The parking lot lines beneath the vehicle faded away, once yellow, perhaps even white. The spot might have even once been for the disabled, but those indicators were long gone, too. He flung the truck door open and climbed out. Before he could take a complete breath, the unwelcome stench of body odor mixed with alcohol seeping from the homeless man's pores hit him. In either a moment of compassion or total hysteria because of the chokeworthy scent, he handed the man a five-dollar bill. "Get out of here. Go buy yourself a hamburger and sober up."

"That's my business, not yours, chump," the man responded in a Yankee accent.

"Excuse me? I just gave you money, and you're calling me a... chump? You're the one begging for dollars. Beggars can't be choosers."

"No, no. That's what everyone else says. I say what I want to say. I... am a chooser. I'm off for another six-pack of *Flitz*. It's the cheapest stuff in town, and there ain't anyone else around here that ever drinks it. I call it the hobo's special. Haha!" The man's nervous laugh lingered for a moment before he spoke again, "We should just call it the official drink of the homeless. I could be their damned mascot if I wanted to."

Todd interrupted before the self-proclaimed *Flitz* mascot could say anything else, "Okay, whatever. Take care, then."

The homeless man trekked behind the pawn shop building in the face of its second-rate graffiti. His exiting self-monologue reflected his ongoing struggle. He walked toward the back of the building and out of sight. Glass shattered.

It's not my problem the bum can't take care of himself. Is it?

He pulled on the worn, jet black door handle — its undercoating exposed and reduced to a champagne color. His obsessive and angered thoughts raced.

The countless filthy hands that touched it and the owners to which they belonged. How many hadn't washed? How many had a disease? How many had killed someone? Hell, they might have even done it with a tool or weapon purchased from this building.

Entering the double-paned door, Todd waved at the shop owner, Steve Renzell, standing still behind the counter of his namesake business. Well-acclimated to Steve's typical standoffish demeanor, Todd walked by with a half-wave and headed to his usual browsing spot. Steve entertained a conversation when he sensed it needed. Still, he was often a man of fewer, more intentional words — the ones he deemed critical.

Todd often entered the store with no particular goal in mind. Despite an innocence to the practice, his compulsive knack for buying grass whackers had become a problem.

Steve called out from behind the register, "Come on now. Do you even have any grass?"

"No, not enough to fuss about. I'll get a weed from time to time, but that's about it," Todd replied, almost sounding embarrassed.

"Well, I guess the weed part fits in pretty well with what everyone else is doing around here, doesn't it?" Steve said.

Get on with it. I've got to get home.

Todd rolled his eyes, ignoring the inappropriate reference, and said, "I'd like to check out, please. Ring me up."

"Going with the sticker price today, are we…? Not even going to haggle or negotiate with me? Gee, Todd, you are losing your touch…"

"Hurry up, already!"

Steve shook his head, speaking at a relaxed tempo to calm Todd's frustration, "Okay, okay. Don't get your panties in a wad there. $54.00 even."

Todd paid cash and walked away.

It wouldn't hurt you to be nicer. Would it, Todd?

"Take care then, Steve."

He reached for his back pocket, unwedging his boxer shorts.

Steve might have been onto something. Ninety minutes in standstill is enough to make any of us antsy.

While exiting the building, Todd observed a five-dollar bill and a note taped to the hood of his F-150 as the parking lot security lights illuminated.

What's going on here?

He removed it, looking closer to examine the scribbled words before a sudden jolt went through the back of his head, knocking him unconscious.

CHAPTER THIRTY-TWO

WAYNE WALLACE and Ramblin' Ron had been radio partners hosting the Dynamic Duds show for years. They achieved notoriety in the area because of their spunky attitudes toward politics and the region's anxiety-inducing government affairs. With local attitudes swinging back and forth between party lines — an exhausted pendulum of aged elephants and pompous asses, they found a variety of ways to make light of situations in every instance, regardless of political affiliation.

This flavor of the week styled approach kept the show fresh, forcing the pair to remain on top of news and information. Dealing with the ferocity of partners and investors in their hunt to get better ratings was far from simple. Their show topped the charts on occasion, remaining in the top five by volume of listeners. Despite this, they liked to lead their audience to believe they catered to a smaller, more exclusive crowd. While wrapping up another episode, the two men took off their studio headphones.

Ron took a sigh, looked his partner in the eyes, and said, "I'm not sure I can do this anymore."

Wayne's eyes widened. "Are you kidding me? This work comes natural to you. You can't leave now."

Ron leaned into the doorframe of the studio, propping his weight against it. "I want to end this thing on a high note. This show has cost me everything. My marriage. My life. My friends. I think I just want to go off-grid for a while."

"Ron, come on. Think it over, buddy. I don't know what they're paying you, but I'm sure we can negotiate better. I need this show as much as you do. Bonnie and Clyde. Siskel and Ebert. Hall and Oates. Wayne and Ron. This is our jam, man. Don't leave me now."

A glassy film came over Wayne's eyes while he processed the news.

"I'm sorry," Ron said. "This is it. I'll give you a few more days, and I'm done. October 21st. That's my last day."

Devastation ran amuck in Wayne's mind.

What will the producers do with me? Without Ron, I'm nothing but a punching bag. I can't be a one-man-band. Nobody listens to that kind of show anymore. It's always got to be a gang or a duo. I don't want to deal with a new partner. My contract is up at the end of the year.

Walking out of the station, he stepped into the street in a state of shock. A homeless man sat out front of the station with a cardboard sign.

That guy looks familiar. Huh.

It was, in fact, Creeper Joe, though Wayne did not recall their being introduced.

The white sign featured permanent marker ink written at a slant.

We all know the world is going to end... Help a brother out.

Wayne reached in his pocket, feeling a couple of dollar bills. "I'm sorry. I don't have any cash," he lied.

"Are you sure about that?" Joe asked.

"Of course I'm sure. My wife and kids took it all, pretty standard around here."

What's your deal? Memorize the guy's description. When he's done with me, I'll go to the cops.

Joe stood up, and his voice elevated, "Guess again, Wayne!"

Dusk approached, and Creeper Joe grabbed Wayne's neck, choking him as he carried him into a neighboring alley. He continued to squeeze tighter and tighter, speaking with an increasing rhythm and volume in his voice as he spewed words, "A lying tongue will get you nowhere. Absolutely nowhere! Why don't I cut it out for you?

What do you think? That might help. You know, take away your...
livelihood. The thing you do best. Blah... blah... blah! I'm not sure you
could handle that now, could you?"

*I can't breathe. Keep my feet on the ground. I'm smarter than he is. Play
it that way.*

Wayne shook his head. "I guess not," he said, clearly winded as
Joe loosened his grip, brushing the asphalt from the tops of his
shoulders.

"Well then, come with me. I'm going to take you someplace you
need to see. If you ever judge me with those haughty eyes again, I will
hollow them out for you! Heh-heh!"

Play it casual. It'll throw him off.

"Fine. I'm coming. I'm coming. What's your name? Haven't I seen
you around here before?"

"I doubt it, Mr. Wallace," Joe's voice eased. "I doubt it. Call me Joe.
Walk with me a little further?"

*Must be a full moon tonight. Why would I? That's right... Self-
preservation.*

Wayne studied the sky. The full moon made his heart sink.

"Sure. Show me a good time."

Silence followed them as they went through the dark alleyway.

*This day's been too emotional for me. When I hit the sack, I'm taking three
crazy pills.*

Approaching the neighboring Oak Hollow District, Wayne spoke,
"I know where..."

He fell to the ground.

CHAPTER THIRTY-THREE

TODD ADAMS awoke in a dark tunnel as a rat ran across the top of his chest.

How long have I been out? Where am I?

He studied the ceiling above, observing its long trail of dim lights and a few bats hanging in the vicinity. Feeling post-concussive side effects, he noted a series of small, multicolored halos around each as it glowed. They billowed gray smoke, burning no brighter than ten or fifteen watts.

The lights are useless. The tunnel's twenty-five, maybe thirty feet high, fifty feet wide. What good are they?

A radio kicked on in the background down the long corridor. The Creepy Nights commercial jingle came through the speakers at an overpowering volume and then transitioned back to the scheduled program.

"Thank you for listening to WGBO 530 AM. The only Riverton station for deplorable people like the dud-heads! I'm Wayne Wallace, and you all know my pointless, breath-stealing accomplice, Ramblin' Ron Richards. Today, we're going to talk... scary. It's October 29th, 1982..."

1982? No. It's 1983. What's going on here?

"Halloween is just around the corner, and I want to give my half-brained buddy, Ramblin' Ron, a chance to tell us a good yarn..."

The radio turned off, and the lights in the tunnel dimmed. Hobbling footsteps neared as they traipsed through puddles.

Where am I? Who's there?

"Hello?"

It hurts to move. Who the hell is flicking my ear?

Feelings and memories of his childhood flashed in front of him, first being bullied, and later, memories of himself being the bully. He never was the bully, so to speak.

These phantom memories aren't mine. Whose are they?

He turned around. A strange-looking figure lurked — his familiar face and eyes glowed a distinct amber. The character shined an overpowering flashlight beam into Todd's eyes.

"You know why I have you here... don't you, Todd?"

"No, not really. Do I know you from somewhere?"

"I don't think so. I'm here to creep on you."

"To what?"

"Creep on you, dummy. Don't you get it? This is my funhouse. Not yours. Heh-heh. Let's set you straight before you end up like all the rest of 'em around here. What do you say?"

His face... What's wrong with it? Is he even human anymore?

"Set me straight? I don't follow."

"You know. Cure you. Cure you of all of your impure thoughts about the 'lessers' around town. Pride cometh before a fall. Did you honestly think that giving them a few of your... hard-earned dollars was going to fix the problem? Why'd they end up on the streets to begin with? It's a broken system out there."

"Yeah, okay, sure. Don't get preachy on me. I get the picture now. Please get on with it and set me straight."

He heard the tug of a weedeater cord, and the unwelcome odor of aged gas hit his nostrils. After sputtering for a couple of seconds, the unit turned over. The silhouetted figure pulled the plastic trigger on the Red Helix weedeater.

VROOM... VROOM... ZZZZZZZ... ZZZZZ... ZZZZZZZ!

Todd still wore his pair of khaki golf shorts, donning a tan that doubled as good advertising for the thriving tanning businesses popping up all over Riverton County. It was irrelevant. Without a hint of daylight in the tunnel, day and night no longer mattered. The weedeater wielding weirdo leaned in closer. Threaded six inches too long, the tight-wound cord cut into the front of his shins as the creep spun it.

He's gonna kill me.

Todd worked to wrench himself away as pieces of his skin flecked off into the floor of the tunnel — some even landing onto the top of his parched lips as he cried out in agony. The torturer kept on. Todd shrieked and moaned as he heard growing amounts of unprecedented laughter coming from the subterranean bully. It echoed down the long tunnel.

"Ah! Ah! What are you doing?" Todd screamed, "That's enough!"

"I'm just getting started on you, Todd Adams. You better roll over. Ha! You know what? We should get the back of your legs matching with the front. Don't you think? Those haughty eyes of yours better stop judging others and start doing something more productive, like God made you to. Don't you worry, I'll go to your house and collect all those grass choppers. Some strange kinds of idols you got. All you financial people are so materialistic, aren't you?" The creep clicked the back of his teeth. "Such a Western problem... we'll get Chris to hang every one of those whackers from the ceiling in one of his exhibits up top. It'll look good next to the hanging cadavers on hooks. Don't worry. They're rubber, of course. Who knows? What I did to you might even end up in a story told over the phone to a self-serving creep up there, too. Heh-heh."

I can't take this anymore.

Todd fainted a moment.

Dear God, it hurts.

The relentless tormenter hovered over his body.

"Fifty-two. Fifty-three. Fifty-four! Fifty-four scrapes on your legs. A perfect number in here. Just like you. What are you going to do about them? Just feel the pain. Learn it!" the weirdo's whiny voice carried through the tunnel. He put his hand on Todd's shoulder, patting it with a peculiar rhythm.

I'm in agony... my legs are numb.

Todd closed his eyes, working to regain his composure.

CHAPTER THIRTY-FOUR

WAYNE WALLACE's relocation to the tunnel was nothing short of unpleasant. Becoming alert, he panicked.

I can't see. I can't see! What have you done?

He tried to scream but could only make guttural noises. Reaching into his mouth, he searched with his index finger as he collapsed to the floor.

My tongue's been severed.

Creeper Joe called down into Wayne's cell, "I save only the best for my worst. You folly stricken people are worthy, aren't you? Fifteen feet deeper than the rest locked away in a cell, Wayne! You deserve it. I know who you are. You're back again to torment me, aren't you? You ruined my life on this earth, and I can't stand thinking about how much you wrecked my childhood. You didn't have to. You didn't have to take advantage of us — always turning to the bottle when we needed you most."

Who does he think I am? I'm a small-time radio guy. Nothing more.

"Don't you find it ironic? Everything comes full circle, doesn't it? Silent film star in the 20s... shock jock in the 80s. I liked you better as the film star. Now you'll be nothing more than a has-been radio star. Think about that for a moment. No one will ever hear you blab with that giant mouth of yours again. Did you ever do anything useful with your God-given gifts and abilities? We'll remind you with some

Dynamic Duds episodes where you trashed others the most with your lying tongue. It seems to me that you wanted to stir up trouble in the community. I can make this place hell for you, you know. Heh-heh."

Wayne's mind raced into the unfamiliar past.

The room was dim as evening encroached. He sat in the back pew of the Oak Hollow Church while the reverend spoke to a bruised Joe.

"Son, you need to honor and respect your mother just like Scripture instructs. She deserves better out of you — giving you one-hundred percent every single day. Even setting these meetings up with *me* to grow you into a better man. You've got to do more to show her you care. How can you do God's work when you act this way? He has a *special* purpose for you, but you have to deem yourself worthy first."

Joe nodded his head as he stood up to leave the room.

"Goodbye, Joe. Tell your mother I said hello."

CHAPTER THIRTY-FIVE

CHRIS WILKERSON's descent to misery followed him everywhere he went as Joe twisted him deeper into his manipulative grip.

I'm sick of the news. Aren't there better stories for them to cover? No big financial scandals or cover-ups? No affairs? Every single night it's more and more coverage on the disappearances. I don't think there's any getting myself out of this mess — twenty kidnappings more than I should have ever done. A chip in the bucket to the fifty-four. I can't rationalize my way out anymore.

He popped a can of *Flitz*, took a big swill, and poured an ounce of *Old Tymer's* into the bottle.

That's a little better. Block it out. Numb the pain. It's the only way to move forward.

Avoiding Joe prolonged the problem as Chris's exits from Creepy Nights lessened and his inaction brought out more reclusive tendencies. Manipulating Joe's victims to kidnap them nauseated him. Doing so amidst their innocence made it agonizing.

The freak's more than capable of performing the captures on his own, but seems to get a rise from involving me. That's a ghastly atonement for sharing the mysteries of Oak Hollow. Whatever those are... They're going to catch us any day. I can feel it. And the worst part is, I went along with it like a freaking puppet. I've got nowhere to run. No longer a matter of if, but when — forever an accomplice. These burdens aren't going anywhere.

The sofa bed couldn't beckon any faster. He surrounded it with a couple of accordion-style room dividers on rollers and closed himself in. It darkened the area well, but that was no match for the struggle. Every night at dusk, he longed to escape his inner turmoil, but the regime was never enough to achieve inner peace.

Exercises to slow your mind. Ice cream flavors. State capitals. Favorite movies. It's never enough.

This evening was no different. Chris anguished over Creeper Joe. He struggled even more over a recent victim that he wrangled with electrical wire and duct tape — feeling ever so horrified to see full pieces of the woman's scalp separate from her skull as he yanked it away. Weeks after the encounter, the memories haunted his mind. With no way out of the toxic agreement, a foreseeable path to relief seemed impossible.

I need to get out, but I'm bound to run into Joe again. I can't. I don't care how high the stakes are. I live in fear, knowing it will lead me to an uninteresting end. I'm not ready for that yet. Everyone deserves a second chance.

His insomnia would cure itself for short periods of rest until he awoke sleepwalking and wandering Level Eight in the overnight hours. He worked with diligence to escape his brushes with hysteria — trying to the best of his abilities to meander his weary mind. He remained unsettled one night as his mind wandered.

Not going to be any trips to Level Zero to clear the air with Joe. The entire Oak Hollow property, both above and below, take on different forms in the wee hours of the night, and it's too unsettling. Joe's done me wrong for too long. Something has to change, but first, I have to learn his pattern. I will no longer be a gaslit pawn.

CHAPTER THIRTY-SIX

TODD ADAMS heard a clicking sound as the voices on the radio grew louder and the tunnel speakers echoed. Further symptoms of lithium withdrawal set in.

I've worked too many hours in my life for it to end like this. My head's killing me. It's like I'm swimming around as I walk.

The lights came back on, and the radio stopped. The creep's stutter-stepping footsteps moved in the opposite direction. Feet clanked on a metal ladder, fading away.

There's some daylight. Where are you going?

The brief glimmer came a quarter mile from where he laid. Todd reached for his shin, examining the gashes and abrasions from the weedeater.

Man, that hurts!

He wrenched himself up to gain momentum as his mind searched for a rationale for his unexpected capture.

I'm not prejudiced against the lessers, the homeless, or the indigent. I'm quite considerate. In fact, I'm nicer than 98% of the other useless people around this forsaken town. Who's he to judge me?

Todd looked at his legs in the dim light as it exposed various aspects of his seven layers of skin.

I hope that's not muscle jutting out. I can't look at the scratches.

He stood and hobbled through the tunnel. As to the direction, North, South, East, West, it was unclear. If there was a burning orb in the sky to light the way and direct him, it served no purpose. Traversing through, others sat with their legs crossed, keeping to themselves. He stumbled across a familiar face.

What are the odds? It's the same drunk I gave five dollars to at the pawn shop.

"Hey, I know you," Todd said.

"Have a drink with me," the man mumbled.

He pulled out two *Flitz* beers.

Is the tunnel some kind of underground society? A better way for them to do life away from the pressures of the rest?

The man's red sleeping bag graced the mixed dirt and concrete floor, accompanied by an underwhelming garden lantern that barely glowed and a small charcoal grill.

A brewski with the character might be just the respite I need – anything to block thinking about the weedeater incident.

"So, you live here or something?" he asked.

The hobo cleared his throat. "I guess I do now. Been panhandling on the streets for a while. Government no longer paying me for my service in 'Nam and times got tough with my old lady. The bag booted me out when the pension ran dry. Haha."

There's that misplaced laugh again.

The inebriated man rubbed the back of his middle-aged head in something of a nervous motion.

Todd shook his head. "Yeah? No money, no job, and a lot of giggles. Sounds like an expedited recipe for divorce to me."

"No. I'm not sure about that. We were bad off... way before that. We had plenty of other problems... I shouldn't have ever done this, but in the winter, I'd heat our unmentionables in the toaster oven. You know, to keep things interesting behind closed doors." The character raised his bushy and unkempt eyebrows, looking to Todd for approval or disapproval.

Todd returned a blank stare.

What are you doing? What am I doing?

They each held a can in the air, popping them open in perfect synchronicity. The man stuck his hand out to shake Todd's. Todd returned with a firm grip.

"Harvey Brown. You can call me Harv."

"Todd. It's nice to meet you... officially."

Is it really? I don't know. What else can I do?

Harvey clanked his can against Todd's.

"To friendship," Harvey said.

"To friendship... I haven't had one of these since... college. Man, now I remember why," Todd reflected aloud, wiping the stale beer from his lips as he gagged some of it up.

This stuff is for the hobos.

"You found anything else to drink around here?" Todd asked. "How about a way out?"

Harv grinned. "Well, you can go over there and stand under those pipes. Looks like they drip a trickle here or there." His coarse laugh evidenced a buzz received from the stale *Flitz*.

"Before you go and while we're a little tipsy, I want to relive a moment with you; from better days... it might make you appreciate men like me a little more. I know you ain't seen a day on the front lines in your lifetime."

"I should get on..."

"Just this once. I need a friend."

Alright, then. Get on with it, man. Don't waste my time.

"Sure... go ahead," Todd said.

Harvey smiled. "Thanks... In '71, I enlisted in the army to help support my ex and the kid financially. It was just the right thing to do. I hadn't left things as tidy back home as I should have. I was what you would call a non-traditional candidate. Imagine a forty-two-year-old in basic training—Fort Knox. It sure whipped me into shape quick, though. There was this ignorant idiot kid, Johnny Welch. I always had a soft spot for the punk. One night we got a little rowdy in the barracks when our lieutenant was away. The troops had loaded *Creedence Clearwater Revival* in the stereo, and it blared through the building, rattling the walls in protest to our impending deployment. The kid kept messing with me as I prepped to turn in for the night.

'Hey, gramps… you need us to change you at night? Pretty sure we hear you getting up at least six or seven times a night to relieve yourself. Do you want to tell us what it was like growing up in the Abraham Lincoln administration?'

'That's enough. I'll have you know, I am in a position to one day take over this entire platoon before your extremities are even mature.'

'Shut up, old man. You don't know what you're talking about. I bet you're shriveled up like an old raisin.'

The men got a little wound up that night. Beds flipped over. Windows broken. Holes in the sheetrock. The cadets were all roaring and howling, louder and louder by the second. The lieutenant was out late, and me and the mostly twenty something group took advantage of our extended liberties.

It didn't take long before I was in the middle of a good 'ol fashioned brawl. Here I am twenty-four years this little guy's senior. I knew better, but I couldn't hold back. He dogged me one time too many, and I couldn't take it. Johnny stood there front and center as the others pushed the remaining beds that weren't flipped over flush to one another and against the walls to make room in the middle as they circled around. I dropped Johnny to the floor. We wrestled and fought for several minutes as the grunts and yells got louder and louder. Props in this… battle for manhood were not a bunch of smoke and mirrors like you see on TV; it was all real. Young versus old, but for some reason, the boys seemed to cheer for me like *I* was their old man.

'Yeah, I'll put down ten on the old timer,' one man said.

'Me too,' another called out.

Another barely sober one made the dumbest joke I can recall, 'I'll bet he falls down and starts the menopause before it's all said and done.'

Some of the more plastered cadets laughed, but the rest just looked at him, agreeing the alcohol made him stupid. I tried to script out my moves to shut the twerp up. Annoying little piss-ant stood 5'3 and weighed 140 pounds. You've seen me. I'm hunched over and frail now, but in those days, 6'3 and 220 looked good on me. I had decades of southern cooking before the divorce. I kept teasing the kid because he rattled my cage.

'I bet little Johnny still eats his lunch in the high school cafeteria when he goes home for the weekend...' I said.

The room roared in laughter, some even applauding. It was my moment of glory. That one time in my life where I had the spotlight and looked like I mattered.

I scripted out the finale. Punch to the left... rabbit punch to the lower torso... duck... uppercut to the chin... southpaw him in the upper torso... duck... and pivot with another southpaw to the jaw... down. Johnny was one step away from a KO. And then I saw it. He was a momma's boy, and it was clear he was compensating for never having a father around to care for him. I could see it in his eyes. The kid deserved mercy, so I tapered off. I held back. The lieutenant was seconds from coming back in and spouting off a list of obscenities no cadet's mother would have ever approved her son to hear. I chose the higher road. Always fight with character... Keep some dignity in your back pocket for the good of everyone else. That's it."

"Thanks, Harv. I know you a little better now." Todd patted him on the back.

"If you're going to get us out of here, Todd, follow that idea... with character. Treat the others in here right, too. I'm willing to bet that a lot of us have had a tough life. Probably a lot tougher than you could ever know, pretty boy."

Easy for you to say... Play it nice.

Todd nodded, maneuvering away from Harv. He pitched another can of *Flitz* to Todd.

"Take one for the road ahead," Harv said. "I'll be in your corner."

I don't want this. Be polite, anyway.

"Thanks. So what ever happened to Johnny?"

Harv teared up. "We got deployed right before Nixon started pulling some of the troops out. Raided a compound in 'Nam and a landmine blew the kid up. He was a day shy of nineteen. God bless him."

He struggled to catch his breath as a tear went down his once sun-kissed cheek.

"I'm sorry to hear that."

"Never take a day in your life for granted," Harv said. "They're all a gift. I may be a little off my rocker, but I have *my* redeeming moments. How about you?"

I can't take any more of this sappy talk.

"Harv, it's been interesting. Yeah. Interesting. I'm sure I'll see you around here again. I know it's a little off topic, but, what did you do with the five dollars?"

"I didn't get to keep that. I gave it away. Someone else needed it more than me."

They heard a clicking sound.

"Shh. Listen up," Harv said.

The voice of Ramblin' Ron came on the tunnel speaker, "Yep, we're here again. 6:04PM. The disappearances in Riverton are on the rise with no clear leads for RPD. It's certainly causing people to look over their shoulder as they leave the office or the house. They seem to go missing after dark. If you have any information on these cases, please call the authorities. This is..."

CLICK.

Todd moved away from Harv toward a quiet corner.

I guess this nook will be my home base 'til I can find a way out. Doesn't look like anyone's laid claim to it.

CHAPTER THIRTY-SEVEN

RAMBLIN' RON maintained glitz in the public eye, despite perpetual struggle under the surface. Beneath the dark shades, the swooped hair, and the thrift-store smoking jackets was a wayward man far from who he longed to be. The radio life had its perks, but it also had its setbacks. He struggled with the loss of his radio partner.

Where are you, Wayne? What happened?

His on-air accomplice had not been back to work since he gave notice to WGBO, nor was he home or returning phone calls. He and the other WGBO staff spliced historical audio snippets from Wayne based on scripted episodes of the Dynamic Duds that Ron penned in the interim. Even with that, he was running out of energy to keep up. WGBO worked to keep the Wayne narrative out of the press. The extra work wore away at him as he neared the self-declared finish line.

Is it quitting time yet? Get me out. I shouldn't even be here.

He cued the commercial break as the show concluded and walked out of the studio, not bothering to greet his relief or the receptionist. Moving onto the street, he crossed paths with an unrecognized homeless man a block past the station. It was Creeper Joe, though the two had never had a formal introduction.

Joe spoke to Ron as if he had a mouthful of spit, "Hey, you're that radio guy, aren't you? I've seen you before."

"Nope, not me," Ron lied. "I'm in commercial appraisals."

That was a smooth lie. Where did that come from?

"I don't know. I take you more as a... self-assured... Messiah type. You sure about that? You *sound* familiar."

"I assure you. Can I show you my business card to prove a point?"

"No. Not necessary. I know better. I'm not going to make you deny it a third time. I'm sure a rooster would crow. Watch out. That lying tongue of yours will get you into a big heap of trouble around here. Heh-heh."

Whatever you say. Just let me get on with my life, and I'll let you get on with yours.

"Yeah, okay," Ron said. "Have a good day."

He continued his walk on Oak Hollow Lane toward the bus stop. An irrational fear of driving and a slew of back-dated alimony payments led him to public transportation. He sat down.

That guy can't afford a bus. What do I have to worry about? He was just riffing. Yeah. That's all.

He looked over his shoulder in paranoia.

Who's watching me?

The bus stop bench annoyed him — its problematic and troubled surroundings only exasperated matters. The stop was just to the east of the Creepy Nights facility and the closest pickup spot from WGBO. Ron inventoried it many times in his waits.

The asymmetrical rows of gum stuck to the translucent plexiglass — random wads running across the top and bottom of the bench. The neighboring, rusting, hunter green garbage receptacle, covered in bird droppings — never lined with a sack — a sorry testament to the lazy workers. Cigarette butts jammed into the cracks of the concrete just below, lingering urine stains... What a mess!

The bus interrupted his thoughts as its air brakes pumped. Ron boarded, taking his usual seat on the fourth row from the rear, window seat, driver side.

What a relief to get away from that weirdo. I may have to rethink my way home. I can't be too predictable anymore. Who knows what happened to Wayne?

A familiar, prominent, alto-saxophone sprinkled *Bruce Springsteen* song came through the bus speakers as he climbed on. His usual ride was about twenty-three minutes, with eight stops — just two miles to his residence, but the trek passed through a lot of high-risk and crime-ridden areas he was unwilling to chance his life on. He considered bicycling to drop the extra weight he carried from getting paid to sit on his ass and jabber away all day, but never followed through. There were far too many drunks and idle-bodied hobos to consider it.

The bus rides were a goldmine for inspiration and material on the show. When he and Wayne were dry on ideas, Ron took excerpts from observations of the ride and his best recollections of the chance conversations that happened on each trip. He would take notes in a small spiral-bound notebook chronicling each day, the passengers, and the mood or flavor of the surrounding conversations. His favorite trips were the quiet ones, though. Even Ramblin' Ron could use a break from time to time.

Bus riders were, at times, a lively and exciting crowd — sometimes too wasted to drive themselves and too frugal to afford a taxi. Other times, it was a homeless panhandler who collected enough quarters to hitch a ride to the other side of town to siphon more. Looking for a passenger to write about, he judged a man across the aisle.

Yeah. You're mismatched, aren't you? Olive slacks and a houndstooth jacket. How long have you been divorced? If you still had a car, you'd probably sleep in the back seat.

He struggled to ignore the body odor of the man sitting to his right while continuing his brief analysis of the other.

I bet the poor bastard got those at a Good Will from some corporate fat-cat lawyer that outgrew his britches. Good for him.

The man in the seat next to Ron clicked the back of his teeth while shaking his dirty finger at him.

No way… how did he get on here without me noticing?

"Oh, Ron, you have *so* much to learn. You ever heard this one?

Judgy wudgy's threads are bare.

Judgy wudgy isn't fair.

Judgy wudgy soon is dead… Soon, you're dead!

You are the picture of SIN, my friend."

Joe bent over and yanked a Bible out of his beaten-up messenger bag as he tore out a page.

"Read it and apply it. You better become a Proverbs 6 man before it's too late. It's already cost your marriage and your friends, hasn't it? Heh-heh."

What an ass. This hobo thinks he can talk to me that way?

"I'm sorry," Ron said. "What did you say? How is that any of *your* business?"

Joe's voice elevated, getting faster by the second, "That's where you are *so* wrong. You have a public life. You're in media, genius! You've got people in every damn dimension of this town listening to you."

"What do you mean, dimension? North side? South side? The places in between?"

Creeper Joe chuckled. "Not at all. Not at all. I can't answer complicated questions off the cuff like that, and neither can… Wayne. Heh-heh."

What does that even mean? Archaic, cryptic, or schizo?

Joe handed Ron an unmarked, white paper sack, twice folded, and soiled at the bottom. Gobs of spit flew through the air as he spoke, "Don't open *this* 'til later." Creeper Joe stood up, walked to the front, and said something to the bus driver.

What are you saying?

The bus stopped without warning, and Joe exited. Ron opened the sack. Just inside, there was a severed, bloody tongue.

Good G…

The harsh odor of the spliced appendage caused him to faint. In what seemed moments later, Ron regained consciousness, observing the soiled paper sack in his lap.

"This is your stop, ain't it, Ron?" the bus driver called through the crackling loudspeaker.

"Yeah, I'm going. I'm going," he said.

How does one react to this kind of thing? I'm not going to say anything to anyone else right now.

He carried the sack under his jacket as he exited.

Upon arriving home, he placed the sack on the tiled floor near the front door.

I guess I'll call the cops. Don't know what else to do.

He collapsed on the couch, nodding off for a moment to escape the stress of the day and its peculiar end. There were three pounds on the front door.

Must be the cops.

Ron got up slowly to open the door, and then there were three more.

Hold your horses.

A police officer greeted him, "Hi there. We received a call on some… evidence you received. I'm here to collect it."

"Yes sir. It's in that sack right there. Forgive me for not wanting to touch it again."

"Hold it. We're not letting you off that easy. We'll bring you in for questioning and work to rule *you* out as a suspect," the officer said.

"What? I gave this to you. Shouldn't that rule *me* out?"

"I'm sorry, Mr. Richards. It doesn't work that way. We've got mounds of missing person's cases around here. Haven't you been watching the news? I don't know what the chances of matching this tongue to someone will be, but we might. Strange as it may sound, a calculated body part removal is almost always *specific* for a *specific* reason."

"You mean… it could belong to someone known to 'abuse' their tongue?"

"Exactly."

"Well, that narrows it to about 540,000. Nice going. All of my hard-earned tax dollars at work," Ron said.

Remaining solemn or cordial looked to be a struggle.

I guess that struck a nerve. He's fuming now.

"Watch it or I'll write you up for contempt," the officer said. "I shouldn't say this, but, I'm sure it is another guy about like *you* — someone cheeky in the public eye. You guys get some weird followings, especially around here. I used to be in Jersey. There were homicides, murders, rapes, common garden variety crimes there. The things you see in the movies. The stuff around here. It's worse, man. Who knows? There's probably a joker somewhere that has every episode of your radio show taped, listening to it before bed at night, and playing your voice in slow motion — all because he's attracted to the way it sounds. Better yet, maybe it's a chick that's got your face tattooed in the small of her back. Think about that as your ugly mug stretches across the top of her fat butt. You never know."

"Nice one. Thanks for the bode of confidence... Officer?"

"Detective... Penske."

"Like the truck?"

"Yep. Just like that. I won't be cuffing you. Let's just take a ride to the station to admit the evidence, and we'll ask you a few questions. Your friend Wayne's missing, isn't he? You guys have pulled some strings to keep that one out of the press, haven't you?" As they walked toward the police vehicle, Ron nodded his head.

"You know, Ron," Penske said, "the case will get a lot more media coverage with the discovery of the tongue. It's just too darn juicy a story not to get some air time."

"Oh my..." Ron buried his head in his hands. "I hope you don't link *me* to Wayne's disappearance. He was a moody guy, you know — a depressed type. One day on cloud nine, the very next — back to his own personal hell. He wasn't miserable, but most of the time, he was bitter. If we're honest with each other, he was just flat-out aggravated. I mean, let's face it. We've all had our moments. Riverton's a depressed place — a miserable town with dark secrets that silently eat away at all of us, wearing us all to pathetic states of mind. I'm sure you've figured that out by now, though."

"I don't disagree. Let's not get bogged down talking about that. As for Wayne, it sounds like you have a good profile worked up on him yourself. Are you a calculating type?" Penske asked.

"What do you reckon, Penske? We worked together for close to five years. The talk-radio scene has changed a lot since we first came online. We have eighteen seconds to get someone's attention before they change the station on us. Our investors are forcing us to advertise mid-segment to avoid losing listeners, and we both hate it. What else can we do with change but embrace it?"

Keep it together. Everyone's had a ride in a cruiser... who am I kidding?

Penske shrugged, twisting his lip with his index finger and thumb and said, "Not much, I guess. If you want to keep a job, I mean. Well, here we are... Precinct Three. You ever been in here before?"

Ron shook his head as he studied the facility,

The building's not much to look at. It could double as an abandoned YMCA from the 60s. Full of vagrants, deviants, and invalids — sloppy stonework by a half-drunk mason. Roof tiles falling off… just dangling from the building. Even the adhesive filters are peeling off the windows. Council's too busy financing its next street-level port-a-john to consider spending any more money on what's needed. Go figure.

"What are you doing? You dazed or what? Let's get the evidence admitted, and I'll escort you back to interrogation room three," Penske said.

CHAPTER THIRTY-EIGHT

TODD ADAMS continued en route to the area the freak exited, still pondering on his conversation with Harv. He studied the tunnel, noting many crevices, hideaways, and various pieces of old furniture strewn about.

My meds are wearing off. This ought to be interesting. I'm due for a change any day now.

He had many thoughts about the tunnel, but nothing seemed to make sense.

What does the creep want with us, and why aren't we dead?

He ran his fingers across the sides of one of the walls, hoping to identify the texture.

It's solid rock. Walls are jagged enough to point back to dynamite. Ouch... A shard of something from the rock must have caught one of my fingertips. There's my blood. Way to go, Todd.

Working his way through, he spotted varieties of burrows, holes, and places for others to reside until coming upon a woman.

Oh, man. She looks like a winner. Probably hasn't showered or changed clothes in months. I bet she's got a better handle on this place. Look at that skin. Not a hint of preservation could save it unless she's going for the leather bag look. And... to perfect the accoutrement, an oversized red men's polo and baggy blue jeans. Such a flattering ensemble. This is brutal. I can't think about it any longer. An imagination gone wild on her can't be good for anyone.

Gazing upon her with care, desperation for community radiated through her eyes.

Her creaky voice spoke, "Hello. Call me Nancy. Have a seat."

Todd sat on the make-shifted bench made from an old, recycled bed frame as it leaned against the wall.

Be pleasant, Todd. Treat her better than you think. If there's one thing this period can do for you, it's to grow you into a better man, right? She deserves that, despite her… non-effeminate elegance.

"Hi, Nancy. I'm Todd. I don't know much about what's going on here. You *look* like you've been here a while. Can you help me figure things out? Where am I?"

Unphased by the candid remark, Nancy said, "It's nice to meet you. We're in Level Zero."

"What do you mean? What is Level Zero? I ran into a bullying creep earlier."

Nancy's face grew pale. "Creeper Joe? He hasn't messed with me in a while."

I wonder why. You might as well have clouds of filth and smoke coming off of you.

"Really?" Todd replied. "From what I've observed, I'd think he would be a real problem to your little 'town.' The creep tortured me with my weedeater and counted my scratches — all fifty-four of them. Dark as it is in here, you probably can't see 'em."

Nancy moved closer to Todd, and he caught a putrid stench exuding from her mouth.

Good Lord.

She spoke softer, "Of course he's a problem. Creeper Joe appears to those he deems worthy. Do you have something to hide? Why's he after you? Are you one of us?"

One of us? What's that mean? I'll go along with it.

"I am."

"Well, I would assume he was just trying to get you… settled in. This is a strange and mysterious place. It can, at times, be… ominous, and other times… completely enchanting. I don't have it mapped out, but I think we're just under Creepy Nights…"

"What a waste," Todd said.

"Watch your mouth. You could have your tongue seared right off talking that way," she whispered.

"What are you trying to say?"

Nancy fidgeted with a small rock she picked up from the ground. "You think I'm in here because I'm homeless? I hate to break it to you, but this isn't a way of life we've chosen."

"It's not?"

"We're his prisoners."

Todd processed the statement. The tunnel walls wobbled up and down as his lithium withdrawal threw him in a topsy-turvy haze.

"Ugh. I'm sorry. I'm not feeling well. Do you mean prisoners of the mind? Isn't that what most you homeless types are?"

"Fair question, but I'm not homeless! Like I said before, I'm a victim… and you are, too."

Screw that. You don't know me or anything about me. Watch it… be nice, Todd.

"Exactly," he said. "A victim of a failed social service system. If these politicians would just quit their yammering and do somethin' for a change, we could get you some help."

Nancy studied Todd. "I see you trying to separate yourself away from me like that. It's not like that down here, mister. If you're in here, you're plagued with it, too."

"Plagued with what?"

"Don't play dumb. I know you see things. Memories you can't explain. Times you never lived."

"What else do you know?"

"That's it. We're trophies."

Oh, boy. This is where stuff hits the fan.

"Well, where's the case? I want to make sure I'm polished and glossy before we get any lookers."

"It was a figure of speech, smart ass."

Todd scoffed. "I think you're just wasting my time now…"

Nancy faked a grin despite the rude comment. Though quite dim, he noticed she was missing three of her front teeth. The others that remained appeared iridescent, yellow, and decaying. A swirl of anxious and uncomfortable thoughts rushed.

Could it get any worse? I'm stuck in the middle of the earth next to the worst case of halitosis I have ever experienced. Dig a hole and let me die, he thought.

His mind flashed to another experience at the hotel.

Creeper Joe stood in the lobby, a well-groomed man, exceptional at disguising his idiosyncrasies, all the while maintaining a charming cunning he finagled with ease.

He spoke to Joe, "I want you to have the job. You're young. You're smart. *You* are attentive. I've known your father for a long time, too. He's a good man, an honorable man."

He could see Joe's distrust in the statement.

All to save face.

"Let me show you around the hotel," the man said. "I know you don't get around quickly, and that's okay. I'd like to show you the highlights. After we conclude, please explore the rest as time presents itself. This place *will* get busier… You know what? I might even invite your folks to stay. What do you think? Totally on the house." He lit a pipe, inhaled, and puffed it out.

Joe grinned and replied, soft-spoken, "That would be great. I'm sure they would have an excellent time."

"Joe, you know about the subway tunnels, right? They are going to run them right through this area, just underneath my hotel. It'll be perfect. Think about it… great access to everything else in town. You know something? This entire facility would make my father so proud. God rest his soul. We buried him back there. You see through that large east window? He's right under his favorite oak tree, right where he belonged. The man loved this place, and he wanted to make sure it remained in responsible hands. Who knows? One day *you* might even be the next man in line? Let's not get hasty, though. I can't just go off of my shallow assumptions now, can I?"

Joe answered polite but plastic, "Well, you could, but that would be… unwise."

The man chuckled. "Well said. We have some staff quarters in the basement. Feel free to make yourself at home, and welcome to the family."

"Thank you, Mr. Wasserman. You're too kind." Joe concluded the conversation and they shook hands with a firm grip. He wandered away to the basement quarters.

The memory ended.

Wasserman… I've got to let that name stick. Who is he?

•   •   •   •   •

Nancy waved at Todd as she spoke, "Todd! Hello. Are you there? You zoned out on me there for a sec."

"Oh, yeah. I'm sorry. You know what happened. You told me you deal with it, too. Please continue."

"I got it. I used to work there, you know?"

Todd's eyes widened. "Work there?"

Nancy nodded. "Yeah, at Creepy Nights."

"*You* worked at Creepy Nights? When? Why are you here…?" Todd asked.

Nancy cut him off before he could continue, and her voice elevated, "Slow down with the questions! I don't multitask well. That's part of why I didn't make it. I worked at the front desk for a while as Chris's assistant. It stressed me out a lot. I started stealing petty cash and drowning my sorrows in the Reese's from the vending machine, and now… I'm here."

"Stress eating? What was so bad about being a receptionist?"

Nancy scoffed. "Everything! You have no idea. It wasn't just the job. We'd get these moments where the building just went a little nutzo. It was unsettling."

"Nutzo? How do you mean?"

"Yeah," she said. "Sometimes, the power would go out. The entire floor would start howling and growling. I'd hear stomping. It would get so dark in those moments we could never see what was happening." Nancy's voice grew more uncertain as she continued,

"This whole property above and below… is some kind of… special — that much I know."

Well, aren't you perceptive?

Todd scratched his head and looked away for a moment. "Wow. Okay, you gave me a lot to unpack. I'm still trying to get my bearings here. I need a few minutes. I'm sure we'll catch up again. Thanks for the overview. It was enlightening. Is there anything else I should know about to help my chances at survival?"

She smiled, toothless, and with the breath of a corpse. "Chances? This place is full of those. Just explore and don't let the claustrophobia get you down. The tunnels are larger than you might expect."

"Thanks." Todd turned around, gasping from the unforgiving odor.

His mind screamed.

Oh my… where can I go to get a breath of fresh air? That was miserable.

Chuckling to himself in slight disgust, he moved away from her. After a quick walk, he collapsed in his self-appointed nook, leaving "Breathy" Nancy, a pet-name he called the homely woman he encountered.

CHAPTER THIRTY-NINE

RAMBLIN' RON RICHARDS finished the lengthy interrogation session. He began his exit after an all-nighter in the Precinct Three building. Walking through the hallway, he caught the scent of fresh coffee in the break room as another officer yelled on the phone in earshot.

As he moved toward the exit, Detective Penske bid him farewell. "Thanks for your time. We'll call you if we have any more questions. Again, we appreciate your cooperation. Please let us know if you hear anything else from Wayne or see something strange. I called you a cab."

How sweet. If you were the one to foot the bill.

"Thanks," a weary Ron replied.

He walked out the door of the piss poor facility, peering at the twilight evening sky. The sleep-deprivation and long-winded questioning had pushed his anxiety to its limits. The yellow cab pulled up, and he climbed in.

"Hi. 3800 Bayshore Drive. Step on it."

"Very good, sir. I'll get you there. I've got a thermos if you want some coffee for the ride." The driver leaned over to reach for it, his head brushing against the fuzzy red dice that swayed back and forth below the rearview mirror.

"I don't know that coffee will do me any good at this point, but thanks for the offer. Forgive me if I nod off for a second."

"I'll do what I can to keep the ride smooth. Bayshore has a few speedbumps, though. No promises."

As Ron drifted, the driver lit a Lucky Strike and smoked it. The car filled quickly as the driver cracked the window.

What a selfish move. I'm the client. You couldn't wait ten more minutes for a drag; at least I keep my smoking in the designated areas. So typical.

Tension overwhelmed his body. The muscles in the sides of his face tingled.

Cynicism lurks in all of us. Control it before it controls the rest.

Exiting the taxi, he paid the cabbie and went inside. He headed to his bedroom closet, pulling out his .38 *Smith and Wesson* revolver from the shoebox under his neckties.

"Dad, I know you didn't give this to me for this, but I've had enough. What else do I have to live for?"

He sat there, frozen and struggling with the image of the tongue laid out and soiling the white paper sack, mere seconds away from falling through the bottom to the floor with its lingering moisture.

It must have been Wayne's.

Emotions compounded into an ugly mess. The tongue, the run-in with the creep, and the countless hours of brutal interrogation, left him threadbare.

Ron Richards. Nothing more than a useless wretch, hopeless and deserving of a meaningful end.

In his moment of darkness, he was no longer a husband, a father, a brother, a son, a radio host, or a friend to anyone — nothing but a failure, and *that* was the only thought racing through his troubled mind. Pulling the hammer to the revolver back, he rested his finger on the trigger, preparing to seal his fate with his only bullet.

TAP! TAP! TAP!

A knock at the door.

Wiping the sweat from his forehead, he tucked the gun beneath a couch cushion and prepared to greet the unexpected visitor.

Oh, the sweet taste of providence, divine intervention. That's what I needed, a distraction, a diversion. Maybe not…

He opened the door, observing another twice folded, crumpled white paper sack on the doorstep. Before unfolding it, he took a deep breath. A slimy eye and a tooth sat motionless in the bottom. Reluctant to touch them, he carried the sack inside and retrieved a magnifying glass from his home office. He went back out to the porch.

I'm not gonna get this crap on my floors. I'll take my chances out here.

Sitting on his rocking chair, he studied the tooth.

There's a serial number on it.

Before he could ponder anymore, he vomited all over the front porch as disgust overtook him. Some of it landed on the scarecrow that stood to his right.

The one thing I got out of the divorce and now it's covered in vomit. Why am I being tormented? I've had a rough enough life on my own.

He called 911. A few minutes later, a dispatch vehicle arrived as he sat there waiting. Detective Penske returned to investigate and collect the disconnected appendages.

Penske yelled at Ron from the window while driving up, "What are you trying to do? Make me earn my pay?"

"I'm sorry, Penske. I just can't right now..."

"Are you okay? What's going on, Ron? Why aren't you saying anything else?"

After a minute of silence, he spoke, "I've got no words. Do what you need to. Bring me in again if that's what it takes."

He vomited all over Penske's uniform and passed out.

"Ron? Ron? Are you with me?"

Ron trembled on the ground but did not reply.

Penske picked up his dispatch radio. "Yes, this is Detective Penske, unit five-tango-four. Send an ambulance to 3800 Bayshore Drive. I've got a guy that may need some medical attention."

CHAPTER FORTY

TODD ADAMS awoke the next morning, continuing to explore the tunnel.

I'm famished.

He walked past a few fire pits and other items that hinted at the tenure of the others.

I can't get over this. It's like a world of its own. Just all the more perfect with Peter Gabriel coming through the speakers. Isn't it?

He uttered a curse as pain raced through his leg.

Dark enough in here. Maybe I can avoid him for a while and get my bearings. I never want to see a Red-Helix again.

A woman sang to herself, but the song was unintelligible.

Just a made-up melody. I hate it when people do that. Unless you're in the business, I don't want to hear you try.

He approached the woman, noting her colorless dreadlocks, pale complected skin, and icy blue eyes. They were albino-like — reflective of the fact she had not left the tunnel in weeks.

"Hello there."

"Hi."

He extended his hand to introduce himself as the woman accepted, returning it with a weak and clammy grip.

"Todd Adams."

"Ebony Ivory."

"Ebony Ivory? That's quite the contradiction…"

"My parents were earth-loving long before the hippies came on the scene. I don't blame 'em for it."

"I get that," he said. "So, how long's it been?"

She picked up a pewter cup and drank from it. After she finished, she tucked it behind a rock. "I don't know anymore. Month or two? I lost track. Diabetic coma did me in for a while and got me feeling all confused when I came back. It didn't take long before Creeper Joe showed up on a street corner one night and told me I had a lying tongue. He dragged me down here."

Go figure. I could have pegged you for a Pinocchio.

Todd furrowed his brow. "Well, did you?"

She nodded. "Yeah. Lying was always an issue for me. I worked in Creepy Nights on Level Seven. Stupid me… I snuck onto Level Five when Chris told me I didn't get the job to spite him. Before the floor supervisor could approach me that night, I busied myself, and picked up a phone as it rang. You want to hear the story I told? It's still locked in my memory like it was yesterday."

Here we go again. Everyone's living in the past. No one looking to the future.

"Sure. Let's see what kind of story-telling chops you have."

"Well, let me tell you about a time that a man lost his eye…

A few years ago, back in 1972, a gentleman lost his job at a bottling factory. There wasn't much to be said about why. He entered the plant manager's office and received the news.

'Herb, I'm sorry, but we're going to have to let you go. I hate that it's the holiday season and all, but corporate desperately wants us to make some cutbacks to meet our numbers for year-end.'

'Rick, that's not fair. I've been here for eight years… I never called in sick. I never said 'no' to a single project that you assigned. Why me…?'

'They decided over my head, Herb. I'm sorry. I like you and all, but we've got to work with younger and cheaper talent. Eight years of raises costs me a good bit more than the fresh meat I can get off the streets does. It's just simple dollars and cents… nothing more. It's not personal… just common sense. You get that, right?'

'I'll take a pay cut. Please… Rick, don't do this to me now. What will my wife say? She's going to think I wasn't up to company standards. She'll be so disappointed… might even flip out on me.'

'I'm sorry, Herb. The decision is final. We'll pay you through the end of the month. All the best.'

'Likewise.'

On Herb's return home from the office, he continued to process the news, knowing Gina would be irate. She warned him this was coming. He hadn't listened. In fact, just a week earlier, she told him as much. He recalled the conversation as he drove.

'Talent comes at a cost, Herb. We both know when large organizations are bought out by corporations, heads are going to roll. I'm not sure you'll have a job much longer. You need to prepare for something else.'

'Oh, Gina, don't sell me short. I am an A-lister at JP and Sons. They're more than happy with me. Rick would never leave me out in the cold like that without warning.'

'I don't think so, Herb. You are on a shorter leash than you think.'

'You're mistaken, Gina. You really don't know what you're talking about. I'm the professional. You're the housewife…'

'Herb, I'm… going to kill you. Mark my words. It won't be pretty either. Rest assured of that.'

'Aww… C'mon, Gina… You know you are overreacting.'

'I'm overreacting?! That isn't fair at all. You are an idiot for thinking you're so safe… remaining employed.'

What am I going to tell Gina? She was right all along. Am I too stubborn? At this rate… I'm just delusional. What an idiot. Yep… I'm a dead man. Here comes the grim reaper.

He entered the door to their small efficiency apartment; Gina was sitting on the couch, folding clothes.

'Hey, Herb.'

'Hey.'

'What's going on?'

'Oh, not much.'

'Really…? You seem quiet.'

'Well, give me a chance to sit down and think through my day before you turn this into a dad-gum interrogation scene, would you?'

Gina stood up and raced into the kitchen where she grabbed the butcher knife from their *Sears* catalog case knife set.

'I'm not going to put up with this nonsense anymore.'

She charged into the room with the knife... Herb blacked out. He awakened abruptly, realizing half of his world had gone dark. Looking down at his shirt, he watched a blood trail run down the side of his cheek and drip to the floor just beneath. He reached toward his left eye. There was nothing there. Only a hole..."

Todd interrupted, "Okay, okay. No more, please."

"That's exactly what the customer said, too — at the same point of the story. I guess I get to hold on to the ending."

"Is it bloody?" he asked.

"Of course."

"Okay. That's all I need to hear," he said.

"So back to that night..." Ebony said. "I finished the call. Everyone else on the floor vanished during the story or left for a dinner break. The west wing of the building and its dark shadows piqued my interest. I moved toward it and looked up at the ceiling, noting a black liquid.

DRIP. DRIP. DRIP.

No bucket to catch it — only the cheap Berber carpet below to absorb. The night cleaning crew arrived, but they ignored me. I was upset... and my stupid streak continued. I found the stairwell and marched up to the restricted floor, Level Six. I ended up covered in gallons and gallons of some kind of black oil. The stuff stripped all the color right out of my skin and hair. I should have followed the rule..."

"What rule?" Todd asked.

Her voice became monotone, "Never set foot where you aren't welcome. Your feet will be quick to rush to evil."

Todd studied Ebony's face a moment until her voice normalized. "I wish I would have listened," she said. "I'm cursed here now. There's no way out."

"I've heard that, but why doesn't anyone try?"

She shook her head and sighed. "The torture. Hasn't Creeper Joe gotten after you? I can't go through any more of it. I won't. He's left me alone ever since he stomped my kneecaps into pieces. I figured something would give at some point. He nursed me back to health with the water and went on his merry way. I snitched this cup from him and he hasn't come back looking for it yet. Probably has a stock of them stored and doesn't care anymore. I went from an invalid to a tunnel athlete. He got me feeling so good for a while that I was jogging from one end of the tunnel to the other. I lost the umph for that, though. Thing is, I think we all get a touch of the seasonal blues in here. We could all use some sunshine. Thing with Joe is that it's almost like he's got another agenda more important. The other thing... every few days, I see a new face in here."

"So what's the deal with Creeper Joe? Who is he?"

"I don't know how to explain," she said. "I really don't know. This is the one thing that will help you. Once you march to the beat he wants you to, he stands down."

Get to the point, then. Or I will. Julie's voice echoed in his mind, *'Remember, everyone has the potential to be a friend before they're an enemy.' What a bunch of poppycock. I'll try it, anyway.*

"So... track star, you haven't come up with a plan to leave? Joe's not that fast. I've watched him hobble around," Todd said. "How many of you are here?"

Ebony shook her head again. "Hard to say, probably fifty something by now. We haven't tried to leave... We're all a little confused — disoriented, I mean. I reckon you are, too?" Her voice got quieter, "We got to watch ourselves, you know. A long spread out tunnel like this, no easy outs, only the bats, the rats, and the other vermin let loose when we're lucky. If we catch and kill the critter, we take it on over to the mess hall and have us a grand 'ol feast now and then." Ebony stood up and stretched her legs. "Talking about the running, makes me want to move. Do you want to? I'll tell you this; I appreciate my legs a lot more after what he did to me."

"Oh, really? No. I'm not there yet. Maybe one of these days."

"You have to be resourceful, Todd. Very resourceful. Survival in Level Zero's far from easy, but rarely does anybody die." She rubbed her hands together nervously and continued, "You look too fresh-faced to have been here long. Your poor legs…"

Fifty-two. Fifty-three. Fifty-four. Flecks of skin and blood.

"I don't know how long I've been here," he said. "I think I was out several days before I woke up. I'm kind of finding myself. Maybe it's a chance for all of us to reset. You know? I don't hate it, but I *am* ready to eat."

"It's about that time. We usually get two large squares a week," she said. "You'll see. As for hating Level Zero, I don't think you can. This place has a way of polarizing our feelings. There's something in the water."

What are you saying?

Ebony locked eyes with Todd, and his heart skipped a beat. The icy blue he first observed in them before now appeared more an absence of color.

"Go find the Spring of Life, and you'll have your own awakening."

His mind raced away to another unexplained vision as he sat in an old chapel. A reverend in black garb yelled at his congregation while he sat next to his father.

"I can't tell you how much it pains me to see folly running rampant here… In fact, it sickens me… It utterly sickens me. Despicable acts by despicable people looking only to seek their own pleasures and treasures… Never once stopping for a moment to respect the Almighty. What does it say? What does it say? These are things the LORD hates! They are detestable to Him… And you know what… from where I'm standing… they are detestable to me… and they should be that to all of you. I need you to be better stewards. God wants you to be gatekeepers for doing His good and stomping out anything evil. It's not about taking care of yourselves in worldly ways when or because it feels good. That's what's detestable! Get out there and make a difference for a change. Hold people to a higher standard for His glory. He won't mind the added enforcement, will He?" The reverend began to pray, "God, send an angel of wrath on this town and remind us of our wrongs."

The stained glass windows rattled through the chapel — almost indicative of the reality they would never shake the same again. The heated sermon choked the life from the room as the attending families exited in silence.

* * * * *

"Hey, where's your head at?" Ebony asked.

"I'm sorry. Got a tinge of Attention Deficit."

"No. I know what was going on. I get 'em, too. I don't want to talk about it, though. I know I'm kind of changing subjects, but since you brought up Attention Deficit, it's only fair."

"Okay. I'm listening. Spit it out."

Ebony made motions with her hands as she struggled to get the words out, speaking after a deep gulp, "Did you ever meet Chris Wilkerson?"

"I haven't. I've heard the name. I've seen the commercials."

"Let me tell you something, I think Joe creeps on Chris in his own unsettling ways. A prisoner up above the rest of us left to rot here below. I saw it before I ever ended up down here. It was just a look in his eyes."

"Deep," Todd remarked.

"Isn't it, though?"

Todd stood up, dismissing himself from the conversation. "I'll see you around. It was nice talking to you."

"Perhaps under better circumstances, we'll get better acquainted," Ebony said.

"There's always hope. Let's make a way out of here. Shall we?"

She patted him on the back and smiled without saying any more and jogged away from him.

Moving on now. That was interesting.

Todd stumbled onwards. A grinding and cranking sound resonated from above. "Ebony and Ivory" by *Stevie Wonder and Paul McCartney*, cued on the tunnel speakers as it reverberated through the tunnel.

What a tease… Someone's there watching me and cuing the music as I go. It's almost like the tunnel's my own stage. Shall I take a bow?

Screams came from every direction, bouncing off the tunnel walls.

"TAKE SHELTER!"

"WATCH OUT!"

"WHAT'S IT GONNA BE THIS TIME?"

Looking up, moonlight shined through from the ceiling, and the cranking sound grew louder. Two animals stood back to back with one another on a lowering surface, suspended by chains.

Boars? Nope, not believing this.

"Is anyone here? What do I do?"

The boars neared the floor, and the volume of the music intensified. Todd moved toward the edge of the tunnel walls, peering around for anyone he could find.

Even help from Harv or "Breathy" Nancy would be sufficient. Think stealth. The boars will catch my scent.

Everyone in the tunnel had disappeared.

"Thanks for leaving the new guy out to dry. I appreciate it," his voice echoed down the long corridor for several seconds as the effects of the sultry tunnel temperature took hold. Though his body temperature skyrocketed, his dehydration left him struggling to sweat.

I'm not ready to be the meal. I'm not ready to be the meal.

The descending grate hit the floor, and the wild and threatening animals exited their cages. They roared in eerie unison.

Man, they're loud. Almost like they got a microphone in front of their throat.

His ears rang as they came toward him at full speed. Collapsing to the tunnel floor, he crawled into Harv's red sleeping bag, tucking himself inside, just out of sight.

Here's to hoping they don't catch a scent of me.

CHAPTER FORTY-ONE

WAYNE WALLACE sat deserted in the bottom of the cell as he heard a click and a familiar jingle.

"Welcome to a special October 29th edition of the Dynamic Duds. I'm Wayne Wallace, and you all know my wanderlust amigo, Ramblin' Ron... Richards! You know we've been doing these Halloween episodes for a few years, haven't we, Ronny?"

"Sure have, Wayne. This year, I want to take things a different route. At the direction of our 'management', we want to explore some unfamiliar territory. Would you care to join us?"

"You know I would!"

CLICK.

I don't remember that episode. What's going on here?

Wayne Wallace sat voiceless and sightless, confined to the depths of his cell.

A scratchy and whiny voice called out from above, "You hungry, fella? Here you go." Creeper Joe dumped a bucket of sweet-scented animal feed from above. "Help yourself."

Thanks a lot. What is this? Deer corn?

Attempting to sink his teeth to split the kernel, he felt it give way, and he spat it out along with a tooth.

"It's not kind to the teeth, is it? What's it matter? It's not like you can taste anymore, you once-babbling fool. Go on. Eat up! Just swallow it whole. Heh-heh."

Wayne munched on the feed while fumbling around until he found a small door.

Maybe there's a way out of here. What gives? I can't see anything.

Walking toward the door, he heard the soft-spoken voice of another man, "I'm Dale. Dale Creensteen, Markets Broker, Riverton Financial. Well, I was."

He spoke through the bars next to Wayne, "What *you* in here for?"

I can't answer you. Don't bother trying to talk to me.

After seconds of silence, he moved toward the man's voice as it became apparent the man could see his maimed face.

"Ugh. What in the name of heaven happened to you?"

See for yourself, dumbass.

Wayne opened his mouth and pointed to his missing tongue.

I know I look wretched, but that doesn't mean you have to wretch. Come on!

"I have a weak stomach," Creensteen said. "I can't do this. Take a drink. This ought to cure what ails you."

Wayne reached toward Dale's pathetic voice, grabbing hold of a pewter cup and sipping from it. The remaining piece of his tongue relieved in swelling, and his eyes grew back.

What in the world?

"That's better. It'll take some time. We're punished, but we're not hopeless. I'm going back to my side. See you later."

Wayne maneuvered around the walls of the cell with his back pressed against it.

His mind flashed to the past.

He sat at the kitchen table, drunk and disconnected as his wife berated their son.

"You see this, Joey? Anytime someone tries to get something out of you, it always ends the same. They heat the water up on you until they choke you out and do you in, son…"

Her eyes expressed an unending dreariness as she took a swill of the *Old Tymer's* whiskey that sat to his right — her matted hair still in disarray from illicit activities around town.

"Life's not fair, is it?" she asked. "I hate this place... this life... this miserable existence, Joey. Don't you ever be the frog in the kettle. Look out for yourself. Choke out the people that crank the heat on you when you aren't ready. Do what you think is justice. Let it be poetic. Let it be harsh. Leave 'em to rot. This world isn't the way it should be anymore."

His mother kept her right hand in the kettle as she held the frog underwater, and it came to a slow boil.

"Pain, Joey. Pain. Experience it. Punish yourself. Punish others even more. Know the pain... It will be sweeter. My daddy taught me that best when I was growing up. He would take me out behind the barn and bruise me senseless. I never did nothing wrong, nothing at all. That didn't matter to him, though. He just took out his rage the only way he knew. That was all. Generation after generation of drinking and beating. One day, you'll be doing the same thing, son. It's just a way of life."

The frog lay immobile as she pulled her withered and pruned hand from the kettle. She flicked the top layers of her boiled skin onto the kitchen floor.

"I'm made new now, brand new. These hands can work again. Bend over. Lift your shirt and show me your back."

She poured the scorching water all over his back and rear end. He shrieked and fell to the floor.

"Now you know the pain, the pain I feel every day. A numb world is a real world devoid of meaning. It won't hurt as bad the next time. It won't hurt as bad, son. I promise."

Tears flowed from Joe's eyes as he whimpered, unable to elicit sympathy from his mother.

"Dry it up... now! Do you ever pay attention to Reverend Selsky?"

"You have more admiration for that hot-headed windbag then you ever did me," the man said. "You're both obsessed with that fire and brimstone philosophy. Maybe you two deserve each other? You been seeing him beyond Joe's counsel? Incorporating some business with pleasure?"

"I've got nothing to say to you, Henry. Stay out of this!"

Joe interrupted as he wiped the accumulated perspiration from his face, "Why... did you ... do this to me?"

"Don't ask me that again, boy. I just told you why. Do you want me to show you?"

"No... No. I don't, momma! Leave me be."

"Get out of here... now!"

She threw the boiled frog at Joe as it splattered on the back of his wet and well-woven white shirt.

"Go!" she screamed.

The woman stared at her inebriated spouse in disgust as she yelled, "Well, don't you have anything more meaningful to contribute, or do I need to boil *you* up a little and set *you* straight?"

·   ·   ·   ·   ·

Wayne came back to the moment. He tried to scream, but there was only a puny guttural sound. His speech would take some time to heal and restore to its original state.

There's something strange about that drink.

He collapsed to the floor, attempting to escape the terror of his current reality.

The walls of the cell crumbled around him, smothering him beneath. As he worked to dig himself out, deer corn rained from above and rats circled around him munching on the feed. Diminishing in seconds, they gnawed away at his skin. Creeper Joe appeared behind them, hissing into the air and they scattered.

"Wayne... Wayne... Wayne... a taste of fame that would only lead to shame."

Joe juggled fruit around, before pitching an apple to him. "These are a delicacy down here. It's time for a fresh start. Take care now."

CHAPTER FORTY-TWO

CHRIS WILKERSON locked the door to the control room and sat down, studying the screens. He found Joe lingering near the north end camera.

Joe jammed a syringe into his arm.

What are you doing, Joe? You still have to get your fix, don't you? Where's Adams?

Staring at the video feeds, he gulped a can of *Flitz* down and activated the camera nearest Todd on the larger screen.

Maybe Todd will be a hero. He has my vote.

The screen flickered as the boars descended from the ceiling. Chris cued the cassette tape as Todd maneuvered across the tunnel.

Okay. So I overdid it a little. Ebony was a pain in the butt, though. The little know it all could never keep her trap shut. Feeding time was supposed to help them, not kill them. The east elevator tunnel's open. A trip to Level Six will do all of you some good.

The boars charged through the middle of the tunnel, hunting their prey. Chris ejected the cassette from the deck.

Level Six. Level Six.

He recalled the renovation efforts on it several months earlier and the setbacks along the way…

•　　•　　•　　•　　•

He walked the floor studying the cubicles and phones installed when a rush of cold air hit the back of his neck. The lights flickered on the floor as the power surged in an unfamiliar rhythm. The buzz and hum of the floor's electricity pulsed in thirty-second increments.

What was that?

He looked back at the police officer walking behind him.

Are you using me as a shield or what? Shouldn't you be the one on the front lines?

As they made eye contact, Detective Jack Herbert broke the silence, "Hey, did you feel that?"

Let's make him feel dumb for a minute.

"Feel what?"

"That coolness. The dampness in the air. There's something off about all of this. I'm going to order an environmental check on the building. It may not be enough to shut you down, but we need to make sure our I's are dotted and our T's are crossed."

"We've had it done already, but I'll be glad to have someone else out here to check. I'm uncomfortable lingering here. We may be better off shutting the floor down altogether."

"That's probably your best option," Herbert said. "So this is where they're dying?"

"Yeah. Another one here in the Southeast corner. Fourth one in three weeks, but you know that by now." Chris patted him on the shoulder.

"You superstitious?" Herbert asked.

"Aren't you? I don't enjoy thinking about people dying in my building."

"No offense, but you know what the hotel's known for, right?"

"Good point. Feels more real now. Not just a distant memory for someone I don't know."

"Death has a way of doing that," Herbert said. "Autopsy reports in my file showed the other three all died of myocardial infarction."

"Yeah. That's what I heard. No one should stay in here alone. They always die when the others go off to lunch. The guy that draws the short straw works lunch hour and then ends up dead while the others are gone."

"Let me ask you this," Herbert said, "do you think someone's killing them?"

"I think some*thing* is killing them. I don't want to believe in ghosts, but I don't know what else to think."

"I hear what you're saying. Given this building's troubled history, I wouldn't rule anything out. Hang in there. I've seen a lot in my days as a detective. We'll get to the bottom of it."

The pair walked toward the exit. Chris pulled the door open, motioning Herbert to exit first.

"My honest advice... lock it down. The environmental regulators and feds may want to look, but I can't imagine they'll find anything conclusive. These unexplainable cases are hard to pinpoint. You may be better off with a priest and some holy water than with any of them."

You have no idea.

"I'll take you back to the lobby. Thanks for coming in," Chris said.

"All for the badge. All for the badge."

CHAPTER FORTY-THREE

Once the aggressive animals ran past TODD ADAMS, he slipped out of the sleeping bag, and located an unfamiliar passageway. A door stood open several inches. He pushed it wider, squeezed in, and sealed it shut.

I guess I'm the last one. I hope so.

A line of others waited to board an elevator in the dark corridor. A description played in the elevator, instructing riders on the proper way to handle a Level Six call. Entertaining a path out of Level Zero via telephone would not be a possibility.

Arriving at Level Six, Todd noted several others, loitering and appreciating the change of scenery. There was a white sign with red capital letters that dangled from the ceiling tiles, APOCALYPSE AND ALTERNATE REALITY. Warnings plastered all over the floor urged caution while taking calls and the impending threat of confinement to a cell if they mentioned their capture over the phone.

No visible windows or doors up here. Weird.

The phone rang. No one moved toward it to answer.

"Well, if none of you guys are going to, then I will."

He picked up the phone and greeted the caller. Gauging by rasp and tempo, the voice on the line sounded to be a man in his sixties.

"I want you to tell me a story," the man said. "Something about an apocalyptic reality."

"Okay, thanks for the call. Let me see now, here we go."

What's happening? I'm losing control.

The story came to him in vivid bursts, inspired by something he could not recall.

"Dale Bostley announced to the 8,000 employee, northern Albuquerque campus of their organization's impending fate.

'After twenty-one years of taking calls of various natures, our board of directors has opted to shut down the west region's office. I want to thank you all for the capacities you've served in and the tireless hours you've put in to keep this place... profitable. As you know, our business is changing as we see the advent of automated phone answering systems and more cost-effective sales options — inevitably... leaving most of us looking for new jobs in sales or retail. Take heart, colleagues. Our portfolio of sister support companies will help you in your quest for your next role. The rest of our clients, as you know, are mainly in New Orleans and Little Rock. Ever since the main interstate corridors of Texas caved in last year, we lost our most significant market of clients. We'll be donating our building's cubicles to a homeless shelter to offer small domiciles to the... lesser privileged in a centrally managed habitat called Cubicle City.'"

The line went dead.

What's going on? Did I bonk or what? What did I do wrong?

Harv came up behind him, shaking his head, as he tapped him on the shoulder. "Didn't you read the sign?" he whispered as he clicked his tongue. "It's one of the Cardinal Rules. I could tell that wasn't your story. You ripped that off, didn't you? I heard it in the tunnel the other day. Never recycle someone else's story as if it were your own. Too easy to have a lying tongue."

Todd scoffed. "Are you serious right now?

Harv glared at him. "Dead serious. Like the commercial always says, CREEPY NIGHTS provides original, scary stories one-hundred percent of the time, or we'll give your money back. We guarantee it!"

In an unexpected twist, the room transformed.

What's going on? I guess this place is living up to its name.

Todd observed a weathered and worn Albuquerque city limits sign. Looking around, he noted that he and the others were now dressed as well-groomed, white-collar office workers. He turned around and saw the sizeable, pink-bricked building of the former Charismatique business firm referenced in his story.

"You all clean up, alright," he said. "Let's go toward the building. I bet we'll find some help."

No one else acknowledged him. Walking toward the corporate campus, it drifted further and further away. Todd stopped and turned around, looking at the group of followers.

Is this a dream or what? I recognized Harv. What about the rest of you? I'm not used to seeing you this way.

The bright New Mexico sun beat down on them with no shade for miles. Todd pivoted around. He walked away from the city limits sign as efforts to move past it remained futile. The group continued east, hurrying into the desert. Minutes later, evidence of heat influenced mirage manifested as their lips discolored and their sweat dripped into the sand.

Looking to the sky, he yelled, "Is this it? Come on!"

Without warning, loaves of bread and flasks of water began falling in an intriguing Old Testament fashion. He indulged, feeling refreshed with immediacy. The others did not.

"Why aren't you guys having any? Don't make me feel like I'm the glutton here. Did I miss an etiquette course or what?"

None of them engaged with him.

This is unreal.

He and the group continued onward.

Creeper Joe's voice called out to him through an invisible garbled intercom, "Watch out! The earth caves in over here. Just like you wanted. Heh-heh."

Todd's mind flashed back to the drive on the interstate, maneuvering through Riverton in standstill traffic.

Joe's voice continued, "You called it a wasteland, remember…? Unemployed hippies? Come on. What are you now?"

Todd looked in the sky toward the sun. "I don't know. Maybe I'm dead. Is this hell?"

"Why couldn't it be heaven? You have bread. Water. Followers. Riverton's obliterated. What more do you need?"

Todd wiped the sweat from his brow and said, "I just want to go home to knock down some blades of grass in my yard with my new Red Helix weedeater. That's it!"

"No, you don't, Todd. You…" Joe's voice muffled as it faded into the distance.

As Todd peered into the sky, it turned scorched, and everything that surrounded became pitch-black. A phone rang in the distance.

He fell to the floor.

CHAPTER FORTY-FOUR

DETECTIVE NEIL PENSKE's recent promotion left him reviewing a variety of case files. His desk stood piled high, folder after folder with stacks of smeared *Polaroids*, chewed up *Bics*, and a pair of matching 35mm cameras. They were all strewn about in complete disorder, with many cases pointing back to families robbed of their loved ones. Handling these issues was a delicate thing and often a path to nowhere on a winding road to perdition. Perhaps it was the undetectable calculation to the disappearances that made them most ominous. They never occurred in a notable or measurable swoop, but instead one at a time and with care — an unobservable pattern that left them appearing coincidental.

"You know something, Jack. I want to sleep again."

"A few more years of bumps and bruises, and you'll get immune to feeling anything. It's a tough road, but you'll get there," Detective Jack Herbert said.

Penske took a sip of his coffee as he stood up from his desk.

"There are just too many weird things around here. I'm ready to move back to Jersey. The families of these people never want to talk to us. It still breaks my heart every time. We're only reminding them of the inevitable. No one wants to relive the fact that their sweetie's dead."

"Most of 'em don't. It's surprising how many don't seem bothered at all. Remember, foul play is never out of the question."

Penske sighed. "Yeah. I know you're right. I never want to give someone a false sense of hope when there isn't one."

"The sad thing is, half of the adult disappearances stem from relationship issues. Depression... affairs... a combination of the previous stated. Blame it on impulse control, I guess."

Penske stared at the map that graced the wall behind his desk. He angled his lamp toward it. Charting the missing was difficult, as there was rarely a consistent or observable pattern. Pushpin after pushpin placed from one area to the next. He left them yellow to indicate hope. They were only red once a body was located, linking that with a small white string connecting the victim's point of origin and their location upon discovery.

"You know, I stare at this map for minutes at a time, hoping for a link to pop out at me in a providential revelation. It never does, though. It feels kind of hopeless," Penske said.

Herbert put his hand on Penske's shoulder. "Well, I hate to break it to you, but it should. Take the night off, and we'll talk in the morning."

•   •   •   •   •

Penske's sleepless night left him searching his mind.

The medical records... They're not identity crisis runaways. They're kidnappings!

He jumped out of bed and drove back to the Precinct Three station, ambitious and confident, running straight to Herbert's desk.

"Hey," he said, working to catch his breath.

"What are you doing here, Penske? I told you to take the night off."

"Good grief. I don't think you ever leave, do you, Jack? Can you give me a few of your missing person's files? I want to check something."

"Sure." Jack picked up the stack of folders and handed them over. "What's going on?"

"I'll tell you in a minute."

Penske rifled through the files for a period before looking up to grin ear to ear at Herbert.

The senior detective approached his desk. "What is it?"

"They were comatose, Jack. Before they disappeared, they were comatose. Some at RGH, handful across town at Northview, others at Southcreek, even a few at Westlake."

"What are you saying?"

"We have a lead. Let me look at the Nancy Helbens file again. We matched the serial number on that dental implant in Walnut Creek Park. She lived with her mother on the east side of town."

They raced toward the home of Bobbie Helbens. *The Scorpions* blared through the RPD-issued vehicle, an '81 Crown Victoria. The two men bobbed their heads, jamming to the music as they drove down the freeway.

Nothing special about this place. Just an average lot and block property in suburbia.

Penske put the car in park and turned the radio down. He took a swig of coffee and popped a breath mint in his mouth before pouring another into Herbert's hand.

"Alright, Detective," Herbert said. "Let's do this. I hope you really are onto something."

They climbed out of the car in haste. The two detectives knocked on the door, and it squeaked open. An elderly woman with glasses dangling from a chain, and a crochet hook tucked over her right ear, stood with a cane.

"Hello, Mrs. Helbens. I'm Detective Penske. This is Detective Herbert. We're here to search your home for evidence regarding your missing daughter, Nancy."

She gasped as her eyes widened. "You're here to what? Where were you two months ago? I'm moving on."

"We understand, ma'am. Humor us, please. We have additional evidence," Penske replied.

"Okay. Don't expect any coffee or cookies from me. I've already repurposed Nancy's bedroom into a craft room. Forgive me, but I've got to move on with my life, and we weren't that close. I only meant her to live here short term before she... before she disappeared."

Cold as a cucumber, aren't you, lady?

"Understood, ma'am," Penske said. "We appreciate anything you feel would be helpful for us to know. Your daughter's dental implant turned up the night before last in one of the parks."

Helbens face remained emotionless as she spoke, "Well, as you may or may not know, Nancy was in a coma for some time before her disappearance. She awoke and seemed to have a massive imagination for life in a different era altogether. The doctors assumed her to have a schizoid-clustered illness or personality disorder after the brain damage. Drunk driver all but killed her. We didn't think she was going to pull through," Bobbie sighed. "You know, some say people have vivid dreams while they're in a coma. I figured that's all it was. That faded away with time, and I got more and more of my 'old Nancy' back, but then... her job began taking her away from me again. I thought she'd drop some weight while she was out... it never happened."

What's that got to do with anything...?

"Just so we can verify with our files," Herbert said, "what was her last place of employment?"

She shook her head and huffed as her crochet hook hit the floor. "Here, just look in the box."

Didn't mean to put you out. Most parents care about their children. Sheesh.

Mrs. Helbens walked the two men over to the corner of the wood-paneled living room, rifling through Nancy's things.

Her eyes glimmered a moment, "This might seem a little off-topic, but I was going to ask if you'd seen those commercials for Creepy Nights."

Both detectives smirked at each other.

"Penske, you take the high harmony. I'll take the melody."

The pair sang the commercial jingle and Helbens chuckled, applauding them for a moment before circling back to the more serious discussion.

We got a smile out of her. What do you know?

"Very nice, gentlemen. Very nice. Nancy worked over there at Creepy Nights. She called me that night and told me they fired her.

Disappeared sometime on the way home. You guys know that already, though."

"We found the car wrapped around a gnarly oak. No body, though. Why did they fire her?" Herbert asked.

"I don't know. Nancy was a good person. Maybe she was late for work? I think the manager's the one on the commercials. Go talk to him."

"Yeah," Herbert said. "He's a piece of work, alright."

Penske extended his hand to shake Mrs. Helbens. "Thanks for the information, ma'am. We'll be in touch."

They waved at Mrs. Helbens as they walked away from the house. She closed the door.

"Man, those windchimes are obnoxious," Herbert said. "Look at those hand-painted garden gnomes. This lady should stick to paint by numbers."

They both laughed as the door to the house squeaked open again. While they approached the Crown Vic, Helbens called out from behind, "I just want to say, I hope you find her. Dead or alive. I don't care at this point. Just bring my daughter's disappearance to a close. This has gone on long enough."

Herbert and Penske glanced at each other for a second and nodded.

"We'll do what we can, ma'am," Penske answered. "Thanks again for your cooperation."

They climbed in the car, and Herbert questioned Penske, "Well, Detective… where do you want to go now?"

"Creepy Nights."

"Do we have to go over there? I've done my time in there already," Herbert said as they headed westbound across Riverton.

"I don't like it either. We need to."

Herbert looked over across the front seat at Penske. His eyes lacked twinkle, worn from years of sleepless nights and no proper outlet for his feelings.

"Penske, you ever think about giving it all up…? You know, just start things over."

"You mean the badge? Life as a detective? City-employee perks? I need some more time in the job before you burn me out."

"That's what I mean. Maybe one day, we just go partners and open one of those frozen yogurt shops. That stuff always sells."

"Maybe so."

Or maybe you do, and I keep climbing the ladder. The chief's up for retirement soon.

"Just a thought," Herbert said.

CHAPTER FORTY-FIVE

TODD ADAMS regained consciousness.

Some kind of nightmare.

Dressed as a call center agent and sitting in a cubicle, it seemed that he worked for Creepy Nights in the moment.

Yes, Todd, you are going psychotic. Floating above your body and watching yourself take a call. Find the padded walls. Yes. This is a real proper… existential crisis.

"Thank you for calling Creepy Nights. This is Todd Adams. How can I help you today?"

The voice on the phone spoke with a notable southern drawl, "Yes, I'd like to hear a story, please, alternate reality."

Todd heard himself speaking as if someone or something other than himself was in control.

"Once upon a time, there was a special property — one full of many tales… Stories, mysteries, and people, but, perhaps, the most interesting part was just beneath it all, Level Zero. It housed fifty-four — all victims of October 29th, 1928 — wayward souls who never left their place on this earth before greedy hands stole away their lives. Their bodies long dead, their souls forever restless. The property protected them because of the injustices they faced. They hovered in and around it, aimlessly wandering…"

Wow. I've officially gone off my rocker.

The WGBO jingle came through the phone.

"Now, that… is an interesting story! What do you think, folks…? Should we tell him? Ladies and gentlemen, how about a great round of applause for Todd Adams? The best storyteller of them all. Manning 'Apocalypse and Alternate Reality,' all by himself and broadcast all over the eighth most-listened-to radio station in Riverton, WGBO 530AM. I'm Ramblin' Ron Richards signing off for this special edition of the Dynamic Duds show. Good night, DUD-heads! Stay deplorable."

My imagination never stops. Time to punch my time card. I'm back in my own skin again. That's better.

The lights in the room flickered, and the ground shook beneath, giving validation that he unsettled things in ways he never should have. Proceeding toward the elevator, he remained confused.

I guess we're all aimlessly wandering until we find our purpose.

When the elevator door opened, he reached toward the button for the ground level to exit. He focused on the chrome-plated wall, realizing the control would only return him to Level Zero without a key.

Not going to pull an Ebony up here. I don't want to die anymore. I'm too intrigued.

He took a sigh and pressed the clear zero on the wall. It illuminated orange, and a familiar elevator ding followed.

Creeper Joe's voice came on the intercom.

DESCENDING TO LEVEL FIVE, LEVEL FOUR, LEVEL THREE, LEVEL TWO, LEVEL ONE. GOING DOWN, GOING DOWN. SYSTEM MALFUNCTION, SYSTEM MALFUNCTION. REROUTING, REROUTING.

Five seconds of silence.

ARRIVING AT YOUR DESTINATION. WELCOME HOME. NOW ENTERING LEVEL ZERO.

The elevator doors opened, and Todd crossed into the sub-tunnel. *One thing's for certain. I now know an alternate reality when I see it.*

CHAPTER FORTY-SIX

RAMBLIN' RON RICHARDS awoke in the back of an ambulance as *Cheap Trick* played a familiar number in the stereo. Blood flowed from his arm into an oversized bag. He yanked it out.

I'm not feeling so great... Where am I? Why am I?

A whiny and scratchy voice spoke from the driver's seat, "Don't worry, sir. We'll get you taken care of."

He looked up at the ambulance driver.

Oh, man, it's the creep from the bus. I can't catch a break, can I?

The voice spoke louder, "No time to chat, Ramblin' Ron? That's your name, isn't it? Heh-heh. I'll get you over to RGH, and we'll get you fixed up. Don't you worry."

I can't take any more of this.

"Excuse me. I just got sick in the heat of the moment. I don't need a hospital, just a chill pill which I already have prescribed. Take me home, please."

The driver chuckled. "Oh, Ron. That would only be possible if you hadn't 'lost' your mind in front of the detective, buddy. We're taking you to the psych ward for your own safety. I'm sure you get it. Heh-heh."

This is not happening. Hold your ground.

"You've got to be kidding. I'm just weak-stomached and fighting an anxiety disorder, not psychotic!"

The driver tormented, "Don't you remember? You confessed to killing Wayne Wallace before you passed out."

"No, I didn't."

"I'm quite sure you did. You're going to have to answer for it now." He clicked the back of his teeth. "We can't reward hands that shed innocent blood. Of course, Wayne was far from innocent. Besides, who knows? He might not even be dead. I digress... We gave you some sedatives to calm your nerves. I hope it helped. Is your world a little underwater right now?"

Where's my mind? I'm too sedated to remember anything else.

"Almost there. RGH is waiting to get their hands on you and lock you up. I'm thinking an icepick lobotomy will do the trick. Dr. Hicks is not known to be the most conventional in town, but he's the most likely to recommend that kind of procedure."

The creep stuck his tongue out at Ron, rolling his eyes and making inhuman faces like a Claymation character. Ron struggled to find words as the ambulance continued toward the hospital.

I don't have great distrust for the medical community, but whatever I can do to get away from this whacko's bound to be an improvement.

The ambulance parked, and the driver exited without a formal goodbye to Ron.

"You're just going to leave me here strapped to the stretcher bed?"

He undid himself and moved toward the front.

This isn't RGH. That's the Bridgewater Restaurant over there.

He climbed out the door, stumbling his way down the block.

CHAPTER FORTY-SEVEN

CHRIS WILKERSON sat in the control room, staring at the video feeds, toggling back and forth between each one. His exits from the space had dwindled in the recent times as he grew more fixated with watching the tunnel residents and the way of life that emerged.

It's weird. They almost seem like they're adapting in there. I don't see any duress. Am I missing something? Look at me, sitting here, watching these people in a strange voyeuristic manner. It's a false sense of control. A pipedream to reality. It's hard to admit I'm numb to the world, but I don't feel anymore. Staring at these screens keeps me from becoming hollow.

His eyes glossed over and he drifted into a deep sleep.

He stood in the tunnel, watching all the victims as they clawed their way up the walls and screamed. As they neared the top, a glimmer of light shined through the ceiling and they roared in excitement.

Veering to another corner, he saw victim number twenty — maimed with duct tape and electrical wire. Smoke came from her exposed scalp as she spoke, "Was it worth it? I hope it was worth it."

He ran away, and she pursued him with a cackling laughter that lingered as it bounced from the tunnel walls.

Creeper Joe dug into the overflow freezer and pulled out some of its stored contents. His brass syringe shimmered. He lunged toward Chris with a W crested dagger.

The door to the control room clanged shut, and he awoke holding a defensive position. He studied the screens.

Where are you, Joe? Where are you?

He swore aloud.

I forgot to lock the door.

Spinning his chair around to leave, it came to a sudden halt as Creeper Joe's foot stopped it.

His yellow eyes glowed in the darkness. "Not so fast. You've got some kind of mouth on you, don't you, Chris? I've been waiting for you to show for a while now. Where've you been? Did you lose count? We've got all fifty-four. The Easter egg hunt is over. You can breathe again."

"I let it go on for too long," Chris said. "I feel so jaded. There's no rush in torturing or kidnapping people. Just a horrible pain in the pit of my stomach and mounds of remorse that I can't come to grips with."

"Those are very human feelings, but, what are *we* really? Dead, alive, or somewhere in between?"

Chris's face grew pale. "What are you trying to say?"

"Life and death aren't so different," Joe said. "It's a state of mind, really... That's why *I'm* still here."

"Do you relish in ambiguity or what?"

"Of course I do. It's not fair for me to have a lying tongue with you... Truth is, I slit your throat last night, and you're with me now."

Heaven help me.

Chris panicked, feeling of his throat. His hands dripped scarlet. "You what?"

"Look down at the console," Joe gawked. "You think all this is, is a bucket of red corn syrup? I did what you needed me to. You failed to keep Oak Hollow in order, Chris. I let you rule the roost a while, gave you a taste of what it was like, and well, you know, it just didn't work out as well as I hoped. You signed the dotted line, but you never delivered."

"Why are you doing this to me?"

"To prove a point," Joe said.

"Which is?"

Joe shook his head in disapproval. "A partnership takes more than one participant. You failed with Katrina. You failed with the building. You failed with me."

"How can I know I failed if I never get a report card?"

"Wait until you see the undertaker chipping away at your headstone. That's always a real eye opener for us."

"What are you trying to say? Am I on the path to Sheol?"

"I think we all are. You and I, we supersede this world now... You. Me. A few others. It's not immortality. Don't misunderstand me. I've struggled to know how to handle you. We're alike now, Chris. Either you're with me, or you're against me."

"It's not always that simple," Chris said. "I don't only work in absolutes; don't put me in that position. You know, I can't trust you."

Joe began digging his nails into Chris's wrist.

Why is there no blood?

"Pick a side, but do it wisely. Oak Hollow will spit you out quick if you make the wrong choice. The ground's only hallowed on the surface. Basement is warped beyond recognition from years of folly. A pit for pleasures and sacrilege so obscene, you can't undo it."

"Screw this! I'm done," Chris said.

"This is the moment where I tell you... you're not really dead, and *then* I slit your throat."

"Say what...?"

Joe lunged toward him with a dagger cutting into his throat. Chris collapsed to the floor as blood gushed from his neck. Joe dropped the storied knife, hurrying to the back of the room. He collected a bucket and waited for it to fill before leaving.

"Chris, it *was* only corn syrup the first time. Some fools never learn," he said.

Creeper Joe exited the room, and the Shadow spoke, "I don't know why you did that."

"His blood was far from innocent," Joe said. "Besides, you know we're racing the clock. It was time."

They walked through the basement, moving back into the tunnel through an unseen point of entry.

"No more," the Shadow said.

CHAPTER FORTY-EIGHT

DETECTIVE NEIL PENSKE pulled the black Crown Vic down the block, noting the Creepy Nights building in the line of sight.

"5454 Oak Hollow Lane. Man, this place gives me the creeps," Penske said. "Who paints a multistoried building that shade?"

"An independent entrepreneur or a colorblind, old lady," Herbert replied.

"Let's stay parked here. I'd like to approach this one incognito if we can. I have a strange feeling about it."

"Good call."

"You have your vest on?"

"Always."

The two men entered the lobby and approached the unstaffed receptionist's desk. Papers, cobwebs, and Reese's candy wrappers lay strewn about. The surrounding walls featured posters of forgotten slasher films and b-movies to mask the dated wall paneling.

"You ever seen any of these, Penske?"

"Na. Not my scene. You?"

"Yeah. I had a few rebellious years back in the day. Not memorable in a good way."

"Those films always attract a certain crowd, don't they?"

"Yeah. I know, I know," Herbert said. "The people that look like they have it together on the outside, but deep down, have something much more devastating within them they're trying to unravel, demented and disturbed."

Penske cocked his head sideways as he looked at Herbert. "Well, shoot. That got dark awfully quick. I was going to say something more along the lines of 'alternative, creative types.' You know, the folks that paint pictures of their mother and put a sheep's head and a cigarette on top of her curvy body... You know the type, right?"

"That sure is descriptive, Penske. You sure you're not one of those creative types? Ha!"

"Back to business," Penske said. "Here's the reception phone. Why don't I see if I can get through to someone? It's obvious no one's coming to check on us."

"Yeah, sure. Go ahead."

Penske picked up the sunbaked telephone handset and pressed 1.

"Space Fiction, this is Mary Beth."

Penske signaled to Herbert that he reached someone and pointed at the phone, mouthing something unintelligible. "Hey, Mary Beth. We're in the lobby. Can you come and speak to us for a second? There's no one here."

Mary Beth responded, unenthused, "Yeah. We prefer to live in anonymity around here these days. Wilkerson won't hire anyone for *that* position. I'll be out in just a moment."

From the far northwestern corner of the room, the door popped open, squeaking and creaking as a heavyset woman in her upper 40s walked in. She was red-headed and pasty cheeked with hints of gray and a different tone of red in her hair from a previous botched attempt at coloring it.

That's a DIY project in the back of a trailer house. The question is... I wonder if she split the box of hair dye with her significant other... or her mother.

She broke the silence, extending her hand to greet the pair, "Hi. I'm sorry. Yeah, we don't get many visitors here face-to-face. What are your names again, guys?"

"Jack," Herbert said. "This is my colleague, Neil. We're doing an article for the *Statesman* and thought some of you or your bosses might be free to answer a few questions."

"Yeah. Sure. Why not? I've got four months invested in this dump."

"Wait a minute," Penske said. "Why do you call it a dump?"

Mary Beth chuckled, looking over her shoulder to make sure no one was behind her. "Chris Wilkerson, my boss, will kill me for saying this, but this place still needs serious updates. It's been going downhill since... since the disappearances. Katrina... Nancy... There are others. It hit close to home. We don't allow visitors into the production areas where we take the phone calls. We have mice and roach infestations like you've never seen. It's kind of embarrassing..."

"I can understand why," Herbert remarked.

"Wilkerson took his eye off the ball," she said. "I can't read his mind, but he must be thinking, 'Nobody can see us... so what gives...?' We're just a call center, right? What's the point of sinking money into building upgrades when you can pay for top-notch storytellers like... yours truly?" She spread her arms wide, motioning toward herself while channeling an awkward and crooked smile.

"How many people do you have working here again?" Penske asked.

"I don't know. About seventy, I guess? We don't come together all at once to have an exact count. Numbers are dwindling. Business is going downhill. We've got no one to light a fire under us. Chris just kind of checked out on us and seems in his own little world these days. He keeps things very... how should I say this? Siloed. We don't talk to anyone outside our own department. I mean, we're talking, full-on, non-disclosure agreement in our contracts. We have to keep our lips sealed about what goes on in here. You know, to preserve the integrity of the enterprise."

Herbert spoke up, "Integrity of the enterprise? You make it sound like you're a damn stockbroker with insider information. Isn't this just an hourly joint? You guys aren't doing that well for yourselves, are you? No disrespect."

Mary Beth took offense to the haphazard comment as she put a hand on her sizeable right hip. "I'm at $5.80 an hour with benefits." She gulped. "It's not terrible."

"I'm sorry, Mary Beth," Herbert said. "Like I said, no offense. It makes sense... I guess. Speaking of Wilkerson, your boss... is he around?"

Mary Beth shook her head as she clamped her eyes closed for an extra second. "I haven't seen him in a few days. He might be in the basement. That's just Chris, a man of many mysteries — like the Wizard of Oz. He's down to earth and everything... but that doesn't mean that he always acts like he is. He prefers life behind the curtain — interesting, but in a disturbing way. It's hard to explain—a man more tattered and torn than I've ever known."

Penske grabbed the sides of the chair to distribute his weight, prepping to end the discussion and said, "Okay. Thanks, Mary Beth. Anyone else you think we should talk to?"

A fly landed on her head atop her altered and synthetic mane.

Look at those discolored roots, wrecked from years of shoddy self-treatments. It would be a miracle if that thing ever gets out of that tangled up mess.

"Wait a minute," she said. "Aren't you guys writing an article? That can't be enough material. I'm not buying it. The information out there in the public eye is next to nil. I'm sure Wilkerson would appreciate a tactful plug from a few other of our more colorful characters around here. What do you say? I'll go grab a few more for you to interview."

Penske stood up, tucking his small notepad in his jacket pocket and moving toward the front door. "Nope. Not necessary. We better get going. We'll see you around. It'll be in the paper in the next few weeks."

Mary Beth scratched her head, looking at the men as if they violated her. "Okay, then. See you later. No grand tour for you guys. I was feeling nice today," she mumbled.

I didn't know if we'd ever get out of here.

They exited the building.

•　　•　　•　　•　　•

The detectives walked out of Creepy Nights down the sidewalk.

"Let's wait a bit, and we'll go back inside," Herbert said. "I'd like to see the basement."

"You would like to see the basement? How about explaining to me why all the sudden we're reporters for the Statesman working undercover?"

"We're incognito to minimize suspicions and we don't want Wilkerson or others to get the idea we're onto something just yet. Just too many strange feelings I get around here. Wilkerson's probably down there now."

"Don't we need a warrant?"

"We have a lead. What gives? Doesn't seem like anyone else gives a crap."

After a few minutes of loitering just out of the building's line of sight, they slipped back inside and got on the elevator, riding down to the basement.

"Huh, that's weird," Herbert said. "They usually mark basement with a B. Not a zero."

"Yeah. Interesting. Then again, that fits the M.O. of this place, doesn't it? There isn't much that makes a lot of sense."

The basement door opened, and they walked around, exploring each of the rooms.

"Not much going on here," Herbert said. "None of the lights are very bright, are they?"

"Might be by design."

"You're right. It very well could be. Keep your hand close to the trigger finger. I've got a strange feeling about this."

"Me too."

"This room off to the side... It's the only door that's closed," Herbert said. "Let's go check it out. See if it's unlocked..."

Approaching the door, they both drew their guns. Penske motioned to Herbert with his fingers.

One... two... three.

They plowed the door open.

"What's with all these screens?" Penske asked. "We've got us a real creep on our hands, don't we?" He grabbed the control, rifling through the camera feeds.

"Way to go, rookie," Herbert said. "Your fingerprints are all over it now. So much for that idea."

"It's Wilkerson's building. Wouldn't matter if his prints were on it or not, right?"

"No. Look at the people on the screens...."

"Yeah. I'm looking. They don't look like they're struggling."

"Penske, your hands. Look at 'em. They're covered in red. Must be on the controls."

Penske licked his fingertip. "It's corn syrup."

"What? What are you saying?"

Penske swiveled around. "There's another puddle of it on the floor back there. Should we swab it?"

"Na. I wouldn't bother," Herbert said. "This weirdo does those wacky commercials, probably just a stupid stunt he pulled for one of those and hasn't cleaned up."

"Well, how do we get to the place on the screens?"

"Judging from the cables connected to the back of them, they're running someplace nearby. We've just got to follow the cords…. Why don't you go back to the cruiser and call for backup? This looks like a much bigger rabbit hole than I would have expected. Get us the paperwork we need to be in here legally and we'll stage it like it's our first time in the basement."

"Go ahead. Send the rookie detective back up top while *you* get to have all the fun."

"I've seen a lot in my career, but this may be as big a bust as I've ever seen. Tread carefully on your way back to the car."

CHAPTER FORTY-NINE

TODD ADAMS observed the corridor outside the elevator as the security light illuminated a path back to Level Zero.

I guess the others found their way out without me. What else is new?

Locating an entry point back into the tunnel, he pulled back on a small, ring-shaped handle mounted to a doorway of granite rock. He pulled the heavy door, squeezing through the small space. It closed behind him on its own, blending in with the wall. He stared at a cascading waterfall and spring just ahead. A small sign stood next to it, SPRING OF LIFE.

I wonder what that means. Sounds a little too good to be true.

Others stood nearby rinsing, cleansing, and in some cases, drinking from the spring, but he did not recognize them.

These people wouldn't know the difference between sewer water and clean water anyway, would they?

Creeper Joe came around the corner, objecting to Todd's thoughts as if he vocalized them.

"Ah, Ah, Ah! No, no, Todd! Remember, we don't permit haughty eyes here…? I thought we were past this."

He came from the shadows and began dunking Todd in the waterfall pond over and over as he teased.

"What do you think?

What do *you* think…?

Is it drinkable...?

Are you worthy of it...?

This could *be* the Fountain of Youth... for all you know, you idiot! You are *nothing*, and I can make you less. I really can!"

Joe dunked Todd's head in the water as he gasped for air. He threw Todd on the ground, kicking him in the stomach, and knocking the wind out of him. Todd coughed the liquid he swallowed all over the floor, its appearance more like a green-tinged mucus than anything else.

Joe raised his voice to a live-theatrical volume and tone, "Get the picture yet? Quit judging these people and love them for who they are. You're one of them now, anyway!"

He spat in Todd's face and disappeared. Todd perused the area, hoping for some help or relief from an onlooker.

Of course. They're all gone. Who wouldn't run?

He sat alone near the mysterious life-giving source, the Spring of Life, facing the irony of all ironies — being used to tease him in a close brush with his own mortality.

He observed the spring welling from beneath, its gush recirculating through in the wash just above. He looked closer at the rocks and objects that lined the wall behind the waterfall, surmising that some of them were skulls from past tragedy. A glimmering light shined through the ceiling. The hole was not larger than the size of a quarter, but the suppressed daylight shining through offered him an unspeakable relief. He took a few moments to collect his thoughts as he studied his changing features in the reflecting pool. He struggled to make out the details in his face, but noted less color in his skin and life in his eyes.

The effects of the spring took hold.

The floor bottomed out under Todd as he plummeted down into a dark hole. Lorrie fell to his right as she yelled, "You are going to pay for this, Todd. You better make your wrongs right and help these people!"

"Lorrie, I... I don't know what to say."

He continued to fall faster and faster down into the abyss, as a barrage of bloody hands reaching to the sky surrounded, and Lorrie disappeared.

Voices chanted in unison, leaving him struggling to identify what they said. Before he could, they faded away.

Creeper Joe rocketed from beneath the black as his glowing eyes hit Todd with a momentary blindness as he returned from the peculiar experience. As his sight returned, he found himself staring at his reflection in the pool.

What's happening?

"Handsome, isn't he? You know... I should just start calling you... Narcissus," Creeper Joe called out.

I've got to get back in the spring. That was remarkable.

He immersed himself. The spring wrapped itself around his body in a method unfamiliar to that of water.

Maybe I shouldn't have.

In a matter of moments, the cuts on his legs healed, and he watched them vanish away.

I guess it is some kind of Fountain of Youth...? How fascinating.

After several minutes of soaking, Todd climbed out of the spring, sloughing off the excess liquid from his body. He felt refreshed as it dripped off and moved with an altered chemistry, density, and viscosity to that of water. Its lingering trail rolled across the pores of his skin.

"I feel like a brand new man. It would sure be nice if I could dry off."

Above the waterfall, a large vent opened and hot air spewed. Sunlight shined through momentarily.

Creeper Joe's voice came from around a corner just out of Todd's line of sight, "Like this? Then you could be a... Hottie Toddie, couldn't you? Heh-heh!"

The entire area became a wind tunnel, drying Todd off just as requested. As his body lifted from the ground, the air from the dryer dissipated.

Creeper Joe walked toward Todd with an uncommon grin. "Yeah. I picked it up from one of those drive-through car washes going out of business and powered it up about ten times stronger. What do you think, Hottie Toddie?"

Todd shrugged and said, "I don't know. I guess I'll be going now."

"Where are you headed this time? Have you already learned your way around here that fast? This place can be a real pain in the arse 'til you figure it out. Heh-heh. Bye-bye now!"

Don't give him the satisfaction of a reaction. Apathy is his worst enemy. I'm not ready for another close brush with death. Gauging from the shine of the sun, this was the south end.

He saw a woman, hunched over, looking short on breath. Moving closer toward her, he realized they were previously introduced.

Katrina, the woman from the Bridgewater Restaurant? What's going on?

"What are you doing in here? Are you okay?" he asked. He came toward her and gave her a hug. "Your ex throw you in here or what?"

"No, it was nothing like that."

"It's great to see you again," he said. "I'm sorry... given the circumstances. I wondered why I hadn't seen you at Bridgewater in a while."

"I've been here just long enough not to pay any mind to life up top anymore," she said.

"Katrina... Katrina... I... I..."

No more of this. I can't handle any more phantom memories. Through the eyes of Wasserman I go.

Kicking the lingering ash aside, he stood next to his father, William, as he laid the cornerstone to the wellhouse, sketching out an uncommon interpretation of the Warnings Against Folly as Cardinal Rules for the property.

William laid a beautiful, custom-made pocket watch on top of the stone. "Son, these rules will be our covenant to protect this beautiful place. Don't you ever forget." Raising the worn riveting hammer in the air, he dropped it toward the timepiece. The image played out in slow motion in his memory — the force of the hammer striking the top of the watch face, the scattering of its glass in every direction, his father's portable clock coming to an unexpected halt, and the unforgettable sight of the man grabbing at his chest and collapsing six feet to the ground below. He breathed his last, and yet, somehow, it still felt right. They looked at one another in a moment of unconditional love. Then, there was the look of the spirit leaving the body, eyes hollowed out and lifeless, as William's life came to an abrupt halt. He looked into the spring as the elevating drip filled the well.

•   •   •   •   •

"Todd, Todd, you there? I'm no stranger to the runaway mind… or soul… or whatever you want to call it," Katrina said. "You want to talk about it? I see it in your eyes… We were all guests of the hotel, and a part of us is still here waiting for a meaningful end."

"And you know this how?"

"Forgive the approach here," she said, "but it's just a matter of summoning…"

Her eyes glossed over, reflecting the gaze of another.

"Don, it's Sylvia. Don't you remember? Come on now."

"It's coming to me in bits and pieces," Todd replied as Don manifested himself. "My fury with Joe only burns hotter with time. I gave him a chance… Sylvia… and he ruined me… he ruined us."

"Darlin', you managed it while you were alive," Katrina remarked as Sylvia kept control. "I managed it after we were dead, and now we're both here tangled in the web. It's like we're meant to beat him together, honey."

Todd forced his way back into the conversation. "I'm not comfortable talking this way. I'm in control of my own life."

Katrina returned as Sylvia buried herself deep within.

"Suit yourself, handsome," she said.

Todd scratched his head as he spoke, "So, what's the point? We've all got baggage, and we're all locked up. To what end?"

"An end only God can know. You best get on. Save your damsel in distress and the rest of them, too. You and me… we could have an enjoyable life together, just like Don and Sylvia would have given the opportunity."

"Yeah? We better get on it then," Todd said. "Level Zero's taking hold of me… and the strangest part of it is that I'm feeling more normal than I have in ages. I can't explain it.

"I hear you, Todd. I'll see you around. Don't get lost."

CHAPTER FIFTY

TODD ADAMS moved on past Katrina, hoping to uncover a deeper meaning and purpose to his being there.

Another rabbit hole… Why not?

Walking down the path through a narrow passageway, he noted a glow of bright lights toward the end. Going in further, he found his way to an archery range as rumbling bass came through a nearby speaker. The room was lit well with targets at varying distances. A middle-aged man stood dressed in black with a tightly tucked ponytail. He stood in the range, focused on one of the targets with his make-shifted bow.

What's that thing made of? Hmm.

Todd prepared to speak, and the man released the arrow as it flew toward the target. Two boars hung by chains on the far side of the room with penetration marks in their neck. Before he could introduce himself or ask, the man spoke, "I got 'em, alright… That'll make for a pleasant change of pace. We don't eat much here."

"Well… I guess I'll start off by saying thanks," Todd said.

"It's nothin'… nothin' at all. I'm sure you'd have done the same for me if the shoe were on the other foot. It'll make for an enjoyable meal. If I can help the rest… I want to."

Todd shook hands with the man as he handed him one of the arrows.

"This is not a traditional quiver of arrows, champ. It's handmade. We get imaginative in here. We have to..."

"What do you mean, handmade?" Todd asked.

"I mean, the arrows are hand bones fused together with a bondin' compound."

Todd looked disgusted as he replied, "You've got to be kidding me."

The man picked up another arrow and said, "Do I look like the kind of guy that would be kiddin'? How long you been here...? There's a whole new meaning to 'sick' in this place. Joe picked the hands because of... because of the number..."

"What are you talking about? The number?"

"Twenty-seven bones in each hand... fifty-four bones for the set. That's Joe's magic number... Haven't you heard?"

"Only fragments," Todd said. "Don't bother trying to explain it to me now. It sounds like I'll have plenty of time to hash it out."

"Whatever you say. The bow isn't any better. I'll leave that to your imagination. My name's Bob, but everyone calls me Livewire. Creeper Joe set this room up for me. Might even say I get a little preferential treatment. I..."

What are you getting at? What's your deal?

"Treatment?" Todd interrupted. "Hang on a minute. You hesitated. If you have something else to say, please do. Nothing's as it seems around here. That much, I know."

"We can crack Joe, you know?"

Todd rubbed his chin. "Crack him? No. I don't. Care to elaborate?"

"You've got to make yourself useful. You know. Be indisposable. Play by his rules for a while. Then, he'll reward you more and punish you less. It's all 'fun and games' to him. I'm sure he's declared as much to you at some point. Haven't you noticed? He'll undoubtedly remind you if not. He loves to make people squirm — to fight against the injustices of the lesser, and self-indulge in... dark humor."

"I don't know if I would call it humor. The things he's done to me so far have been horrifying. I'm not sure I'm ready for what may come next."

"Well, it sounds like you have some more observin' to do around here. Like I've already said, he's got his own rules. This place is his town, and he might as well be the sheriff... Every sheriff can be bought for a price. Can't they?"

"Oh, I don't know," Todd said. "I've known some loyal lawmen committed to the badge, no matter what."

"You are just ignorantly goin' through the motions, aren't you?" Livewire fired another arrow at the target and hit the bull's eye.

"Winner, winner, chicken dinner! Nice going, Livewire," Creeper Joe's voice came blaring through an intercom speaker as both men looked at one another, reaching to plug their ears.

Livewire tried to downplay the noise. "Yep... Joe's watchin' us alright. I'm a good enough shot to keep the weirdy's attention. Here, why don't you try it? What did you say your name was there, champ?"

"Todd. Todd Adams."

"Alright, Todd. It doesn't fire quite like a traditional bow and arrow, as you can imagine. Aim higher than you think would be accurate."

Todd lined up his sight and looked at the target. Creeper Joe's face appeared right in the middle. One of his eyes aligned within the yellow circle that surrounded the bull's eye.

"Go ahead," Joe yelled. "Put me out of my misery, mister!"

Todd released the bow, and the arrow flew into its center.

"Jackpot... Jackpot... or maybe I'm a Crackpot!" Joe said with a chuckle. "Oh, wait. I'm sorry, folks. Forgive me. I misread my 'line.' Crock pot. Ladies and gentlemen, a crock pot for Todd Adams. Let's have a round of applause and celebrate."

"Ebony and Ivory" cued again, interrupting the other song, and a crock pot lowered on a suspending chain into the archery area.

Livewire patted Todd on the back and signaled a thumbs up.

"There you go. You earned something in Level Zero. Nice job."

"What the hell am I gonna do with a crock pot?"

Creeper Joe spoke from the face of the target, "Uh... I don't know. Cook! Duh!"

His face faded away.

"Listen here," Livewire said. "We all have jobs, you know. Joe lets us rotate them around. Your first assignment looks like it's going to be cooking. The mess hall is down the pathway you just came down and on the opposite side."

"Thanks. This was 'enlightening.' Hey, speaking of... how did you get the bright lights in here?"

"Simple. I just asked for 'em. Let me tell you somethin' else. This whole tunnel's wired... in every way that you can imagine. Did most of it myself. Joe likes to rearrange the scenery, but he don't know I have this." He turned around and lifted a large rock. Underneath it, there was a large hand-drawn map. "You're going to have to be careful with it. If he catches us, we might both be goners. I'm guessing you've gathered that there are cameras and microphones everywhere! I sit under this spot because I've got a few zones in here where I miswired 'em, and to my knowledge, they are still that way months later. Of course, I did it on purpose. Call it a 'consultant's guarantee' to ensure that they can come back to work to squeeze more money out of you, but you didn't hear that from me."

"Thanks. This might be helpful. I'll tuck it away for safekeeping. I better get on my way."

"Take care of it. There are a few places in here that few have seen or been to. Tread with care."

CHAPTER FIFTY-ONE

Approaching the Crown Vic, a half mile's walk from Creepy Nights, DETECTIVE NEIL PENSKE noticed a trembling man sitting in the passenger seat. The intruder's mannerisms reflected his fatigue. Penske drew his gun.

Just another druggie strung out. This city sure has gone to shit.

He tapped on the glass, and rather than seeing fear in the intruder's eyes, he observed relief.

Ramblin' Ron?

He pulled the door open. Ron sat in the passenger seat.

"Thank God, Penske. I hope you can help. They kidnapped me. Some weirdo drugged me and left me to rot. You've got to help."

"Slow down. Don't act like we're friends. You've just unlawfully entered a municipal vehicle without precedence."

Just gonna give him a scare. It's almost Halloween, after all.

"Didn't you hear a word I just said? I need your help, not incarceration."

"Not my problem. You broke the law when you came into this space. Didn't you notice the license plates?"

"That's why I got in. I thought I could have confidence in you! I made the mistake of assuming you people would help. I guess that's where I went wrong."

"What I'm seeing and hearing is that you entered an RPD vehicle without precedence."

"Ha... Ha... You're quite the comedian," Ron said. "You could even take your act on the road and quit your day job."

"Don't flatter me."

"Go ahead. Lock me up! Do whatever you have to do, but please send someone to look out for this guy. We were in an ambulance. He must have stolen it before he kidnapped me."

Alright. Time to stop busting his chops.

"Ambulance? You should have said that sooner. That changes things. We have totally different protocols for different situations, as I'm sure you can imagine."

Ron rolled his eyes.

"Please move to the back seat," Penske said. "I've got to call something in. It's big."

•   •   •   •   •

Penske put the car into motion, driving back toward the Precinct Three station as he questioned Ron.

"Why were you in an ambulance? I try not to be on a first-name basis with my... clients. I'm almost certain we have a serial situation with these disappearances. That's about as much as I'm at liberty to say right now."

"Really? What makes you think that?"

"A new development. That's all you get to hear for now. Let's say the tongue you turned in was Wayne's... why is he on the hit list?"

"I think in Wayne's case, it's because he so candidly made a fool of himself in the public eye. A disgruntled listener probably did this to him. I bet he's holed up in a basement somewhere being fed pigeon food because that's all he can stomach."

"Well, based on *that* theory, he can't taste much. Seems like he would have bled to death."

"There's one way to cut a tongue out and keep a person living — to sear it shut with heat. Only a calculated creep would have known that," Ron said.

"Well, what does that make you, Ron? That method sure seemed to roll right off of *your* tongue."

Ron scoffed, wiping a tear from his eye. "I used to study serial killer profiles. Give me a break. I pay my civic duty to the community every day on the airwaves."

"Oh… you studied them that closely? We'll need a full verbal and written statement of all you heard and saw. I don't want to put *you* in any harm's way."

Ron shook his head. "Please forgive me. That guy I was with was an odd one. You ought to track him down and lock him up. He didn't seem quite right in the head."

"Are you a radio guy or a shrink? I've heard enough of your… 'crap' shows. You're not stable enough to assess the health of anyone. Especially if Wayne Wallace is your definition of a healthy baseline."

"Hey, I never said Wayne was stable. I just worked with him."

"Sometimes, the truth is sitting right there in front of us. We just need the right details to come in focus," Penske said.

CHAPTER FIFTY-TWO

Preparing to enter the mess hall for the first time, TODD ADAMS waited for Creeper Joe to give orders as he stood in the center of the tunnel near its entrance

"Hey, Todd," Joe called out. "Report to work at 0600 and whip us up some vittles. We eat twice a week. Sometimes three times if you're lucky. Steamed rat, fried bat, maybe even a boiled toadie frog... or two. I've got 'em stored away. Don't worry; I'll bring them to you. Hunting day is on Wednesday."

"Are you kidding?" Todd asked. "Aren't they diseased? Besides, how would I know what time it is?"

Joe grinned. "There's no disease in here. The Spring of Life keeps everything vital, including the vermin. Anyhow, I've got a clock in the mess hall. I'll walk you over. It's active when I feel like turning it on, and that's that. It's not like time matters for you. I didn't say it was accurate. You're not going anywhere! Heh-heh."

Todd stopped the overextended laugh. "Joe, that doesn't help matters one bit. Does it? Can you just quit with the teasing and get real with me? What's going on, and why am I still here?"

"You're not ready... not even close. Why don't I just 'mess you around' a little more?"

"Not ready for what?"

"Just forget it."

Todd entered the room and looked around.

Kind of like a medieval version of Oakdale High. Not ready to go back there. Only a few things missing — the clinking from the kitchen, the stressed banter of the underpaid workers, and the unending chatter of the students.

"What do you think?" Joe asked. "Up to your standards? Don't let those haughty eyes make you cast judgment on my handiwork... Don't you dare have a lying tongue either! You know what will happen if you do, right?"

"It looks good," Todd said. "I'll give you props on this. Reminds me of a trip to Carlsbad I took a few years ago. Never in a million years would you expect a cafeteria to serve cold sandwiches in the middle of the earth. It feels sterile. 'Government-managed,' but precisely the room for me to get to work on giving you the best doggone fried rat and steamed bat that you can get around these..."

Creeper Joe interrupted, "Ah, ah! You've gotten it wrong. It's 'fried bat' and 'steamed rat.' Don't forget about the toadie frogs. Oh, lookie there. You only have seven minutes. You better get cooking. I'll ring the bell in a bit, and you'll see the others show up faster than a mosquito to a bug zapper."

Joe left the room as Todd explored the kitchen area. He had many utensils at his disposal — forks, knives, wooden spoons, loads of miscellaneous tongs, meat cleavers, whisks, and stainless steel plates. He read signs mounted all over the kitchen.

REMOVAL OF ANY KITCHEN SUPPLIES FROM THIS ROOM WILL LAND YOU on the NORTH SIDE of the TUNNEL in a CELL for MORE TORTURE. DON'T TRY YOUR LUCK.

•　　•　　•　　•　　•

The large vat nearly spilled over as Todd swirled the bat around the grease and steamed the rat above the boiling water in a neighboring skillet. Another pot boiled behind it with fifteen frogs.

The odor of the creatures is a lot more likeable than I could have ever imagined. I must just be that hungry. I'm ready for the day we can serve up that boar.

He finished firing up and cooking the meals for the hungry inhabitants of Level Zero. Shortly thereafter, the bell Creeper Joe mentioned rang. The creep's voice piped through the entire area on the loudspeakers.

"Wake up. Wake up, my children. Time for some grub grubs so you can have some chub chubs! Heh-heh."

The unlikely army of transient prisoners began their walk to the mess hall area, lining up single-file just outside the room as their anticipatory chatter remained minimal.

Todd spoke to the group as they approached, "Come on in, you guys. I'll be serving your meal today."

Harv was at the front of the line and chimed in, "Let me guess, fried bat and steamed rat, right?"

Todd smiled, almost welcoming the sarcasm. "Right on the money, Harv. Don't forget about the boiled frogs... for the select lucky few."

The best way to cope with the struggle is to have fun with it. It'll help the rest do the same.

After all went through the chow line, Todd prepared his own plate. Once the others sat to eat, he carried his meal into the main seating area. He struggled not to fixate on the sounds of munching and chewing while the forks clinked across the tops of the stainless steel plates. A table of unfamiliar women sat together, but none looked up or acknowledged him.

"What's going on, ladies? No love for the chef?"

They returned a cold stare in stone silence. Todd turned around and studied a sign on the wall: NO DRINKS IN THE MESS HALL.

He and Livewire made eye contact.

"Hey there," Todd said. "What's the word, buddy?"

"I'm not going to talk to you right now," Livewire said. "The mess hall must maintain order at all times." He pointed to a sign that read the same in red blocked letters on a white backdrop. "Joe will tolerate nothing less. We don't want the sprinklers kicked on. It's too easy to gossip around here. This is just about the only time that we're all together. We can't be stirrin' up trouble in the community or pourin' out lies like a false witness."

"Gossip? About each other? About Creeper Joe? Oh, come on. Are the sprinklers that bad? At least everyone could have a sip of water with dinner, right?"

Livewire shook his head. "You're thinking too casually again, like we're above the surface. What do you think sprinklers full of *bleach* can do?"

"Burn skin and poison food?"

"You got it. One of many demented ways to keep us from rallyin' together and rebellin' against what we're governed by. The poison's never enough to kill us, but it'll do a good bit of harm to your innards. You'll be beggin' for a trip to the Spring of Life."

"Which is? What are we governed by?"

"I can't answer that. These guys are old-fashioned. If the women even utter as much as a peep in here, they get accused of gossipin'. Men talk about their... trade. Women talk about their... relationships. That's what Creeper Joe says, anyhow. Let's park this conversation, and we'll pick it up when we are in a safer, less public spot. We might as well be under a microscope while we're eatin' in here. Assume nothin'. Instead, just recognize that you're in Joe's wheelhouse, and you must follow his rules, and play *his* games, *his* way. Did you notice anything else that's different other than our delicate and gristly cuisine?"

Todd shrugged. "No children?"

"That's right. None."

Harv turned from another table and chimed in, "Don't even think about procreating with the women here. Anyone that's tried ends up self-volunteered to castration."

Todd's face turned pale. "Thanks for the tip. I hope *you* didn't have to learn that the hard way."

Harv smiled and said, "That's between me and God..."

Todd laughed. "Fair enough... anything else?

"I've said enough..." Harv said. "We'll talk again at the appropriate time."

After Todd bit into the coarse and undercooked meat, he had a strange and unexpected feeling of both relief and community hit him.

I don't know if it's laughing gas they pipe through the vents around here or if it's something else, but I don't enjoy feeling this way. I know my positive feelings about this place are irrational. It must be some kind of Stockholm Syndrome...

CHAPTER FIFTY-THREE

DETECTIVE TERRY HERBERT was unwilling to wait any longer. He explored the basement of Creepy Nights for a while, unable to find a path into the area he and Penske had seen on the video feed. He went outside and explored the back of the property. Walking around for several minutes, he found an access panel near the storage building.

Need to jimmy it loose.

He opened up the building and found a crowbar.

I'm surprised it was unlocked. There we go. This is perfect.

After lifting the top of the panel cover, he shined his light in the hole.

Now or never, old man.

He descended into the mysterious area just beneath, stepping several feet down the rebar ladder. Looking upon the hatch that separated him from the space below, he noted a large "0". It had a keyed padlock on it.

We've got a lock pick in the Crown Vic, but I can't go back over there now. Where's my backup?

Without warning, a commotion came from beneath it.

I've got to get the heck out of Dodge.

No one arose from the tunnel hatch. After several minutes, Herbert cascaded back into the mysterious area. This time, the lower level access panel was open.

Alright. Who's in there waiting for me?

He drew his .38 special, pulling the access door further back to enter the area. He peered below. The drop to the ground was about thirteen feet.

Just drop to the floor. Your back can heal. Workman's comp otherwise.

No one else was in the immediate vicinity.

All for the badge. All for the badge. This is what it's all about.

He walked toward the south end of the tunnel until arriving at the first notable area. He spotted a white sign that read SPRING OF LIFE.

Why do I feel like I should drink from this? I can't help myself.

A whiny voice called from the shadows, "Excuse me. Don't do that. This is an exclusive club here... Heh-heh."

"What's that?" Herbert asked. "Exclusive club? What is this place? Some kind of sewer?" He studied the secluded waterfall and spring area. A figure shoved a brass syringe into his own arm, showing an ecstatic satisfaction. An excess of blood trickled down the side of it onto the floor.

"What the heck are you doing?" Herbert asked.

"What I have to. You wouldn't understand."

"You bums can't figure out how to make it up top, so you end up here doing the same thing you do everywhere else. Bottom feeding off all the rest?"

"Something like that. Rather than classify me by my looks, why don't you call me by name. I'm Joe."

The spring glows. I've got to...

Herbert bent down toward the spring, cupping his hands together.

"You don't understand what you're doing," Joe said. "You aren't welcome here."

"Aren't welcome? I don't get it. How am I any less welcome than you are? Are there others?"

"Why should you get it?" Joe asked. "I wouldn't expect *you* to. You're better off knowing less and getting out of here before it's too late. Don't let yourself fall for it. I see you making the self-serving assumption you can enjoy the spring like the rest of us *bums*... as you call us."

Herbert scoffed and motioned toward his gun. "Go ahead and blabber away like all the other 'street philosophers' I've met in my life. Relevant one minute and irrelevant the next. I could make you go away down here and no one would know the difference. What good are *you* doing for our town?" Herbert washed his hands and face in the spring, drinking from it as it wet his parched lips.

Creeper Joe shrugged. "Good question. You don't deserve the answer, though. When the spring dries up because of your unclean hands and your haughty eyes, don't you come crying to me."

"Okay, then. This conversation is over," Herbert declared. He pulled out his finger and motioned toward his head like a gun, mimicking suicide.

"That's no way to look at how precious your life is. Now get on out of here before I change my mind." Creeper Joe proceeded to the waterfall, pressing in on the third skull to the left, and a passageway opened. The spring began to dry up. He turned and faced Herbert as its decaying state became more evident. "Take my word for it. Go down this tunnel and never turn back. You know what happened to Lot's wife...? Don't turn around. It's not worth it. You've had your *sweet...* taste of it already. It might benefit you if you can keep it to yourself."

Herbert rolled his eyes and turned around. "Fine. Maybe we'll meet in the next life... street philosopher."

"I wouldn't count on that," Creeper Joe said. "Your heart's too impure. I don't think it'll matter, though. Not for long... Heh-heh."

Herbert exited. He continued through the passage behind the Spring of Life as it continued to dry up, a lasting consequence of his forceful and unwelcome entry into the place.

That was too weird. Not only do I need a colonoscopy, I also need a CT scan!

He sloshed through to another tunnel that became city property as its rank odor became more pronounced.

The spring's contents took hold on Herbert.

He fell into a puddle of the flowing sewage as it rose to his neck level. The Shadow appeared to him in a ghost-like fashion, communicating from the end of the sewer passage in an unfamiliar voice, "Never speak of this place or return to it again. It isn't for the unworthy. If you do, unending torment awaits in this life and the next..."

Detective Penske's head floated down the sewer, staring up at him as it went by. He spoke to Herbert, "Shouldn't have meddled around. It would have been better if we'd left it to the feds."

"What are you saying?" He stood up lunging toward the head and it disappeared. Herbert continued to move through the sewer passage as the torrent of gray water pushed him onward.

His late wife stood further down, waving him on. "Come home to me, Jack. Dinner's ready."

"Honey, I... I... it's so good to see you."

"I wish you would have said that more before I was gone. Always working and never home." She washed away under the sewage.

"I'm sorry, Marie."

The spring influenced mirage of scenes ended and the torrent from the sewer reduced to knee deep water. He continued through the sewer tunnel for several minutes until finding a way out.

Come on now. Find a distraction, old-timer. That was worse than any bender, wasn't it?

The chilling voices lingered in the back of his mind, leaving him unsettled to the extreme. He climbed the exit ladder, pushing up on the lid and surfacing in the middle of Clairmont Avenue just west of Oak Hollow Lane.

I'm going to open that frozen yogurt shop. I'm done with this.

He hoisted himself into the street as a taxi cab sped by. It plowed him over in an unexpected sweep. The trauma to the head killed him on impact as he faced the sky motionless.

CHAPTER FIFTY-FOUR

TODD ADAMS made his way back to the archery room. The lights darkened and dimmed as white noise came through on a nearby speaker.

"Livewire, you in here?"

He looked around. A voice whispered from the corner, "Come over here."

Moving toward it, he came closer and saw a burly, red-headed man.

I saw you at RGH. Wait a minute… you're Wilkerson.

"Chris, is that you?"

"In the flesh. What's left of me. I woke up next to the SPRING OF LIFE. All of my wounds were sealed up and healed. I must have angels watching over me. If Joe sees me, he'll have my head."

"Why are you still here, then?"

"We've got to get you out of here. I discovered something about Creeper Joe."

"Why bother with us? Aren't you mixed up in all this?"

"I need a clear conscience."

Get on with it, then. Joe's gonna pop out any minute.

"Fine. What is it?"

"He's a Creeper," Chris replied. "You know what that means?"

"Not really."

"Joe's youth is fleeting. He's getting weak… much weaker than you might realize."

"How do you mean?"

Chris looked over his shoulder as if he feared being seen. "I never heard of such a thing before Joe, but the best I got it figured… Creepers can only remain for so long. You may have heard that Joe's dead, and that's mostly true, but that doesn't mean he can't disrupt the physical dimension. He does it all the time. He's no spiritual being, but he's sure not a full-on physical one either. You have to get to him a different way."

"How does this help me any?" Todd asked. "You're just spinning your wheels. Why should I trust you?"

Chris slicked his hair back nervously. "You act like I had a choice. I never had a choice. If I wanted to live, I had to keep on."

"Not true. You have the right to make every choice. Why let a goof like Joe keep you in his grasp?"

"I don't have time to discuss that. It's more complicated than right and wrong, or good and evil. There are too many layers to examine anything at face value."

"Okay, Chris. So, what's going to help me here?"

"Creepers feed off of two things. Blood and fear. You've got to do everything in your power not to permit either of those. If you aren't afraid, he can't haunt you. If he can't haunt you, he can't bleed you."

What a weird thing to say.

"What? Bleed me? What are you getting at, man?" Todd asked as a puff of air came from his nose. "You're not going to send me on a vampire hunt, are you? Come on! This just gets dumber by the minute."

"No. It's nothing like that. It's much bigger. It's a state of being. You get it?"

"Can't say I do."

"Creepers are indebted to the devil for their love of the dark arts," Chris said. "The thing about it is, Lucifer's caught admiring his own handiwork, despite there being millions ripe for the reaping."

Todd stroked the side of his cheeks as he pondered the comment. "So what are you trying to say?"

"I'm saying..."

A rush of energy pulsed through Todd's body as a flashback came through the eyes of Wasserman.

He spoke to a much younger Joe. "You found your way to the basement, I take it. I hadn't thought about that cornerstone for years. I think it's an excellent idea. The Oak Hollow Hotel should be a place where we can uphold and affirm more righteous living. I like it."

"Thanks, Mr. Wasserman."

"Mr. Wasserman was my father. Call me, Don. You feeling okay? You look peaked."

"I'm fine, sir. Thanks for asking." A nefarious twinkle glimmered in Joe's eyes.

•　　•　　•　　•　　•

Chris shook TODD a couple of times, whistling as he snapped his fingers to get his attention.

"Todd, you there?"

"Yeah, I'm sorry. Drifted for a second."

"What I was saying was... you got to catch Joe with his pants down... so to speak."

"You know this *how*? And if you're that remorseful and really care about the rest of us, why haven't *you* done that already?"

"He already bled me. I can't. He's got blind spots. You follow?"

"Really?" Todd asked. "How do you know he has blind spots? He doesn't seem to miss much as far as I can see. It seems like he's just there waiting to pounce most of the time."

"I've watched how the other one treats him... and how he squirms."

"Other one?"

Chris leaned in close and spoke quieter, "Yeah. I don't know as much about him. He seems to be more of a 'watch the world go by' type. He's never lifted a finger on any of us since I've been around. He's spoken to me a few times... Who knows? The way Creeper Joe acts around him is enough to remind me that Joe has limitations."

Todd disagreed, shaking his head. "No. I'm sorry. What makes you think this 'other one' as you call him won't jump in front of us and attack if we try to get Joe out of the way?"

"It's a feeling I have. He's not happy with Joe. He's more emotional… and caring. I think he saved my life."

"An emotional Creeper?"

"I don't really know what or who he is. He may not be a Creeper. I think he's watching over us in a way… not looking down on us. There's a difference."

"Why is he allowing this to happen?" Todd asked. "As much as *you* seem to know… are you telling me you're one too?"

"I don't think so. It's only a season. Vengeance is inevitable. Creepers can see a whole hell of a lot, but the thing they want most is the deepest part of the soul. They'll spend years trying to shape a protégé, only to find out it was all in vain if they're not careful. I guess that's what separates 'em from the demons. It becomes a total waste when they find out God's in there somewhere protecting their hunt from consumption."

"Man, there's an interesting thought. This is terrifying stuff."

Chris nodded his head. "Yes it is. Let me tell you something else. Joe's got a supply of blood in the overflow freezer at the end of the tunnel. I've been watching him on the cameras for a while. He goes in, gets a load, and pops out like a brand new being every single time."

Todd scoffed. "I'm sorry. This seems unbelievable, but I guess I've got nothing to lose."

"Do it while you can." Chris's eyes glowed.

Time to go. Time to go.

"I think I'm going to turn in for the night," Todd said. "I'll check it out in the morning."

"Just remember," Chris said, "No fear and no blood." He motioned toward Todd to move on. "I need some space before I get myself sick. I've been getting a little claustrophobic."

"Got it. Good night."

CHAPTER FIFTY-FIVE

A familiar feeling hit TODD ADAMS as he stood in a dark corner of the tunnel, relieving himself. *The memory overwhelmed his mind.*

He glimpsed the inside of Wasserman's elaborate suite on the sixth floor, all pointing to an obvious reflection of his pride in it. He looked himself over in the mirror, walking out of the room toward the elevator, and proceeding to the eighth floor. As he got off, he walked past a young Joe and tipped his hat. The eyes of Joe Bonsall glowed uncharacteristically to Wasserman's recollection. Joe extended his hand.

"Mr. Wasserman, I just want to say thank you for everything. I'm looking forward to the party tonight."

"As am I... I've got to get on. I'll speak to you later."

Fragments of the memory seemed jumbled. The memory flashed forward. Joe lunged toward Wasserman as he dropped to the floor in a large ballroom. Joe smiled at him, cutting into his arm and wringing the blood out into a large pitcher taken from a nearby table.

"I know it's not much... but it's what you said you needed from me to show me more," Joe said.

Wasserman faded away as a shadowy figure lurked behind Joe.

"There was no need for this," the figure said.

The memory ended. Todd collapsed onto the floor of the tunnel, raking his fingers on the ground. He pulled clods of the worn surface beneath his fingernails as he yelled in unspeakable agony.

I can't... I can't handle this anymore.

Julie's voice rang through his head, *"Neutralize the worst parts of yourself when you're out of sorts and capitalize on the very best of yourself when you're on top of your game..."*

He ran through the tunnel in a fit of uncontrollable rage as his anxiety skyrocketed.

"I want out! I want out!"

The Shadow approached Todd as he struggled to remain conscious. His heart pounded as his body temperature rose.

I'm going manic. I'm going manic.

Todd ran toward the overflow freezer, forcing his way in.

If he catches me, he catches me. At least I'll go out trying.

He threw all the freezer's contents in the tunnel in frantic frustration. The associated commotion echoed.

Only a matter of time before he's on the prowl for me.

After emptying all of it into the warm corridor, he turned the stored buckets and containers of blood upside down to pour out and ruin as they thawed.

If he has no supply... he will cry... or kill...

A shriek came down the hallway as Joe's stutter-stepping footsteps grew louder.

Todd slipped out of sight, running back to the usual spot he retired for the night.

Just play it casual. No one has to assume it was you. There are others in here equally capable.

CHAPTER FIFTY-SIX

CHRIS WILKERSON watched chaos unfold from the video feed in the control room.

Get rid of him once and for all, Todd. I know you can.

Joe ran through the tunnel, startled by the commotion. Others drifted that direction. Joe ignored them as his attention remained diverted by the unexpected chaos. Chris flipped to the Spring of Life camera.

It's gone bone dry.

Blood covered the floors and walls of the tunnel near the overflow freezer. Joe studied its aftermath, pacing back and forth in an unfamiliar panic.

Diving to the floor in desperation, he extracted remnants from puddles of wet blood in his brass syringe and jammed it into his arm. The compromised blood merged with elements of the dirty tunnel floor. Chris activated the neighboring microphone, eavesdropping on the conversation as the Shadow appeared. His silhouette resembled a round framed man in a top hat, though no other defining physical features stood out.

"Not as pure, is it?" the Shadow said. "You're a little impure yourself. Always judging others and enforcing the rules your own way despite your own leanings toward self-gratification."

"It's not like that... it's not like that at all," Joe replied as his breath remained elevated.

"I think it is, Joe. Your eyes are far off the target. The deal was simple, fifty-four years of isolation, then fifty-four years to play. Lest you forget. The problem is, you haven't heeded my warnings, and you've continued to wreak havoc. I know some of these people defiled the covenant, but so have you. Don't you remember? I showed the Cardinal Rules to you on the cornerstone in the wellhouse room when you first arrived all those years ago... before you did it... You warped. You manipulated. You even used them to stir up trouble within 'good' people."

"That's not fair," Joe said. "I've hunted for you. I've provided for us. I did everything in my power to keep the Creeper alive."

"I'm sure you did, but the house rules were simple, and one of them far outweighed the others. 'Never shed innocent blood.' Wilkerson may not have been the picture of morality, but he wasn't one of the fifty-four. You crossed the boundary lines. You know something else? Todd Adams is a different kind of special. Maybe I chose him to teach you a lesson. You better watch yourself... because there *will* be hell to pay. Make it right, and I'll stay out of your way. Do it wrong, and I fear for how bad your end will be. Remember, you made *yourself* the troublemaker and the villain. I never told you to hunt for me. I never needed it."

Chris deactivated the camera.

I can't breathe. What's happening to me?

Standing up from the chair, he moved toward the door, and the room spun in circles.

I need fresh air.

He collapsed on the floor of the basement.

CHAPTER FIFTY-SEVEN

TODD ADAMS awoke with a massive headache after his manic tear in the freezer the previous evening. Floating orbs encircled him as he came to his senses. His mind raced at an uncontrollable speed as Wasserman's life flew by in seconds. An unexplainable jolt coursed through his body and he sprung to his feet. His manic phases had always been different.

Maybe this crazy cycle won't be such a bad thing.

The walls of his mind caved in around him as panic overarched its limits. His mind flashed back to the fated flight.

Lorrie's eyes were ravishing emeralds, and her hair was gorgeous. Riverton became smaller and smaller as they went higher and higher.

"These medications are messing you up. Let's get you back on the ground, and we'll get you some help."

"I'd rather be in the ground..."

Todd's inner mania ricocheted back and forth from wild to tame, and he sprinted through the center of the tunnel. His senses intensified as a glowing aura to the other residents materialized. *They seemed insignificant in the moment until his mind flashed back to the party in the penthouse of The Oak Hollow Hotel.*

Bits and pieces of Wasserman's missing memory returned. The ballroom was lit in exquisite incandescent fashion as its guests wore only the most elegant dresses and three-piece suits. The room was full of life and joy as its subjects celebrated a momentous occasion. He looked around, attempting to read the celebratory sign draped across a banner at the top of the room. The words remained incomprehensible. In the corner of his eye, Joe Bonsall stood young and full of life. The entire room carried on with the party. Each of the guests scoffed at him as he hobbled. The guests' inebriated demeanor and high-class sophistication looked to wear on Joe as he clashed with them. His eyes burned red as they teased and hurled insults.

"Look at the fool. Wearing that outfit for this event. What a travesty, Don. What a disgrace," a woman said.

"I didn't invite him here," he lied.

Another woman began chattering away about her husband to another. "It was hard not to make light of the idiot. Such an imbecile… and the worst part is… I'm married to him…" She stirred up trouble in a moment as the other man laughed aloud, "Let's go up to the room."

A quiet man stood in the opposite corner of the room, scheming a wicked way to loot the hotel's cash register.

He made eye contact with Joe's mother and father. They both looked away.

An immoral man ran across the room, lunging toward a buxom woman as he grabbed at her.

He continued to be a false witness. "The sad pity for the lad was, he was nothing more than a pet project for Sylvia to tease. I led him on like he would be my protégé. Fixed up a little broom closet in the basement and told him it was an executive suite, and 'hop-a-long' went for it. Like he was royalty… answering to some kind of higher power…" laughing aloud as he imitated Joe's limp. The others in his company chuckled loudly.

Joe barricaded the exits with chains he lifted from the basement while the rest remained too busy to notice. His eyes glowed an unfamiliar and inhuman color that changed as his fury intensified. He sprinted toward Don, yanking the dagger from under his shirt…

•　　•　　•　　•　　•

Todd gasped for air, coming back to his senses and feeling as if the emotional burden of the memory stole a piece of him. It unfolded in slow motion as "Breathy" Nancy Helbens came around the corner.

Her yell and odor permeated the air. "Oh my gosh! You're pale as a ghost."

She grabbed his arm, leaning in closer toward him. He pulled away.

Ugh. Get a breath mint.

He turned his head from her to dodge the path of her lingering breath as it hit his face.

"Whatever you say. What's the word?"

Before she could reply, Creeper Joe appeared behind them, kicking her down into one of the cell areas below.

Laughing aloud, he said, "Nancy will fit in better down there, won't she? What do you think? Nifty, eh? It's all fun and games. It's all fun and games!" His voice projected much quieter than it had in their previous encounters.

Chris was right. You are weak.

"Joe, are you missing something? I see it in your eyes. There's a hollow emptiness in them. They don't glow the way they used to, do they?"

Joe pivoted to a new subject, "I see you, Todd. You're a sorry excuse for manic, aren't you?"

That tactic's not going to work on me.

Todd shook his head. "You didn't answer me, Joe. What do *you* have to gain by keeping us all here?"

"It's my own little kingdom. I would have thought you'd figured that out by now. My house, my rules. My hunt may be over, 'Mr. Fifty-Four,' but my escapades have only just begun."

"I don't think so," Todd said. "The Oak Hollow Hotel chewed you up and spit you out, didn't it? You were unpalatable. The sad truth of the matter... all of us were, and we all got what we deserved, didn't we?"

Don Wasserman's eyes shined through Todd Adams. Creeper Joe's face sunk as he backed away. The Shadow appeared behind Todd. Todd turned around and fell facedown in an unspeakable reverence.

The Shadow spoke, "Joe, your math is a little off."

"What are *you* doing here again?" Joe asked. "You said you would leave me alone."

"Todd isn't victim number fifty-four. He's number fifty-three. I guess I'm as guilty of wicked scheming as the rest of you. I left a decoy on the list I gave you. I never saw you as my equal. You should have known that, though. We're all bound to come under judgment at some point because every last one of us is folly-stricken. You're a poor enforcer because you're drenched in it, too! I was a fool to think I could take on such a lofty task." The Shadow vanished away into darkness. The cell doors flung open, and all of the once confined prisoners exited toward the tunnel's center.

Todd's manic hysteria remained stuck on a loop, *Crazy is. Crazy does. Crazy is. Crazy does. Crazy is. Crazy does. Get him.*

Todd lunged toward Joe, grabbing him by the throat. "It's all fun and games. Right? Now, it's my turn. No fear... no blood... no fear... no blood... no fear... no blood!"

As he peered around the tunnel, a slew of Creeper Joe's victims circled around in a vivid glow. Enlightened by an unexplained epiphany, they raised their voices, chanting and repeating the same in unison.

"No fear, no blood, no fear, no blood, no fear, no blood!"

"You may have bled me out," Livewire said, "but you got it wrong. I ain't one of 'em... I never was. Sure, I had my share of mental health issues, and I ended up here like all the rest. I went along with the charade because I was on the brink of homelessness and divorce, but at some point, you've got to face the fact you feasted on *my* spoils in vain..."

"What are you saying? This is my tunnel... my tunnel," Joe said as his voice continued to weaken. His jet black hair fell in globs as he raked his fingers through in a rush of panic. His epidermal layer chipped away like his skin was nothing more than rubber cement.

"You've been outnumbered a while," Katrina declared as Sylvia manifested. "The right pieces just had to fall into place for us to strike."

"Shut up! I can't take it anymore," Joe said. "This is too much for me... right now... Who is number fifty-four? Who is it?!"

"No fear... no blood... no fear... no blood... no fear... no blood!" the group chanted.

Katrina scoffed at Joe. "How would we know? You're the creep..."

"Chris is gone, witch. I slit his throat myself. Now, Creepy Nights is your headache to deal with."

"I never signed the dotted line. Not my problem," she said.

"No fear... no blood... no fear... no blood... no fear... no blood!" The chant became stronger and louder.

"You threw law enforcement a bone all right," Nancy said. "It's only a matter of time before they dethrone you forever."

Joe collapsed on the floor, scraping his head against it as he shook in a nervous compulsion. His blackening eyes showed sheer terror.

"Your sadistic pleasure was too much," Livewire said as he kicked dirt into Joe's eyes.

"I never should have burned up that Oak Hollow church. I was just a boy... and I... The reverend stirred up trouble in my community... He prayed for an angel of wrath. What kind of sick person does that? It..." Joe gasped.

"It... what?" Todd asked. "Tell us now!" He kicked Joe in the stomach, leaving him reminded of his finite limitations.

Joe struggled to reply, "It wasn't hallowed ground." His voice softened to a whisper, "it was cursed."

Todd towered over Joe as the creep neared defeat.

The Shadow emerged as a glow shined upon him, revealing his identity. It was Don Wasserman's father, William Wasserman. He was middle-aged, balding, heavyset, and pale. His hair was graying with hints of the carrot tones that once graced it. His mutton chops were razor tight and well-kept — an appearance frozen in time since his death, October 29th, 1910, the date he became one with Oak Hollow.

He spoke with authority, "Joe, somehow, I knew my son would be the end of you — one way or another. You've tormented long enough. I never meant them to be a jar of lightning bugs to tease... just poking holes in the top of it and watching 'til they die. I guess I twisted my own little game into this mess and gave you more autonomy than I should have. It's time to let the old souls leave in peace, and for the rest to live their life as God intended."

Joe's not breathing anymore, is he?

The others came closer together, circling around the body, and tearing away pieces of Creeper Joe. When they finished, there was nothing left but part of the right side of his head, with a lingering ear, and a flickering eye that faced the ceiling.

CHAPTER FIFTY-EIGHT

The others moved toward a bright glow at the end of the tunnel. WAYNE WALLACE's missing senses restored to full strength and his tongue had grown back. His voice returned milder and softer spoken than before. In the sobering moment, he stood still, reflecting upon the creep who stripped him of his livelihood as he studied Joe's remaining eye.

A troubling vision interrupted.

His intoxication was clear while playing baseball with Joe. He chugged more *Old Tymer's*. He saw Joe's fear as his own alcohol enraged anger burned with ferocity. The troubled boy struggled to stay in touch with reality as evil manifested itself deeper and deeper.

The memory faded away, and Wayne stood in silence as his mind wandered.

There was nothing right about that. Nothing at all.

Todd approached Wayne. "I see you lingering for a second. It's an honor to meet you in person. I've loved the Dynamic Duds for years."

Wayne remained lost in thought.

I'm tortured by the memory. A hell no man needeth endure.

Wayne was slow to respond, raising his finger to Todd as if indicating he wasn't ready to speak. "I just need a moment," he whispered. "I'd love to chat more about the show when the time is right."

"I'll give you a few minutes. I don't think we should stay close to him for long. I don't know what to expect."

"I agree," Wayne said. "I'll catch up soon." He watched Todd study him a moment before walking away to converse with some of the others. He spoke a quiet word to Joe as he allowed Henry Bonsall to manifest, "I'm sorry, son. The way I treated you and your mother wasn't right."

The flicker in Joe's eye dimmed away as the rest of him crumbled to dust. Wayne found his way back to the group.

CHAPTER FIFTY-NINE

TODD ADAMS and the others proceeded to the end of the tunnel. The south tunnel exit was open (behind the dried up Spring of Life and its accompanying waterfall). The Shadow stood next to it as they walked together and into the connected sewer tunnel. "My children," he said, "find rest in this world. Take a deep breath and drink it all in. You've paid your penance for your folly. Now, live as you've never lived, and cherish every second. For those of you long separated from yourselves, prepare for a peaceful death — one without agony or struggle and a lot more harmony. Be blessed! Your time in here has ended." He walked away, disappearing into the shadows.

They looked at each other in amazement and astonishment. Katrina walked in step with Todd, holding hands with him in an unspeakable bond that transcended the past and the present. The release gave the souls of the risen coma patients autonomy to live life just the way they had before, but with a much broader and wiser perspective. Assimilation would be a challenge, but they had a chance for a new beginning. They followed one another in a single-file line through the sewer as they climbed the rebar steps toward Clairmont Avenue, a block from Honest Steve's Pawn and Loan.

Ebony yelled at Todd and the rest and said, "Hold on a minute! I don't know if I want to go back out there yet."

"What are you trying to say?"

Several of the others argued, urging Todd to lead the way out.

"I don't have a livelihood to return to," she said. "What's so wrong with staying put?"

"In the tunnels?" Todd asked. "Ebony, let's talk about this once we get everyone out of here."

"I'll just go back to Creepy Nights. Chris had a floor for us."

"Okay. Well, here goes. Remember our pact." Todd lifted the manhole cover as they came to the surface.

CHAPTER SIXTY

TODD ADAMS returned to RGH with several others for a full medical and psychiatric evaluation. The sporadic flashes and glimpses of their unfamiliar past seemed to have dissolved upon their exit from Level Zero and the separation of the souls. He and Katrina held hands. Katrina looked into Todd's eyes, whispering into his ear, "You know, Todd Adams. I think we'll clean up just fine together."

"I agree," Todd said. "A fresh start sounds like just what the doctor ordered."

"Absolutely! I'm glad they aren't keeping all of us overnight. It's already been a year... a year since I... since we woke up."

"Sounds like Wayne may be here a few weeks," Todd said. "Joe must have really rattled him. They committed him. Dr. Hicks isn't my favorite guy in the world, if I'm honest."

"Too bad for him. I'm glad we're okay, though." Katrina pulled Todd closer toward her. "I bet we are some kind of anomaly, two former coma patients shacking up like this."

A wheel squeaked in the background, distracting the pair. Todd looked up, and a nurse pushed a cart down the hallway away from them as she moved with a pronounced hobble, and the rhythm of the wheels rolling startled him as it crashed into a wall.

What's going on here? This isn't happening.

He stepped back from Katrina in a moment of paranoia.

"That nurse. Katrina, I'm sorry. I... I thought..."

"Thought what?" she asked in a stern tone.

"It's nothing..."

"Oh, come on..." she said. "You can tell me."

"I'm just dazed from the tunnel. Probably a little PTSD... Don't worry about it.... my meds will calm me down. I'll take my script from Dr. Hicks and be on my way... Hopefully, they haven't leased my place to anyone else yet... I prepaid the last three months in advance. Why don't we take a night to ourselves and enjoy the comforts of home tonight and catch up tomorrow? Dinner and drinks sound okay?"

Katrina smiled at Todd. "That sounds great! That'll give me time for a fresh cut, a long hot shower, and a chance to don a little black dress just for you." She poked him in the stomach.

"Sounds like a plan. That I would like to see," Todd said. "I know it might seem a little strange for me to propose it given where we've been, but I think Bridgewater would be kind of special."

"Alright. Well, take care of yourself. Get some rest, and we'll meet up tomorrow night. What time?"

"I'll pick you up at seven."

"See you then," she said. "Kiss me goodbye?"

Todd leaned into Katrina, embracing and kissing her as they carried their discharge papers toward the hospital exit.

Katrina hailed a cab, and Todd watched her ride away as Livewire also exited the hospital.

"Hey, Todd."

"Hey, Livewire. You're looking better already."

"Thanks. What's on the agenda now that you're back up and at 'em?"

"I suppose I'll go clean myself up and reorganize my apartment. I'd like to give the pickup a good washing. That's assuming I can find it. I'm sure they impounded it by now."

"Yeah... Good luck with that."

"And you?"

"I don't know," Livewire said. "My old lady still wants nothin' to do with me. Julie was always psychoanalyzin' me. It pushed me to my limits. We were separated a while. Imagine that, even a dad-gum therapist can't fix the problems of the world. As for what's next, I'll probably take a vacation. Chris left me a pretty decent payday before I... we disappeared."

Julie? What are the odds? It's a small world.

"Alright. Well, all the best," Todd said, extending his hand to shake Livewire's.

"Likewise. See you around... or if I don't.... that'll be okay too... not the fondest of memories we have together."

"Good luck. If you ever want to get investing in the markets, I'll probably try to get my job back at Riverton Financial."

"Maybe so. Take care."

CHAPTER SIXTY-ONE

CHRIS WILKERSON laid on the floor of the Creepy Nights basement. He remained immobile as his mind continued.

I've been stuck here a while. I just have to come to grips with it, but why am I still here?

Detective Penske and Officer Abram Markel came into the basement as he stared up at them.

"Chris, Chris? Are you okay?" Penske said as he checked his pulse. "He's gone. I guess the guilt was too much for him to handle."

"What was his goal with all this?" Markel asked.

"I don't know. This... he takes from the cradle to the grave."

You don't understand. It wasn't my doing. It never was.

Penske bent over and patted Chris on his cold shoulder. "I always had a feeling that there was something a little off about this place, certainly, with this guy. Was that your doing?"

Of course it wasn't. Can't you pick this place apart a little before jumping to conclusions?

Penske stared at Chris as he remained motionless.

"It's kind of weird, isn't it? That glow in his eyes."

"Yeah. You make a good point," Markel said. "When I look at him, I don't see life, but I don't see death either."

Control yourself. It's just a phase. It'll pass. You'll move on to greener pastures. Just give it some time.

"I'm not going to call this in yet," Penske said. "Let's barricade the basement with some caution tape."

"Why not?" Merkel asked, brushing some dust bunnies off the back of one of the old pews. "You should never leave a dead body to rot. I learned that at the academy on my first day."

No, you shouldn't. Maybe the embalming ritual will seal the deal for me.

"Don't get smart with me. We'll come back in a few minutes. Did you want to see the control room?"

"Sure."

They walked toward the area and studied the empty tunnel on the monitors, kicking a bunch of *Flitz* beer cans to the side.

"What a slob," Merkel said.

"He watched all of them like some kind of freak...some of them for months."

Channel your emotion before you can't anymore.

"Too sad. Are they going to shut this place down?"

"I guess it's up to the ex. She was one of the victims. Somehow I don't see it opening back up anytime soon..." Penske said. "Let's go grab a bite. We'll come back in a bit. Wrap the basement with caution tape, would you?"

I'm still here. Don't forget.

CHAPTER SIXTY-TWO

TODD ADAMS drove the extended driveway toward the Reinhold estate in his once impounded pickup.

Wow! This place is nice.

Katrina stood out front, waiting for him as he approached.

He honked the horn in a playful rhythm, climbing out to open her door.

"Curbside pickup... for the most beautiful woman in all of Riverton."

She donned a huge grin as she leaned in to kiss him. He was clean-shaven, fresh-faced, and his hair swooped and coiffed neatly to the side, sporting a three-piece suit saved for weddings and funerals.

"Thanks for picking me up. You look handsome." They both climbed into the truck and Todd wheeled the vehicle around toward the gate.

"Thanks," he said. "Look at you! Those legs hadn't seen the light of day in ages, and you're still breathtaking."

She punched him in the arm as they exited the driveway. "Was that a compliment or a jab?"

"There are many layers to Todd Adams. You'll just have to wait and see." He leaned across the seat and kissed her as they arrived at the gate.

Why do I feel nervous? It's not my first rodeo.

"You really look gorgeous tonight. This is quite the lovely property you have."

"Thank you."

"I watched the ten-o'clock news last night. I'm sorry to hear about Chris. Are you sure you still want to go? I should have called earlier. Do they know what happened?"

Katrina shook her head. "Yes, I still want to go. They don't know what happened. They found him in the basement. They'll clean him up as best as they can at the funeral home, and we'll wish him well. You're welcome to come with me. Maybe it's a little morbid, but at the end of the day, we weren't on the best of terms, so I don't care."

"I heard they're pinning the kidnappings on him postmortem since they found no evidence of Creeper Joe."

"That's the way it goes," she remarked.

"And you're okay being associated with that? Are the paparazzo's after you yet?"

"Not yet. We made a pact," she said. "Let's let bygones be bygones. You mind if I smoke? I haven't had a good puff in ages."

"Go right ahead. Hey, there's a new cassette I picked up just before... well... you know. Do *you* mind?" Todd asked.

"I love *AC/DC*. Go for it."

Todd inserted the cassette, and they cruised toward Bridgewater with the stereo blaring and the windows down.

"This is great," she said. "Hey, what's going on? Did you see that?"

"See what?

"A guy looked like he was sprinting toward that port-a-john over there. Maybe we should check in and make sure he's okay."

"I've already been a hero once this week. I don't know that I'm up for it again."

"Oh... just be a good Samaritan. It'll score you points with me later," she smiled, massaging him on the shoulder.

"That might just be worth it. Let me pull over." Todd parked the F-150 next to the street-level lavatory. "Wow, this *is* pretty fancy. I hadn't ever stopped this close to one," Todd said.

"Don't take too long. We don't want to miss our reservation. I just want to make sure he's alright..."

Todd climbed out of the truck.

Why do you have to be so attentive? Do I want you bossing me around the rest of my life? It would probably be good for me.

He approached the stall and tapped on the door. "Hey there. We saw you running. I just wanted to make sure you were okay in there."

"I guess so. I pissed off a panhandler down the street. He chased me down the block with a case of *Flitz* until we got over here — kept going on and on about being a mascot for that crap. The guy split like rubber when we got close to Creepy Nights," the voice said.

"Well… why are you still hiding then?"

"He told me something I didn't want to hear."

"Which was? You sound awfully familiar."

"He said *I* could be their damned mascot if I wanted to."

That's good 'ol Harv, alright.

Todd laughed. "I got it. And that prompted you to hide in a port-a-john…? Ramblin' Ron? Is that you in there? *You* of all people? I heard the episode where you trashed council, man. I'm thoroughly disappointed in you. I'm going to have to give an anonymous tip to the station."

"Shut up."

"Alright," Todd said, chuckling to himself a moment. "I'll leave you alone…"

He walked back toward the truck and opened the door.

"What was that about?" Katrina asked.

Todd smiled. "Oh. Nothing at all. Just another drunk roaming the streets. Let's get over to Bridgewater."

•   •   •   •   •

TODD and Katrina concluded their evening meal as they held hands atop the white linen table cover.

"Katrina, what do you think? How was everything?"

"It's been great. Wonderful company. Great ambiance. An attentive server. All the makings for a spectacular evening. The snapperfish was even better than I remembered. How was your steak?

I've never understood how you men can eat them so bloody and rare like that. Chris liked his the same way."

"What can I say? We have good taste," Todd said.

"So what's next?" Katrina asked. "Back to Riverton Financial?"

"Yeah, I reckon. Suspect they'll let Creensteen back over there, too. Lucky me…"

"Was he that bad?"

"No. Just annoying. If Creeper Joe had taken him out, that would have been okay with me."

Katrina glared at Todd. "You're not serious. Are you?"

Todd smirked. "Of course not… Just don't expect me to give him any *World's Greatest Boss* coffee mugs. What about you?"

"I know it might be a little forward, but I was going to ask you if you wanted to move in with me? Mother's place is too much for me all by myself."

"A go-getter," Todd remarked. "I like that in a woman. We've got nothing to lose. My lease is up next month."

Todd paid the bill and stood up. "Well, why don't we just go back to your place then? I make a killer caffeinated nightcap."

"That sounds great. I love a good coffee."

They headed home and finished the new cassette. Several minutes later, Todd pulled into the garage of the Reinhold estate. A parked Mercedes stood out amidst a slew of horror movie memorabilia and props.

"That's not the mask from *Freaky Fred*, is it…? Oh, wow… You weren't lying, were you? *This* is the famous Mercedes?"

"Oh… that… yeah. That's it."

"Looks like they got the deer's blood out of the upholstery just fine," he said. "I'm sure *that* cost a fortune."

"It did. Let's go inside. I didn't dress up this nice to talk about my dead mother's car upholstery…"

CHAPTER SIXTY-THREE

TODD ADAMS took a swill of his coffee as he and Katrina prepped to board the plane early the next morning.

Looking a little nervous today, aren't you?

"Are you sure you want to fly today?" he asked. "I've got the rental for the next three days if you'd prefer to wait."

"Of course I do," Katrina said. "I've never been on a private plane before. They terrified mother. Todd, I..."

"I, what?"

"I've been trying to wrap my head around it all. If there were fifty-four of us and Joe only had fifty-three, who did he miss?"

Who did he miss? We can only wonder.

"Hmm..." Todd mumbled.

Pondering the question, Todd lifted the plane off the ground as they soared over Riverton overlooking the Oak Hollow District and Creepy Nights.

"No more talking about the fifty-four business," Todd said. "We made a pact, remember?"

"You're right. Fine," she said. "Hey! Is that Ebony sticking her head out the window at Creepy Nights? I guess she made herself right back at home just like she said she would."

"What a strange little woman..." Todd said. "What do you think about the view? It gives a whole new perspective on Riverton, doesn't it?"

"It sure does, Don," she said, grinning ear to ear, reaching to grab him by the hand.

Todd looked at Katrina, "You mean... Todd."

Katrina looked back at him with an unfamiliar gaze. "Call me Sylvia."

What's going on here?

"Fair enough, Sylvia. I made us a 'special' mimosa. Drink up..."

She leaned in to kiss him.

"Can I teach you the controls? Why don't you steer the plane for a little while? I'll help you."

"Never when I'm manic, honey... Never when I'm manic," a voice called from behind.

A pair of burned arms came over the back of the seat and began strangling Todd. Katrina panicked, attempting to rip them away from Todd's neck. Lorrie emerged from the back seat of the plane. Her maimed and disfigured body was a testament to the flames from her plummeting descent with Todd and an act of God saving them both. She reached for the plane's control column as the plane dropped toward Riverton.

"Do you believe in second chances?" Lorrie asked.

"I do..." he gargled, his airway still recovering from the momentary strangling.

"Know the pain. It will be sweeter." She smiled, easing up on the control column. She opened the hatch door from the rear and leapt out of the plane as air rushed through the cabin. Katrina wrapped her arms around Todd in terror as the suction grew stronger. She hugged him tight while the Percocet and lithium mimosa cocktail she sipped on took hold.

"What's going on, Todd? Why am I feeling this way?"

"You'll find out soon enough, sweetheart. You'll find out soon enough."

CHAPTER SIXTY-FOUR

RAMBLIN' RON prepped to turn in his keys to WGBO, packing the rest of his belongings as he removed the final Dynamic Duds poster. Detective Penske opted not to turn him in for unlawful entry into a municipal vehicle in exchange for the information provided.

He walked past the new receptionist. "I'll see you later, Nancy. Tell the new guy I said to break a leg tonight."

"He's already in STUDIO B if you want to tell him yourself..." She hurled a Reese's peanut butter cup in her mouth.

Ron shook his head as he noted the silhouette of a hunched figure behind the hallway glass.

"Na. I don't want to give him any bad mojo with his new job. See you later."

"Bye, Ron. Good luck."

As he walked toward the bus stop, flames engulfed the once pastel Creepy Nights building as a small plane dangled from the side of the building. Sirens surrounded as first-responders worked to put out the fire.

Ron ran back to the studio. The ON AIR sign activated as a voice came through the speaker.

"There's an interesting development in Riverton, folks. In what we can identify as a plane crash with an excess of collateral damage, the once hallowed and iconic hotel continues to blaze. It's not looking good. The Oak Hollow Hotel... now known as Chris Wilkerson's Creepy Nights, may turn to rubble before our very eyes. Unfortunate as it is to see this fine institution up in flames; it is something of a poetic justice, isn't it? The place best known for telling scary stories itself ends in a scary story. We'll catch you later on the next edition of WGBO's newest show, Total... Madness."

·   ·   ·   ·   ·

The mortician prepped CHRIS WILKERSON with similar care to that of Helena Reinhold. Lying on the table, motionless but alert, Chris remained stuck in a transitory state of being. Despite multiple attempts to seal and cover his eyelids with more makeup, the glow underneath shined bright.

"Can't get them to look right. What's going on here?"

Tapping echoed across the room from the back door.

"I'm not expecting anyone," he muttered, stomping his feet across the floor.

He moved toward the door as another series of taps grew louder.

Opening the door, a round-figured man in a top-hat stood outside smoking a cigar and holding a pewter cup full of liquid.

"Hello there. I'm here to tend to some unfinished business. Do you mind if I come in?"

THE END

ABOUT THE AUTHOR

Dan McDowell developed an appetite for writing thrilling and chilling stories to escape the left-brained confines of Corporate America and dive headfirst into the right-brained universe of fiction. He and his family reside near San Antonio, TX.

NOTE FROM THE AUTHOR

Did you enjoy *Level Zero*? Leave a review online, tell or share it with a friend, and don't be afraid to tap into your right brain from time to time yourself. It's okay to let your imagination run wild. You have my permission.

Creep On!
Dan McDowell

Thank you so much for reading one of our **Psychological Thrillers.**

If you enjoyed our book, please check out our recommendation for your next great read!

The Tracker by John Hunt

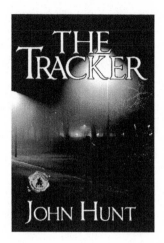

"A dark thriller that draws the reader in."

–Morning Bulletin

"I never want to hear mention of bolt-cutters, a live rat and a bucket in the same sentence again. EVER."

–Ginger Nuts Of Horror

Made in the USA
Monee, IL
27 July 2021

74369989R10152